TO MY BELOVED KATHRYN

To My Father, Ralph Kushner
Who always wanted me to write
The great American novel
And felt that watching
The human escapades
On the corner of Elmwood and Utica
In Buffalo, New York
Was a good place to start

To My Mother, Thelma Kushner
Who sang like an angel
And always had a song in her heart

To My Daughter, Kaitlin Kushner

To My Step-Daughter, Elizabeth Rose

To My Sister, Lauren Ruel,
My Brother-in-law, Bernard Ruel,
and my niece and nephew,
Kimberly Ruel and Steven Ruel

To Jan and Art Brennan
of Casa de Snapdragon LLC
Your kindness, compassion, and professionalism
Precede you

Oh, do not ask "What Is It?"
Let us go and make our visit

T.S. Eliot
"The Love Song of J. Alfred Prufrock"

Prelude

I remember hearing a funny story some time ago. Forgive me if I am not narrating it exactly. An archeologist went to visit a secluded monastery in some far off land. The monastery was reputed to have a library filled with ancient manuscripts. Many of them were said to predate the modern era by millennia. It was said that one could experience a real epiphany just being in the presence of these precious manuscripts. They were reputed to answer the age-old conundrums of the meaning of life, and how to experience heaven on earth.

After a long and arduous journey the archeologist finally arrives. He is well-received. Visitors are not very frequent here. He is full of expectation and desire. Maybe now all of his questions will be answered and he and all humanity will live in a state of grace and bliss forever.

He meets the head monk and all of the novices. They are a quiet and somber bunch, all dedicated to the ancient practice of study, hard work and celibacy.

Many old manuscripts are available to all in the library. Some are written in prehistoric dialects and arcane symbology. They reflect an early peoples' understanding of the universe and the Divine's creation of it. But, there are certain manuscripts that are available only to the head master. They are the most ancient, and due to their advanced age, they are in need of immediate copying. Even though they have been copied many times over the millennia by skilled monks, the head monk could not resist the temptation of reading and copying the original.

The head master set about his task with great verve. He remained a recluse working in his little cell day and night. The closed, heavy wooden door gave the very distinct impression that he did not want to be disturbed.

All the head master took for nourishment was a small bowl of gruel once a day. After several weeks, however, the monks and the archeologist began to become alarmed. The head monk would not leave his cell, nor would he respond to inquiries about his well-being. By a unanimous vote, one day the monks decided that when his bowl of gruel was being delivered to him, the messenger would audaciously ask the head master of his state and whether he could be of any assistance.

On his way down a long and winding corridor the young monk delivering the gruel thought he heard some sounds. The walls were stone and sound easily carried. As he walked further down the corridor he was sure he was hearing a moaning. Hearing this he moved fleet of foot to see what was the matter. Finally, he arrived at the head master's cell. The massive wooden door was closed-and the heavy iron apparatus was firmly closed. The situation did not appear inviting. Still, the moaning was now so loud that the young novice took it upon himself to knock on the door and then open it without waiting for permission. Oh, what he saw when he opened the door.

The head master was repeatedly banging his head against the stone wall, almost oblivious to what he was doing. The distress on his face was unmistakable. It was as though some intense tragedy had been brought to light and the head master could not bear it.

The young monk then looked down on the head master's work table. On it was a most holy and ancient manuscript, and a very cherished copy. The young monk was stupefied when he saw that the Head Master had actually circled something in the original in a heavy red line.

The young monk looked back at the head master who was now saying, "Celibate. Celibate. Celibate. The fool left out the 'R'!"

And so it goes.

Whatever was missing was here all the time. And, it is not necessarily what is here; but what we think is here – and what we think about that.

Thoughts can make the same life either a heaven, a hell, or a dull meandering waiting for the inevitable lapse into the great Void.

The one beautiful, but frustrating thing about epiphanies is that they appear to be spontaneous. They cannot be forced, trained for or predicted. They either happen or they don't. And, there is no going back.

One moment you are in the fog, the next, you are cascading in the verve of newness which you hope will be forever-after.

Introduction

I have frequent dreams. I am on a journey. Somewhere. At some time. I am standing at a distance. I am looking at beautiful, rolling hills in the distance. They are somewhat inverted in the center, giving the appearance of having been volcanoes in the distant past. Now they are smooth and verdant with soft green grass and a welcoming sense. They are so lovely to look at and so familiar. They seem to say, "Don't you remember me? Don't you remember this place?"

The sky above them is a brilliant, metallic blue with rich, bountiful clouds drifting across the panorama. The scene is so complete in every detail that it looks like it came out of a filtered photograph with perfect lighting and shading. Tufts of trees and bushes appear sporadically to give depth. The cloud formation may have been designed by an artist whose intent was to convey the image of angels and angelic beings in every way, shape, form and contour. I am looking at it. I feel an absolute sense of Peace. The scene is, in other words, Perfect!

As the scene shifts, there is a beautiful white farmhouse in the distance. It is very inviting. I walk towards it and am trying to remember something, but it seems just out of reach. As I step onto the porch and walk towards the seasoned dark brown door, there is something I am still trying to remember. My entire attention then focuses on the worn, round brown doorknob. Something about this seems so familiar. There must be something beyond the door! My hand touches the doorknob as if to start turning it, and ... I am wide awake!

With a deep sigh, I wonder where the dream starts and stops. I know I can only go there involuntarily, so to speak, so I have reluctantly stopped wanting to go there. When it happens, it happens. But, the dream seems so real; like I am really there experiencing it. I sometimes wonder if I am really witnessing this beauty in my real life, and that this reality is only a dream. Sometimes I get so confused that I wonder if I am dreaming about a dream in a dream.

At other times, I visit a seaside town that, in my dreams, I have visited many times. To my knowledge, I have never been there. In my dream, however, I know I am very familiar with this place. It is truly special. I have many connections with it, over many lifetimes, and that I truly love it. I take the same route to get there, stay in the same hotel, walk along the same boardwalk. Each time, however, feels fresh and alive, like it is the first time. I feel as though I have made a major discovery. Ah, how enchanting my life feels. Sheer life force flows so abundantly when I am experiencing truly innocent joy; joy, that is, which savors like a young child experiencing joy.

Upon awakening I try to remember where this town is, as if I ever really knew. I have stopped looking for it on a map, but I know I can only get there via means not yet manufactured by our transportation barons.

It is almost like I am living different lives at the same time, and the same space. As if there is a calling from another realm, another reality; here, but not here. In the same space, but yet, so different; so far removed.

I do like a good story. Please join me. Before we can get back to the other side, where things make more sense (because we accept them and do not think about them), we are going to have to go through the zone where things often do not make any sense at all; where confusion reigns supreme, and where darkness poses as light and is accepted as such.

Like a stranger walking through an unknown, threatening city at night; so we walk day-to-day. We have learned how to package ourselves. We have adopted methods to communicate; to get by. But the frightened stranger, cowering at the unknown forces seemingly surrounding him, is locked inside. A damsel in a dark tower, waiting for prince charming. Even when we know we should and that – we can – leave; the fear of the unknown defeats even this escape. Death, the greatest fear, keeps us from opening the door to certain freedom. And so the strong, belligerent thought forms continue, unabated. Root thoughts mutate into branch thoughts, and branch thoughts propagate into still finer and entangled thoughts. The jungle, the labyrinth. Until we say it once; until we say it a million times. Stop! Enough! No more! This is not right. This is not the way. There is a way. I know it. I knew it at one time, and I will discover it again. I will look every moment for the rest of my days if need be; but, I will find it! And so, a sense of calmness descends. And with the calmness, slower breath and a sense of wholeness, quietude, and peace. A kind of middle way – between here and there, before and after.

I

Last night I dreamt I was dancing. In fact, I was engaged in a slow waltz with the love of my life in a darkened, chandeliered ballroom in some forgotten city in a corner of the world that never ages. It was the turn of the 20th century. I was dressed in tails, of course; my rich necktie firmly placed – a statement in itself, against a backdrop of a shimmering white linen shirt. She was dressed in a long, flowing white gown, with lace fringes and a low-cut front. Her long, luxurious dark hair was rich and buoyant, and her bright green eyes – rich green; were the color which only appears in photographs. We were turning slowly, around and around, and this was the only movement in the entire world. We were turning the world and it was turning with us. I looked into her eyes and she into mine. Slowly, oh so slowly we were turning, turning as if nothing else in the world existed.

I could feel the soft skin of my beloved; the airy gentleness of her hair. I dwelled in the perfection of the moment as the soothing aroma of her perfume wafted from her slender, graceful neck.

The beauty and clarity of the dream remained with me even as I soon faded into the fogginess of the day. And not just mental fogginess, but, that evening, an actual, thick impenetrable fog.

From my sixth story window in the Elliot Square Building I am watching a fog which is covering the entire downtown. The way it is just strolling in, it is like a living presence. Walking. Easy. Slow. Assertive and complete.

The beauty of it is that it stills everything in a shroud of quiet, comfort and peace. But, perhaps not enough if you are at the end of a commercial day, and you're tired and just want to get home.

On the street corner below, I can hear the "hawker" in the newspaper kiosk, whose name is Petey, bellowing his litany of the day's events. I have known him for years, and can picture him standing there, all 5 feet of him, and somewhat heavy set – sort of squat and square – in a threadbare overcoat. If I could actually see him, I know he would be wearing an old, faded winter hat with earflaps and old, stained once-leather gloves with the fingers cut off at the knuckles. He would be sporting a two-day growth on his face, and yes, a stogie would be indelibly glued to the right corner of his mouth. I opened my window to get the feeling of the fog. In these older buildings you can still open a window. "Pontius Moon Missing," I could hear him say. But, I couldn't see him, so in this fog, his voice was disembodied. This startled me. My friend, Ponti Moon – what could this mean, I thought, as I kept staring into the fog.

The moisture molecule-flakes of the fog feel tingly on my face. They seem to burst into full glory at the first touch, and then, they are gone forever. Back into the essence that created them.

I feel caressed and nourished by the moisture of the fog and its soft flowing nature. It seems to speak of things that cannot be described in words, for words would only insult the moment.

The fog is so thick that I cannot even see the Pilliam Building across Main Street.

Evening has descended so quickly tonight. Normally there is a momentary interim, an interlude between the end of day, and beginning of night. The "still point" as the poet T.S. Eliot used to call it. Not tonight. No gradual transition where piercing colors paint the sky in the manner of some mythic processional. Tonight there was a very blunt and unceremonious descent. It made me feel "packaged" and introspective.

I am a psychologist. I would have gone into psychiatry, but knew I'd never have gotten though the medical courses at school. Blood makes me very squeamish.

My office is on the 6th floor of the Elliot Square Building. Many decades ago, it was called the "E" Square Building and sometimes still is. The "E" is from the days when the buildings at the foot of Main Street had letter designations. That changed somewhere between the Spanish-American War and World War I. The "E" remains a connection to what many consider a more gentle and romantic age.

Normally, I have a clear view of the lake to the west, where the Sun makes its daily transit into eternity. The fog has dictated otherwise tonight.

I have always loved this city at night. The restraining cylinders that put a tight cap on the emotions of the day are loosened. In some cases, it is an explosive release of pent-up G-d knows what. Stagnant energy is often the curse of civilization. Unbridled explosions can be the opposite problem.

The night brings out the magic in some people. It also brings out the tragic in others. Darkness and electric light help cancel people's inhibitions. A time to act in the perceived safety when one no longer feels exposed, when the senses reside in a different person. A time for anonymity, of ritual celebration, especially in the mask of the fog. The streets become avenues for the Pucks, Pans, pranksters, players, panderers, and those just in it for a momentary interlude. Lovers walking in a universe of their own making; lonely romantics waiting for their bite at the apple of love. Then there are the "bag people" who can now take over, unimpeded by the daily throngs of commercial humanity. The pickings are juicy at evening time, especially during a fog. But, the vast majority cannot be pigeonholed into any category. They are simply the lost. They make up the pawns of civilization, the fodder of society, grist for the mill as it is sometimes said. People who use other people, people who are used by other people, and finally, those that are just browsing through life. Some of them are my clients. Most of them are my subjects. They make up the primary ingredients in this little stew bowl of desire we call our world.

Many think something is missing in his or her own life. They want it. It consumes all waking and sometimes sleeping moments. Whatever it is; no matter how deep it is; no matter how abstract or concrete it is, they want it, and will not cease until they have it. Life becomes a myopic and isolated adventure to find the something – which even if obtained – would be unsatisfying.

In other words, they are most in need of Beauty. Like the dark angel who fulfills its mission, the world is effective in making people pray for light when there appears to be none.

The true experience of Beauty brings with it both stillness and a full-bodied experience of circuiting energy; like an open door through which the primal energies of our realm course without opposition, or even a thought of opposition. And, Beauty is the most wonderful thing in the world if you are ready to receive it. If you are not, it goes unrecognized in the same way as pebbles skipping in a clear pond simply sink to the bottom. After they make a few brief, surface contacts with the water, they disappear as if they never were. Back into the void.

I have known many people who have suffered a great deal in their lives. Many have told me that there is nothing more important than to enjoy the beauty in life, whatever that means to you. Such advice coming from combat veterans or concentration camp survivors immediately passes the litmus test of authenticity and truth. And to do this, I was told, you have to look for things to beautify. You cannot simply remain supine in your easy chair and mentally whisk the darkness away. To start, you have to become your own storyteller; to mold your life as if you were working with a lump of moist clay. You have to tell yourself the story of your life, and in so doing, open the gate for the master clay maker to infuse your creation with life.

When I experience this kind of fog, it puts me into a deep reverie. I am often reminded of a daydream I had many years ago as a young child. I would sit in my second story bedroom and pretend that I was gazing upon a beautiful hillside near a pristine, clear body of water. In the blink of an eye I would will into existence beautiful homes on the hillside for all who needed them. The homes would be stark white on the outside, like in a virgin Mediterranean scene. The creation of something from nothing. It didn't feel strange or magical; it felt like this was the way things really were – we just didn't recognize it any more.

I like to search for things which appear to be hidden, and figure out what seems to be unsolvable. But, in the search for the answer in these enigmatic investigations, I am also looking for something which is very personal to me. I pretend that I am a sailor on an adventure to the new world; that I am looking for answers where no one has ever looked, in a way that no one has ever searched.

I am an explorer of sorts. I have been a psychologist and counselor for almost 30 years. An investigator; helping my clients bridge the distance between who they are and what they were doing. Like a sailor on a mythic voyage, thousands of stories coursing around a central theme, leading to an unknown both promised, and unproven.

In all my years of counseling, I have come to know that everyone is secretly hoping someone will help him or her find out who he or she really is, and give them the love which is so desperately craved. It is almost like one life is being lived in so many variations, all of which are experiencing the same primal theme. How alike we are in all of our differences. Everyone acts like a baby that didn't receive the nurturing it needed as an infant, and has been acting out ever since.

Everyone wants light in his or her life. Everyone wants love, and in his or her own way, to give love. Everyone wants nurturing. Everyone wants to walk outside the fog of uncertainty into the light of acceptance and certainty. Most do not know how to go about it. Most are too beset by normal daily obligations to seriously contemplate it. But, some have done it. How? Even with explicit instructions, it seems difficult, if not impossible, to replicate. So, how do we go about it? Why do we go about it? Because we have a lust for adventure. As if we all know the end of the story – that it is going to be a success, regardless of how it now seems. And, we all know that we are on the long road home. We only have a vague idea about home. We hope and pray that we are getting ever closer.

Even knowing this, normal life can be hard and demanding. Only the most saintly are unaffected by the pressures of the world, and love at will.

The World, in short, is often a reverse mirror-image. That which is good, if even contemplated, is often disregarded or down-played. That which is not good is often heralded and promoted. The "bad" things often come in the prettiest packages.

If this World were nothing more than a transparent bubble, and we were at the very edge of the curtain of the bubble, at the literal still point of bursting – then the choices of times past would be absent and irrelevant. This means that all the choices, all the options, all the variations that perpetuate life in the bubble have already been done and are no longer available. To try to stay in the bubble and replicate what has already been done throughout recorded history, and perhaps, long before, would be nothing but surplus. As much as the Universe always fills a vacuum, it also rejects waste. The state of the world does not need repetition. History is replete with repetitive acts.

A conquering nation eclipses the conquered culture, takes the aspects it wants, and prohibits, figuratively or even literally, the practice of balance. Thoughts, like evil forces from a distant and greedy land, come out of nowhere and do everything in their power to eclipse and annihilate a happy moment.

Many have said that our minds are the battlegrounds on which are waged the eternal and heralded battle between good and evil. Each, in his or her own way, must walk through his or her own, City at Night. I suppose that as we get older, we just become more of who we are.

History is replete with Masters who have acknowledged that the only true path is the path of Love. You cannot enter the Kingdom of Heaven without kindness, we have been told.

But, what is the system, the technique which allows us to bridge the gap; to go from a tormented, struggling human being, replete with an emotional spectrum going from godly love to abject hate? How do you change this person into a loving being worthy of respect, even, in cases, deep admiration; and finally, divine light?

The ancients said there would come a time when the cycle of time would start to unwind. Not another cycle in the endless circles, but ... freedom from the tyranny of an endless cycle.

Bezalel is mentioned in the Book of Exodus in the Bible. At the Creator's command, Bezalel created the Tabernacle shortly after the Children of Israel commenced on the Exodus from Egypt. The Talmud relates how he knew the secret behind the letters of the Hebrew alphabet, and knew the combination of letters which created Heaven and Earth. In other words, the secret of manifesting miracles in the material world. Bezalel knew the codes to create what is thought to be impossible.

Excuse me. We have been talking for a while. Let me introduce myself. My name is Michael Cushner. It is a fanciful name. Michael asks a question which both asks and answers a question which cannot be answered. It is Hebrew for "Who is like G-d?" Cushner is Hebrew for "A Candle in the Darkness."

My earliest years as a child were surrounded by gamblers, namely bookies and horse track betters, affectionately known as "horseballs." By the time I was five I was already working at a drug store selling the Racing News, cigarettes, cigars and Copenhagen snuff to guys on their way to the race tracks. As a perk, I also got to read Playboys. I never really cared about the races or the tobacco. The Playboys, however, were worth the price of admission.

Well, it's dinner time and I have to work tonight. I also need to find out what Petey was crowing about. I will talk to him as I head for a restaurant named Cravens which is right down the street. Cravens is a nice place to go for dinner or at least a drink. The fog is still dense. I think I will just stop in and wait it out. For the players in town, Craven's is a breeding ground. I was and am still happily married. For me, going to Craven's is an opportunity to miss the rush hour traffic and get a good dinner and a drink. This gives me a chance to think – not that I need any more time to do it.

I often remember that my father told me that the most important things others relate to you can never be related in words. This is why the real transmissions from the real masters could never be codified in a book. In a much more pedestrian way, the regulars at Cravens treated each other as an extended family; their lies were kept to a minimum. I also remember my Uncle Duke and all the stories he told me about people he had encountered. He was a real character!

I put on my vest and suit coat and walked down the five flights and out the revolving door into the world of fog. Immediately I became encased in what seemed like a dark, opaque bowl with patches of illumination cast by streetlights. While it is a bit dismal, the moisture has a tingly aliveness to it. Following my instincts, I carefully walked the thirty-six steps from the glass revolving door of the Elliott Square office building to the corner and bought a newspaper from the "voice" I was listening to just a short time ago.

"Hey, Petey, what's this about Ponti Moon?" Even at two feet away the fog made him appear vaporous and distant.

Petey is about 5 feet tall, and almost as wide. He has probably been bearing the same toothless grin twelve hours a day since he started on the corner of Edward and Main in 1921. Nothing going on around here gets around his field of vision, even in a fog. His blue hat with a strap and ear flaps looks permanently attached to his head. His herringbone overcoat has gone in and out of style so many times, it is worthy of an entry in the Guinness Book of World Records, or a showing at the Smithsonian.

To say that Petey is a permanent fixture on this corner would be redundant. He's seen more and heard more standing on this little block of concrete than most people have in a few lifetimes. He's been a witness to flappers coming out of speakeasies, mobsters running roughshod over Main Street, GIs walking arm in arm with their girls, urban blight, hippies, and urban renaissance. Like he's in a perpetual state of meditation, he looks and listens. As far as I could tell, it hasn't changed him at all. Like the Archangel Gabriel with his trumpet, Petey proclaims the headlines as if a voice on high were not only giving him a mission, but also speaking through him.

"Oh, Misshe Cushnah; ha ya be?" he replied in guttural overtones. He had to remove his cigar butt from between some remaining teeth to his half-finger gloves. "I cud'nt see ya too well in dis hear fohg. Yeah, ain' zhat a shame 'bout Misse Moon! Wondaful guy he was. Sometimes would walk from the museum jus to buy a papah fwom me. Made me feew weal proud, he did. A weal gentleman, he was." He shoved the stogie back into his mouth and continued talking with it in tow (I think it helped his pronunciation) – "So how 'bout you, Misshe Cushna?" He gave me a toothless grin. I'll never know how he actually picked up some British affectations in his speech and I was not going to ask.

Petey always meant well. He liked to flatter his clientele. Sometimes he would accidentally embarrass you by what he said, or how he said it. His intentions were good. But, after spending virtually 60 years as a semi-hermit on a street corner, those mental barriers which are usually present in diplomatic or commercial conversations, were gone; absolutely gone. Thoughts, ideas, statements – what have you – would simply drop – full bore – from the top of his head to his tongue without reflection. He gave a new dimension and expression to "stream of consciousness" thinking.

"So what do you hear lately, Petey?"

"Oh, not much. Eveyone jus twyin' to get home wight now. Dis fohg's weally somp'n, ain' it?" He paused. "An', if you wanna know the simple twuth, it kinda gives me the willies; what with Missa Moon missin', and what with that weihd show he was plannin' jus' down the street. I heah it's gonna open anyhoos."

"I know what you mean Petey. It's more than just a fall chill in the air. Well, I best be off now; I've got some work tonight."

He winked at me.

I smiled in response. "You be good and I'll see you tomorrow, Petey." I tipped him as I usually do.

"Thanks Misshe Cushnah. You'se OK, you ah. Some people might t'ink youse a little weird with dis head schwinkin, hocus pocos talky stuff, but Ize bet you got some real moxie too!"

Cravens was only a block down and I had time before my 7:00 p.m. appointment. This one wasn't in my office. I had to meet a client at the Angel's Haven. Of all things. This was a favor for an old friend of mine. He insisted that my counseling could only help if he were really in the throes of anxiety. Seeing his wife with another man would surely do that, and my presence nearby would prevent him from otherwise engaging the guy.

This was certainly a first. I said "no" to his requests until he pleaded with me. I laid down the conditions. No engagement with the couple. No confrontation. No violence. Peep in, see what he knows he will see, and step out. Then, and only then, we will talk.

He was a funny guy, in that we both knew that what he was doing and what he was going to get was all too predictable; but that really didn't matter at all. I also told him that I knew that he was "stepping out" as well. He was more upset that she started an affair before he did. Once competition rears its ugly head, it can infiltrate every aspect of your life. Your life just becomes a game where no matter what the cost, you are going to win, even if it kills you. I told him repeatedly that his best option was to try to repair the damage and restore the relationship. Heaven only knows what a jackass he could be to live with! But, ego has a funny way of exerting itself. Once it does, your world becomes very small and condensed. You versus the Universe. Now, when that happens, who do you think is going to win?! In the final analysis, there is little or no imagination in these "affaire de coeur" cases, if the heart has anything to do with it at all.

The fog is keeping a lot of moisture in the air. It's getting into my bones now. The way it is moving, it feels like a living presence. I can feel its breath penetrating my overcoat, and crawling under my shirt and up my back.

Normally I enjoy walking in a fog. There is a type of unreality, a privacy, a safety it casts. What is hidden in it appears only as an apparition. Tonight, however, it just doesn't feel quite right. It's like there is something in it, and this something either wants me to pay attention to something, is warning me about something, or may even have a negative intent.

Fear is often the product in the realm of the unknown. Fear of the unknown is likely greater than the fear of Death. Many will accept the sinister in an attempt to not have to deal with the unknown.

Perhaps it's because the fog is so incredibly dense. The beams of car lamps are muted and shrouded; surrounded by halos. Streetlights are transformed into luminous bodies encircling Main Street. Buildings are lost in clouds of vapor. The world has been recast in a type of vaporous illusion.

Something does not feel right. Something is missing. Or, something that shouldn't be here is here. Instead of second guessing it, I have learned from hard experience, just to let the feeling alone. If I just leave it alone, it will lead me to where I need to be. When I have done otherwise, I have often acted unwisely. For instance, if I felt that something in my life was missing, but just couldn't put my finger on it, the movement I made was often the wrong one. Movements to quell an internal hollowness before it becomes a vibrating fear are often actions which you have to do over, later; sometimes with more difficulty that when you had the first opportunity.

I often notice how people made a lifetime habit of either suppressing or expressing fear. Neither is a good option. They either mobilize you to move for the sake of moving or immobilize you from any movement whatsoever. Energy suppressed is hell enough. In my own private theology, suppressed energy is the entrance to hell.

What is it?! Something I have not felt for a long time. In one sense, it feels like a part of me. Yet, it is so foreign. The more I try to get rid of it, the more I experience it. Sometimes it makes me feel like a pinball; bobbing between bumper pads, at the whim or control of some foreign power.

Ponti Moon is certainly on my mind. He surrounded himself with a bit too much controversy. And, he loved the notoriety. In the world of ordinary and cookie-cutter, he was definitely Art Nouveau. But, his exposure made him an easy mark. I just don't feel he was missing at all. Where is he then? Did he just want to get out of town for some rest and relaxation, or is his absence involuntary?

Even his real name was a gilded work of art: Pontius Aloysius Montefiore! Pontius was meant to be pronounced in the proper Roman fashion: Pon-Tie-Us; not the unartful slang of centuries which pronounce the name as Pon-shus. He dropped the Aloysius because he felt it made him sound like an 18th century whaler. He changed Montefiore to Moonrising after an experience in a Native American sweat lodge in a New Mexico pueblo. After crawling out of the hut, which consisted of heavy wool blankets over a strong birch frame, in the middle of the night, a huge full moon, in dazzling white and gold, had almost obscured the horizon. For a moment he wasn't sure if he was on the moon looking at another planet, or whether the entire solar system had changed while he was in his personal transit in the pitch black, smoke filled hut. That moment of serendipity was so profound that he felt his very soul linked to the moon for eternity. Hence the name change; but, people adopted it as Moon instead of Moonrising since it was easier to accept a name which sounded Oriental as opposed to some drug-induced hippie name. This gave enough familiarity to be acceptable. He accepted that change as being a token of love from those who admired him.

With a name like Ponti, he had to go far, or that was the logic behind it. Not wanting to be too obvious, his parents avoided a middle name that even remotely sounded like Pilate, or thereabouts. They wanted him to be the man to make hard decisions when the fate of the world depended upon it. They intended this to be in the world of politics, not the world of art! Maybe he was so named to rectify the blunder of his name-sake so many centuries ago.

As I left Cravens and resumed my walk in the thick fog, I overheard a woman saying that it was a pity Ponti Moon may have been taken before his time. I agreed. I wonder if she ever connected my voice to a body. It was as if two bodiless voices were communicating with each other.

I think it was the poet Robert Frost who said, "The quickest way out is through." Tonight that is a significant challenge.

The fog continues to thicken. Traffic is crawling and cars are proceeding like drugged participants in an involuntary processional.

Downtown is engaged in its motor exodus.

II

Humans can be really very silly. They will fight to the death to be included with the majority, if this means they will have a comfortable home, more than enough food, and entertainment. The latter may be more important than the former. It is one of the only things that helps them forget the torment they go through in order to be accepted by the great mass. But, in order to preserve their self-worth and assert their right to individuality, they may jump from one sizeable camp to another, especially if they spy the possibility of a new majority being formed, and the possibility of their being at the top of the heap. This gives them yet another opportunity to avoid dealing with their real problems. They can also hope to reap the glory behind the specter of even more wealth.

Notwithstanding the legends of souls who have lived for thousands of years, or maybe forever – it is commonly understood that the every human being is going to pass on one day. There is the distinct probability that the human body will get tired and wear out. One of human's greatest fears is the Fear of Death. It's not as if death is something new! It's not as if no one has been anxious about this ultimate voyage; this greatest voyage into the unknown.

In my practice, I have seen time and again, that the fear of death, and hence the fear of the unknown, is the underpinning for every other fear, anxiety and psychological disorder ever known to humankind. It is treated as an irrevocable testament, an acknowledgment that we truly are separate from G-d, and that one day our very existence will simply cease. It is the principal reason for the endemic restlessness so pervasive in modern, civilized society. Its counterpart, but also diametrical opposite, is the desire for life; but not just life: youth, passion, and material abundance. Little heed goes to the myriad spiritual masters who have told us over the millennia that we have everything already; all we have to do is let go of the trauma inherent in daily living, and receive what is already ours. By this time in our collective evolution, it is apparent that many, if not most, of the human race enjoys the little dramas in which it is involved, and would fight to the death to avoid being relieved of them.

The Angels' Haven was in a different part of town. The fog had dissipated – which was a little disappointing. I enjoy the otherworldliness, the escape – albeit it temporary – from the regular world of routines and schedules. Routines and schedules. Little boxes which ensure that you never really look inside to determine who you are or what is your real purpose for being here. Often the routines are the least expensive method of pain avoidance. Until the deathbed, one need not deal with any of the real issues – if at all.

As I drive along the freeway, the streetlights in the distance form an entrancing parallel pattern. Are they leading towards or away? Pattern of lights. Figurative. Symbolic?

I remember meeting Ponti when he started as the assistant curator at the Hall of Antiquities—I always liked the name "Hall of Antiquities." It added some European charm to the establishment. We also shared an interest in ancient cultures and the spiritual. I met him professionally over the years. His personal business is none of yours, so I won't disclose anything here. As a favor, from time-to-time he would allow me into the Hall, open some of the cases, and actually touch some of the artifacts. Not the atmosphere-sensitive ones, but some truly rare Egyptian scarabs, a Roman breastplate and helmet, and artifacts from the Temple of Delphi in ancient Greece.

As many will agree, artifacts retain the "energy signature" of their owners. I have known people who can feel an object and know where it has been in the immediate or the deep past. I have been told that some felt like they were in the hands of very reputable and sincere people. Others felt as if they were owned and used by scoundrels. Nothing has changed over the millennia; only the centers of political power.

As a young child I was so sure the ancients knew secrets we cannot even fathom today. I wanted to know them. I felt that studying ancient history would give me the answers. It was interesting and intriguing, but the secret of secrets was not imparted to me. There were as many mystery schools in the ancient world as there are societies, cults and self-help programs today.

Ponti was daring and innovative. He had some interesting and controversial approaches to otherwise routine exhibits. The controversy made me think that the headline "Missing. Foul Play Believed" was a good conjecture.

Shortly after he became chief curator of the Hall of Antiquities, he announced his intention to arrange an exhibit with artifacts not only from the great museums of the world, but also from certain archeological expeditions whose integrity could not be confirmed. It was also rumored that certain prehistoric pieces among the exhibits, from undisclosed locations, might shake up modern notions of the backward and unsophisticated nature of early peoples. They might even be from civilizations never conclusively proven to even have existed, such as Atlantis, Lemuria, and Prehistoric Central Asia. Civilizations that might date back hundreds of thousands or millions of years. Our recorded history only goes back seven thousand years. The press was quick to quote an "undisclosed source" about the exhibit; but, it quickly became sensationalized when this "undisclosed source" indicated that the emphasis was going to be on the spiritual and metaphysical beliefs of these early civilizations – not on the artistic achievements, or even the material comforts or technical knowledge they enjoyed.

The Board of Trustees made it clear that the end result of the exhibit had to be respectable, notwithstanding the sensational approach to its advertising. The artifacts which Ponti disclosed to the Board were reviewed and scrutinized. Ponti was given the okay. Secretly the Board was delighted in the publicity. It would assure a monumental sale of tickets, especially on the first day.

Ponti was no stranger to publicity, and always promoted it. He would neither confirm nor deny the rumors. He knew the mystery posed by the press was the best leverage he could buy, and being for free, it couldn't have come at a better price!

The exhibit was to open in two weeks. It had been years in the planning and Ponti Moon had been the central force behind it. He worked tirelessly to create and maintain a driving impetus in his circle. "Circle" is used pretty broadly here. All the components knew that no one other than Ponti really knew the whole picture, or the details behind the controversial exhibits. Enough of the possible sensational exhibits were downplayed to ensure that the Board of Trustees of the Hall would be satisfied that this was an organized exhibit of reputable merit. But, the complacent silence promoted by the Board was more for marketing rather than for a cover-up. So, this became somewhat of a double blind experiment with the possibility of the Board being the most duped. It must have worked. Rumors and expectations were running unbridled. Whatever expeditions or discoveries were the source of the new artifacts were still a rumor. To keep this lid on, some people must have been paid very well.

The staff at the Hall was exceptionally well-trained each in its own aspect of the exhibit. All the known arrangements had been catalogued in such minute detail that the exhibit catalogue read like a code of civil law. But, as it was now becoming more apparent, there was an undisclosed portion of the exhibit which had been done entirely in secret by Ponti. The Trustees only discovered a part of this at the last minute when an aide reported uncatalogued boxes which had been placed deep in the storage area. After sequestering the ones he wanted to hide, Ponti showed them the artifacts and assured them of their repute, even though some had never been seen in any museum before.

It was too late to seek the counsel of noted authorities; and, by a majority vote, the Board voted to let the sequestered artifacts be seen. They reasoned they would be on the cutting edge if everything went alright, and could claim they were duped if it didn't. It certainly seemed to be a win/win for the Board.

Ponti and I met by chance several years ago in a small bookshop off of Pearl Street. Small, eclectic and noteworthy for carrying spiritual and occult works not stocked by the larger bookstores.

I recognized him from pictures I had seen in the newspapers. As we were milling around the shop we struck up a conversation about the knowledge of the ancients, and the real meaning behind their art. I admired him because he was always willing to take a risk. His exhibits delved deeper than most. The Board of Trustees knew only too well the advantage of having just enough intrigue to fuel ticket sales, but not enough to engender organized criticism from public authorities and other funding sources. Privately, funders were also delighted with enough subtle controversy to make their investments profitable. Ponti knew how to capitalize on the greed of some of his backers and the altruism of others.

I enjoyed discussing spiritual practices from yesterday and today and the use of intuition in daily life. I told him of my love for ancient art and history. I complimented him on his exhibits, especially the study correlating the Mayan and Egyptian pyramids. This exhibit was in conjunction with an anniversary of Thor Heyerdahl's successful trans-Atlantic voyage in the "Sun-Ra," a replica of an Egyptian thatched reed boat. It has been speculated that the Egyptians used such boats to cross the Atlantic at a very early date.

After we talked for a while he revealed that this was but the first of many exhibits he hoped to present on the "metaphysical" inclinations of the ancient peoples. I was a little stunned that he was sharing this with me; a perfect stranger. He must have seen me as a kindred spirit, or at least someone he could trust. I treated it as any other confidence ever given to me. All the other confidences he shared with me professionally, of course, are just that: confidential.

Over the years, we met for coffee many times. I became a confidante and "sounding board." People often remarked that we looked alike. Like brothers.

He kept abreast of the major ramblings and rumblings in the museum circuit. He also had connections with many dealers in artifacts whose reputations were not stellar. Recently he told me that there were rumors from an "undisclosed source" that certain unique amulets and other spiritual objects had been discovered and were being stored somewhere. He did not say what or where. The inscriptions were apparently unique as were the characters used to write them. The only letter that was recognizable, after a microscopic examination, was the Hebrew letter Aleph א, the first letter of the Hebrew alphabet. All the other letters or symbols were seemingly "dancing" around this letter. Images for light beams cascaded from the א out beyond the other letters and encased them. He could not divulge where they were found or whether they even resembled ancient Hebrew or any other ancient language at all. All he could tell me was that from the initial attempts to decipher them, they may have had something to do with the spiritual origin of man. I was brimming with excitement. How startling! Cautioning me that what he was telling me was in the strictest of confidence, he said that they may have been involved in some way in some sort of reincarnation or transmigration of a pre-Abrahamic people. He could not tell me how he knew this, nor could he disclose their age. All he could say is that they predated artifacts from the historical era by more millennia than most could fathom.

To this day, I do not know if, in fact, they exist at all. Nor do I know how Ponti came upon this knowledge. If he was successful in acquiring them, I could only presume that the upcoming exhibit was to be their unveiling. But, I thought, what good was it to unveil yet more artifacts of the ancient world without a testament to their experiential value. There are hundreds of thousands, many millions of books written over the millennia with the secrets of this or that. When the experience is sought, little, if anything is experienced. No. I knew that the mere unveiling of a hard object had to be just the tip of the iceberg.

After seven years, Ponti Moon left a legacy in the museum world. He quickly learned the political and bureaucratic ropes in arranging loans of artifacts from the great museums around the world.

Exhibits started with rather routine loans of coins, vases, statues, and jewelry. They gradually grew to an exhibition of some of King Ashurbanipal's Nimrod Palace gates and other monumental artifacts and wonders. Regardless of the notoriety he garnered, I knew he wanted more; something beyond the exhibition of the mere physical.

In expectation of even greater successes, the museum trustees approved of a massive reconstruction of the museum. The job was undertaken and completed with public and private funds. The work transformed an urban-blighted replica of the Greek Parthenon into a stunning tribute to a rejuvenated inner city area.

If I were ever asked to describe him, I would say that he was obsessed with antiquities. He often said that the study of the past was a critical step in discovering man's primordial past, which he felt was steeped in spiritualism. We agreed on this. He also believed that the ancients easily and naturally could project themselves from one reality to another as easily as we change clothes.

The new exhibit was to be the maxim of his life's work. His exhibits were really a veiled cover-up to explore the very source of creation, as if this was once known and is now lost. Not the mere attempt to manifest things in this physical reality, but to merge with the very creative power itself of the Universe. What some seek through religion or secret societies, Ponti Moon was trying to do through antiquities.

And, if he was right, what then? And why was he so intent to go public with it? One would think that given the dimensions of the discovery, it should not fall into the wrong hands.

There was something really important that he was not or could not tell me, even in the strictest of confidence; perhaps to safeguard me! But, to see someone in the conservative establishment advocating it was both entertaining and invigorating. You always need some eccentric blood to spice up an old house. Religions and political organizations, however, like all living organisms, will go to any length to survive. This usually means to avoid change. The ultimate fear of death is inherent in each and every life form.

It seemed as if he were poised at the actual entry into a system so powerful that its existence and use may have been intentionally hidden for untold millennia. Allegories were not for him. The direct truth was his goal.

He also argued that this exhibit was not different than any other previously shown at the museum. While his approach may have been different, he argued that in the ancient world "religion" was interfused with every aspect of life. He bypassed discussions about the possibility of the art form being carved into a chondrite, a form of meteorite, as this had already been mentioned in one of the unauthorized "disclosures." And what of the symbol?

The spirituality of the ancients was displayed in what we today call "art." But, he argued, their religion was not merely a worship of hybrid human-animal forms conveniently classified in a neat and organized pantheon. It was an intended spiritual exercise designed to maintain contact with spirits they thought resided in higher astral planes, and who helped mold human events. Hence, in order to try to represent the work which was being displayed, he felt it was also necessary to give the viewing public a glimpse of the ideas and the spirit, if not the very experience, behind the creation of the work. To this extent, he offered to exhibit mostly well-known pieces, albeit with a different focus, along with some lesser known pieces of "some interest in the field." At least publically, he asserted that they would be offered in the spirit of artistic and archeological inquiry only.

After several years of arguing, cajoling, politicking and assaults on his position, Ponti finally prevailed. He then began the complicated and painstakingly bureaucratic process of arranging loans from the British Museum and other major sources of antiquities. But, he did have a plan in mind. He was intending to piece something together from the pieces which were being loaned and from the other pieces to which he had access. In many respects, he had ceased to operate as a curator, and was acting more as a visionary archeologist or anthropologist on a mission. His mission being entirely different than one in the classical field of archeology, and more akin to the concretizing of a theological theory: that there is more than just a spiritual basis for our existence; that we are the very gods of myth and legend, and behind this, we are the Creator itself in a glorious masquerade.

If there was any otherworldly aspect intended for the exhibit, it was never entirely clear how Ponti was intending to substantiate his claims. How does a limited being prove the unlimited? The very question breaks the bank, so to speak. It didn't stop the question from being asked on many occasions, however. Was he going to put forth an archeological exposition which would serve the entire community, or channel his efforts in a display of paranormal claims which would only serve a few? Perhaps I should not call them "claims." For purposes of the exhibit, he knew well enough that they could only be "suggestions."

In any respect, virtually no evidence exists today which describes psychic experiences supposedly exhibited in the ancient world; unless, of course you are into allegory. The Books of Daniel and Ezekiel are high on the list. But there is always someone with another explanation; a "normal" explanation. There is always someone who will give a "weather balloon" explanation with respect to a UFO sighting, be it ancient or modern. As many have said, we are limited beings and our consciousness begins from and ends at a limited perspective. How then can we, without training, intuition and foresight, see beyond what we can say with certainty, is all there is?

Anyway, as far as proof goes, Ponti used to say that if you believed in psychic phenomena, no explanation was necessary. If you did not, none was possible. But this did not stop him from trying.

As expected, the mood surrounding the exhibit remained sensational; stirred, no doubt, by Ponti's love of using the media for his own purposes. In fact, the mood resembled a proverbial "Roman Circus." A reputation was either going to be made or broken here.

Now his "disappearance." All of my senses said this was not correct. He was "here" and I knew it! I was going to find him. Well, in a manner of speaking. I may have meant it theoretically, but practically? That is a different story.

Already the papers were insinuating that the forces which criticized Ponti's project from the beginning were trying to delay and, if possible, cancel it. Rumors were circulating that Ponti's disappearance was intentional; the consequence of making inquiries into areas better left untouched.

I was supposed to meet him on Sunday, two days before the opening of the exhibit. He had something to give me and could not tell me about it on the phone.

And what of the primary exhibits he wanted to exhibit. The rumored amulets, the Aleph א symbol, supposedly produced before the so-called "dawn of civilization," perhaps intimating a highly advanced and spiritually adept society long before the dynastic periods of ancient Egypt and Mesopotamia; perhaps hundreds of thousands or millions of years old.

He had a message, what was it?

III

My car is like me, it is a little finicky in moisture. After I got her going, I drove about a half-mile to Chagrin Boulevard. The fog was almost completely cleared. The air had a crisp coolness to it. Fresh. Invigorating. The feeling of having passed through the great unknown to the other side. Neon signs in the evening now assumed the role of the Sun; each one uttering a luminous command or entreaty. On Chagrin Boulevard, they were evident to the horizon.

The "Angels' Haven" was next to a bakery in a comparatively new strip shopping center. It was also ironically located near a Laundromat. The bakery stayed open late on Wednesdays and Fridays to accommodate the munchy crowd. It did a thriving business. The laundry no doubt provided the backdrop for the exchange and eventual laundering of more drug money than city counselors, the police department, and the D.A.'s office cared to think about. But, it was only one of many; enforcement was next to impossible, and there were certainly bigger headaches to deal with in the city.

From what I was told, the Angels' Haven is not what you would call one of your trendiest discos. But, it was not a downtown sleazy slum bar either. A shiny heavy metal door announced to the world its predilection for the less refined, almost "Devil worshiping" aspects of rock n' roll. I always say a prayer when I go by a place like this. Between the alcohol, drugs and sexual overtures, all of these places eventually take on the aura of Sodom and Gomorrah. I wondered how many low spirits who have departed life, but not this realm, were waiting to attach to unsuspecting "patrons." Low spirits wait for patrons on whose energy they can feed like parasites. Places like this provide the perfect opportunity. I chuckled over the name, Angel's Haven. Haven for what?

I parked. My client knew my car. I saw him as he came into the parking lot, parked and walked to the door. For a moment, he hesitated. "Good," I thought. I knew from this that he would be more circumspect. If it was intended to be an invitation for me to accompany him, I stayed put and declined. Many masters have said, in their own way, to avoid people and places such as this.

He came out about 15 minutes later. Thankfully he came out under his own volition and not accompanied by a beefy bouncer.

"So how did it go?" I asked.

"As expected," when he could finally vocalize.

"So why did you do it?"

"So you could see me when I'm really in pain."

"You don't look in pain," I said almost sarcastically. "You look frozen. Take a breath for heaven's sake!"

He did and then just began to talk. I didn't interrupt and just let him go on.

"I thought more than once about not going in," he said almost dreamily, as if he was peering into a mental recording, "but my curiosity and jealousy got the better of me." He paused for a few seconds and then continued. "I opened the door and felt like I was walking into a movie theater that was pitch black and with nothing on the screen. I felt really old and stupid for being here in the first place. I almost left again, but figured I came this far, I might as well see it through. So, taking real short baby steps I took a few steps inside. I knew it was going to take a few minutes for my eyes to adjust to the subterranean darkness so I just tried to stay out of everybody's way. I was uncomfortable to begin with, and this situation didn't make me feel any better. Then I wondered what the hell she was doing here, and I really started to get pissed off."

"I felt like I was in a battle zone. Even if I wasn't going to come out alive, I sure wasn't going to go down easily. This really started to get my blood boiling!!!" he said with a tight jaw literally frozen in space and with beady, eclipsed eyes.

"Breathe," I commanded. "You look like you're going to implode. Breathe, dammit!" I said. Being in this close proximity to an emerging Neanderthal can be frightening and sobering.

When his chest muscles started working again, he started talking. "The music was loud enough so that I couldn't think. Thinking was no competition against the loud, pounding bass and the nether-worldliness of the synthesizers. I was just standing there almost dumbfounded. The boom-boom literally pounded all of the sense out of me. I actually saw people talking to each other. How in the world are they doing that, I wondered? Anyway, my job was to look – only to look," he said with middle age angst. "My vision was hampered by the clouds of cigarette smoke, and my senses were being assaulted by the sweet, acrid smell of contraband. The place was so packed that people were just burning each other's clothes with cigarettes."

"I didn't see her. After I got my bearings, I started to walk around. It was a big place. There was a large inner area reserved for dancing. The perimeters were elevated and had small round cocktail tables and two long bar sections."

I could tell he was really getting into this. Giving detail meant he was a witness and at least an amateur investigator, and not just a jealous husband. I didn't interrupt. He continued, "The dance area was large and circular, with a mirror ball beaming polka dot spots on the people below. The dance floor was brimming with people. A lot of motion. It was hard to pin-point anyone in particular." He then said with a sly smile, that "waitresses in tight aquamarine body tops and snug skirts of the same color were parleying around the area like butterflies flitting from table to table."

"As I looked around, I noticed that at least half of the people there were 'white collar' from their early 20s to middle age. They were still in their work clothes so I didn't feel too out of place by how I was dressed." Then, he paused and a calm, analytical look was coming over his face. "Anyway," he said calmly, if not stoically, "I was looking for Penny Matron. But, then again, everyone there was looking for a nameless someone. You could tell, too," he said almost dreamily, and with passion, insight and sadness, "that everyone was also waiting to be found."

"A woman standing near me was yelling 'Dollar; need a dollar to buy my friend a drink.' She was wearing outdated disco jewelry with bulky gold glitter stars, tight jeans and a dungaree jacket. The guy she was with looked young and embarrassed. Apparently, he hadn't begun drinking yet," he said with his first laugh. "The guy was turning away in order to stroll on. She obviously did not know him. She grabbed his arm, pulled him close, and slobbered something in his ear. This apparently coaxed him to stay." Now he was starting to sound like a tour guide. "She had found a 'friend' whose name she would never learn, or at least not remember in the early a.m. hours when he got up to leave. I had found the 'Angels' Haven.' The only angelic thing about it was the glittering dust which was readily filtered throughout the crowd."

With an almost professorial air, he added, "commerce in the human marketplace can sometimes flow on rank generalities." I think he was finally getting the point.

I just let him go on. Instead of a brief summary of betrayal and proof, he continued on with a kind of travelogue description.

"The bell rang. The bartender got another tip. The crowd cheered. People walking, bumper-to-bumper; flesh against flesh."

"'Comfort on the rocks,' I said to the bartender when he finally looked in my direction. Now that he had gotten to the part of getting his liquid courage," I could tell he was really going to get into descriptive adjectives. He continued. "I could continue to bump and shift through the dark, fuming innards of the bar looking for my Penny Matron. Maybe I would not even recognize her, I thought. This was her play time. Fantasy puts a new face on people."

I sat and waited for him to continue. "Disbursed among the crowd were various 'air pockets;' no-man's land, so to speak, for crossing over to the other side. In this case, the other side of the crowd. Crossing over, I got a glimpse of someone who looked like my Penny. I did not want to get too close, so just looked as best as I could. The profile seemed to fit. Long nose, smallish round eyes, and fleshy cheeks. The brunette hair had been blow dried ad infinitum." Then he stopped, took a breath, exhaled, and continued. "Her beau," he said sheepishly, "could not have been over 21; barely old enough to legally drink. He was facing Penny and had his right arm around her waist. His left hand was conveniently placed just below her right breast. He was young. So was the night. It was then that my blood began to really boil and I thought I was going to lose my cool. Thankfully I took a few deep breaths and caught myself. I summoned all sense of courage and fortitude, and left."

In retrospect, he said "It was a miracle that I was able to restrain myself. Frankly, I did not know what was keeping the young beau restrained. It was obvious that there was no moment of daring that the young one was going to have to wage in his encounter with Penny Matron tonight," he said with a sigh. "I would have said 'my' Penny, but I think that is in the past now," he said ruefully.

"I had seen enough. I never really got over feeling like a 'Peeping Tom,' but it was frankly hard not to notice many other people looking at them."

We talked in my car for a few minutes. I wanted to make sure he was okay to drive. We decided to meet for coffee at a quiet diner. We had a private booth in the back where we could talk. Not the best venue, but the only one available right now.

Sullen, but composed, he told me how he felt. Like a fallen warrior whose better days were behind him, he resigned himself to realities of what he had seen and experienced. That was the best session we ever had.

For the first time in his life, he allowed himself to really feel the pain. All the pain behind the competitiveness, jealousy, control, manipulation, anger and rage. All without going through the throes of logical explanation, I introduced him to the powerhouse of emotion he had been storing for as long as he had been alive, and possibly longer. Without doing more, I had him just feel it; just stay with it – not try to understand it; not try to suppress it; not try to express it. Just witness it – and let it go. Just be with it. And, he did. Like the pressure cooker whose lid was loosened, it just let it out – without design or manipulation.

After about 15 minutes I saw new life come to his face. Like the torment which had been driving him for so long just dissipated and left – leaving him feeling like a new man.

He looked at me, smiled, thanked me, and left.

I wasn't sure if I should have called the police. Either he had dissipated the fuel which was mercilessly driving him, or he had the mental acuity to premeditate his next move. The latter might not be good for Penny or her beau. I decided to take a chance on his recovery.

I finished my coffee and left. A soft breeze began to blow when I started to walk back to my car after picking up some groceries. Very unusual that so soon after a fog the air would be this soft and comfortable. It was this kind of romantic breeze that slides around and against you like silk. It also had a sweet aroma that I just couldn't pinpoint. The combination stops you in mid-thought and takes you away. It happens so quickly that you do not resist. It doesn't matter whether your destination is reality, memory or fantasy.

IV

From the elevated extensions of the freeway, the great cosmopolis lays beneath me. The conglomeration of lights shimmer like a polished jewel in the night; a prized possession for some; an arena of unrequited torment for others. From a distance, a city surrounded by a sense of quietude and peace; but the peace is only an illusion created by distance. During the day, the city offers little peace. It offers only exposure. It compresses all in its wake in categories and containers. We make of it what we will.

This modern behemoth is composed of hundreds, thousands of neighborhoods, like cells of some primordial beast yet to evolve, but growing by continuous division. Spirited by commerce, countless buildings have arisen to create a new horizon. A new and different pedestal to the stars.

On my way home, I remembered that Kathryn and I were meeting for a late dinner.

It is around nine and I parked in the first available space. I then walked a block up to Stilborn Avenue to go into a familiar late-night restaurant named "Korsky's."

"Hi, Jack," I said to the night manager, and owner for that matter. Jack Korsky insists on working the 9 p.m. to 4 a.m. shift. His customers are his life and in this respect, his life is quite picturesque. He has that hard and withered look acquired by his voluntary imprisonment in his business. Short, stocky, impatient, but with a quick wit and a full smile; there was always a cigarette within reach. He had that singular sense of charm that all night proprietors must possess for the after-midnight crowd.

Korsky's was not a casual place. You had to be appropriately attired; a blue blazer at the least. Jack, of course, had his maître de tux, properly pressed.

As I walked through the entrance, I heard "Michael!" from behind me. It was soft, but assertive. Startled, I turned around. No one was there. In fact, it had become so completely quiet that it seemed like G-d had muted the sound function of the Universe. It was then that I again smelled an aroma I have never smelled before. An aroma which made me come alive, as if in an instant!

I turned around. It took a few moments to realize that I was staring right into Jack Korsky's eyes, which – I finally noticed – had become very wide. The "here and now" can take a different meaning when you are on a reverie. Jack was literally holding his breath. When I acknowledged him, he seemed to give a sigh of relief and got directly down to business.

"Hello Mr. Cushner. A table or are you just going to sit by the bar?"

"Kathryn is meeting me here. I take it she has not arrived yet. Any window table that's open will be fine," I replied, looking around to see if I could see any familiar faces.

"Certainly," he replied gutturally. "Follow me, please."

I am not sure if he smoked the cigarettes, or after all these years they were smoking him.

"Have you seen Kathryn?" I asked. We are having a late dinner.

"No, but I will tell her where you are when I do see her."

We took a meandering route through the crowded mid-section of the restaurant and finally arrived at my table. I was tired and felt like it had been a long journey. I had a ground level view of State Street and Luciani's Liquor Store. "Please let Kathryn know where I am when she arrives," I asked. He characteristically replied, "Certainly" with a crisp bow, and went on his way.

I sat staring out the window and slowly slipped into a state of being quiet and mesmerized. I was thinking of the Angels' Haven and its aftermath and happy for my friend and client. Breakthroughs are always happy times for clients and therapists alike. It is what makes it all worthwhile, I thought, hoping he did not backtrack to confront his wife's beau.

At moments like this, I can hear myself think. I can even talk to myself. But, what is funny is that when I talk to myself, I do not always hear my voice talking back to me. Sometimes it is the voice of someone I have never met. I hope to meet the voice one day. Some of the things it tells me seem so foreign; others like they are coming from a higher form of me, one that knows more and sees the big picture. This is the one I want to talk to. Sometimes, it is the other one. This other one knows very little about beauty.

All of us have thoughts going on all the time. Tireless, boundless conversations that seem to go on regardless of our presence or attention. We just seem to focus on them from time to time and hear bits and pieces of some epic story, or drama, in which we are playing the host or the victim, but are not always a participant. I often wondered what my life would be like without this relentless stream of thoughts, words and related pictures and feelings pulsing through my body and mind. How calm, uncomplicated and peaceful it would be.

How easy it was to then focus on Ponti's disappearance and the upcoming exhibit. Did the Aleph amulet truly exist? If so, why was it not heralded as the major discovery of the millennium?

In Kabbalah, the book of Jewish mysticism, it is often said that the letters of the Hebrew alphabet are not just letters, but representations of energy; the energy of creation. He who knows the secret can literally create something from nothing. But, the caveat is that it must be used for the greater good of all, rather than for selfish acquisition.

Kabalistic masters would recommend that with the proper guidance, one could meditate on the letters of the Aleph-Beit and receive information not obtainable from any other source. In other words, one would be communicating directly with the spiritual forces which may be in this realm, but are far beyond it. In Kabbalistic theory, higher forces can descend to participate in this world; but, the lower forces of this world must shed their limitations in order to ascend. But, the irony is that the movement of ascension could only happen in utter stillness and calmness. And in the stillness, the masters said, miracles are created.

Was there an amulet? Did its inscriptions have anything to do with transcendence? Was Ponti aware of this?

The voice then started talking to me, unconcerned about my little reverie, or maybe in spite of it. But, this time, I did not pay it any mind. I knew there was something deeper going on here. I just didn't know where to start. And, I knew I could not figure it out just by thinking about it.

But, just looking out the window without being interrupted put me very still. I felt something touch me on the shoulder, and a tingle thundered up my spine. It made me shiver. I slightly turned. No one was there – at least that I could see.

While in deep thought and repose, I thought of the great masters of many traditions. Each in his or her own way instructed that you could actually experience eternal life when the energy flowed through your body without hindrance. Each said that the unrestricted flow of the life force is the flow of Love. Eternal Life is the display of Love. Any restriction, regardless of the reason, creates a blockage. A blockage creates a past and future and a deep desire either for something or to avoid something. The choice was mine, and in each and every moment, there was always a choice. Either eternal life in the experience of Love, or the pain of temporal life with no permanent benefits whatsoever. Or, in the most common experience where no choice was made, life would just seem to happen.

All the philosophies, the psychologies, the systems, the dogmas, all boil down to one standard, and only one: Think Good. Do Good, and in the process, be kind to yourself and others. Then you will live a wonderful life. How many people do you suppose are actually kind to themselves on even a sporadic basis? I thought of Kathryn and my heart opened wider than ever before. I then thought of my friend Ponti Moon. Again, I ruminated that I was going to find him even though I really had no idea what this meant.

I remembered Ponti talking briefly about the Aleph sign on the amulet. He seemed to become more and more vacant when I told him that the Aleph is the first letter of the Hebrew alphabet and that it represents the formless primordial taking form in the creation epic. It stands for the creation of the universe. Everything begins in the Aleph. Literally, something from the vast Nothing. One of the names of G-d in the Torah – the Five Books of Moses – was Elohim. The source of all that is. Elohim begins with the letter Aleph. In Jewish cosmology, the Aleph energy exists even before the beginning. The source of all miracles in our realm. Genesis 1:3 puts it very succinctly, "God said 'Let there be light, and there was light.'"

In my mental vacancy, I did not realize that Kathryn had been sitting at the table, waiting ever so patiently. She was kind enough not to jolt me while I was on my little reveries; or maybe she did- something made me shiver? Apparently from the look on my face, she decided to remain quiet until I came out of it. She moved her chair close to mine and briefly laid her head on my shoulder affectionately. "Where were you just now? You were so far away."

"Just thinking. Troubled about Ponti. It doesn't feel right. I don't think he is missing. I think he has been abducted or is stuck somewhere and can't get out. Someone must have thought he was dangerous for some reason. "

"It does seem odd and unusual. But, who would really want to do something so outrageous over an art exhibit?"

"Someone who may have felt extremely threatened by the message behind the exhibit, whatever that is. The age-old story of maintaining control. This is a perfect example of the difference between the expansive feeling of the unrestricted flow of love in an ever broadening universe, or the constricted packaged feeling of slavery."

Kathryn and I had a light dinner, and talked for a while. The softness of her voice and her gentle touch helped to soften the hard edge of recent events. That ended when Jack, in his usual perfunctory way, brought the check. We loved him just the same.

V

Life can be a wondrous adventure, full of ... well, life!

Life can also be a crucible and it is easy to get hardened if you are not careful. At one time or another, we all think we've become adept at hurdling the obstacles modern society imposes. In reality, all we do is suppress fear and anger, and get on as best we can. Society has structured immediately replaceable personalities, so that on the expiration of one viable entity, a replacement can be fitted very quickly. Society insists on standardization. Power depends upon it.

In this process of refinement, many are led to believe that they no longer need, want, or can afford human affection. This exterior is usually easy to pierce. Often, even the receipt of one act of genuine kindness, however, burns that exterior away faster than tissue paper over an open flame. No matter what kind of a relationship you are in, if the elements of kindness and compassion are non-existent, or are covered up by other personality traits, it is time to leave. But, the key is for you to be able and willing to actually receive the kindness which comes your way.

Life does not have to be a complicated process. With little more than a positive belief or intention, and a willingness to receive only the goodness of life, one can be a magnet for immense goodness. Life, the process of creation as experienced by us in this dream of G-d, is waiting for the opportunity to give us what we need.

Kathryn is the kindest person I have ever met. Being with her is like being in the well of unconditional love.

When we got home from Korsky's, we sipped a glass of wine and talked, laughed, joked, and became really giddy. Kathryn and I would frequently have a drink late at night when the rest of the world was asleep. It was our time; the time to give free rein to our souls.

She has thick, dark hair and light green eyes. Her face is heart-shaped, gently narrowing at the chin. Her skin is olive-toned and her smile is genuine and unblemished. The spark of touching sentimentality glistens in her eyes. Her smile would ignite the stars in her eyes, making her absolutely alluring.

"Sailor" was her pet name for me. I guess it was her way of adding a little comedy to my mental voyages. "If you ever learn how to go back and forth in time, I may never see you again," she said in a kidding tone of voice.

We were talking, and the classical radio station was softly playing in the background. Then, apparently, suddenly, I stopped – completely arrested by some music, a waltz. It was not that it was just beautiful – hauntingly beautiful – it was, and so much more! It was turning, and I was turning with it. The music was both telling a story and leading me on a buoyant journey. It was telling me something. In an uplifted state of mind, and receptivity, it was telling me something I could not have heard before. It was saying that the seemingly disconnected pieces were actually connected in a beautiful and elaborate pattern; that everything was alright; I had nothing to worry about, that everything was working together very nicely; and, that this combination of events was more than a coincidence.

Although I had listened to classical music for many years, I had never heard this before; or, if I had heard it, I never heard it like this.

It took me. It swept me. Perhaps it was the time of night, the lack of sleep – but tears began to gel in my eyes. It was as if I were confronting some deep-seated memories let loose by this winsome rhapsody. I didn't know what or when.

I listened intently when the piece stopped. In fact, everything had stopped. I even forgot I was not alone. The gentle softness of late-night classical radio hosts can also be hypnotic and soothing.

It was Dvorak's "Serenade in E Major," the announcer said as if gently birthing me into a distant reality. Then, as Kathryn must have seen color returning to my cheeks, she looked at me and said, "Are you okay? One minute we were talking, and having a very enjoyable time; the next, you were off in an alternate reality. You do sometimes take mid-sentence vacations?" she said kiddingly.

It was the soft time of night. Ravel's Pavanne was playing. Life is a dream when it drifts.

I had a difficult dream that night. I was in a tunnel and could not get out. Maybe it was a dark, sinister forest; I was not sure. There was enough light to see contours, boundaries and barriers, but no openings. I wasn't trapped because I could keep moving, but I couldn't get out. There was just enough movement to keep from going into panic, but not enough to feel relief. I was alive, but was living in a bag of uncertainty and anxiety. My breathing was shallow and quick. I was afraid of something really horrible. I just didn't know what it was. But – it felt almost natural – like the way things are normally.

I awoke with a quick start at 4:00 a.m. My T-shirt was soaked and I was disoriented. It took a minute to recognize my surroundings. I laid there hoping that by not getting up, I would drift off again.

I remember a little. Something about this beautiful tower; brilliant to the sight. The image of a person was inside. I could not tell whether it was a man or woman because the image changed. Sometimes like a man, sometimes like a woman.

I fell back to sleep and woke up at 6:30 feeling relatively well rested. I could not remember anything other than snippets of the dream, but enough of it to feel chills running up and down my back. I saw Kathryn and felt safe.

The newspapers still spouted the news about Ponti Moon, as well as the wide meandering of suspicions, all of which were based on conjecture. Even Petey, who has seen everything, looked worried. He has a good sense about him.

Some people live in the shadows as if they were living in the light. They accept the deep, dark crevices as if they are the universal boundaries of life. They act accordingly, only learning too late, if at all, that their entire lives were just minimalist lies. Yet, deep within even them, is a spark which they resist, since it will upset the futile norm which they have come to accept, nourish, and even love. In this downward spiral are the dramas perpetrated in this realm we call home. And, even if we sometimes recognize this fictional drama, they have become so habituated to it, that it is difficult, if not impossible, to vaporize. Vaporizing will evaporate all the delicious little dramas they feed on and feel are filling their lives with substance. That substance is real and palpable. It is called poison.

We have been told, again and again, by beings we consider superior and otherworldly, that love is all there is, that it is the answer; the alpha and omega. Yet, the overwhelming majority of people nourish the clutching which comes from fear, worry, anger and hate; and fight to the bitter end to protect this identity.

What would it take to correct this? Haven't there been enough blessed, blissful beings who have tried to point the way with the light of consciousness? What does it take to wake up in the morning and not filter into the world of anxiety? It takes an opening. A space. Once open, it takes an intention and a choice. Then, it takes little more than being watchful and persistent. A constant journey between the sacred and the profane.

There is something very pressing in my thoughts, but I do not know what it is. Something is trying to get my attention.

Late one evening, Kathryn and I moved some pillows to the floor in our living room. Her back was up against the couch. I leaned against her and laid my head beside her cheek. Even after all these years, our most effective communication is silent and knowing.

Whatever made us do this, I do not know, but almost instinctively we moved so that our backs were pressed together, and we – almost like bookends – sat balancing each other. We did not say a word. We sat, breathing until our breathing reached a resonance and we were breathing the same breath, together. In this stillness, in this silence, was one of the deepest, most heartfelt conversations I ever have had with her. Not a word was spoken, but it seemed to stir on forever. It was almost as if, we were in this silent conversation, this universal conversation, without language, without beginning or end; a continuous, eternal conversation, and we have just became attuned to it and immersed in it.

There were no pretensions, no goals, no need to explain. Just clear understanding.

After a while, I came "awake" enough to realize that with my eyes closed, I had absolutely no sense of my body. I simply felt like a mass of passing thoughts and feelings. I also felt the stirring of a feeling I would have to call true Love. It was not about me. In fact, it had nothing to do with me. I was neither a victor, nor a recipient of any worldly goods; just a passageway for the flow of whatever it was that was flowing through me. In this place, I had no hope, nor desires.

And then, slowly opening my eyes, I became more awake. I then realized that I had not been thinking. And, this is why I felt so grand!

This was one of the most powerful realizations I have experienced. We are so trained to be the director of and container for thoughts and feelings, that when they are radiated back, we think they are, indeed, real. So powerful is this belief that untold billions have lived in both fear and desire of thoughts and feelings.

Then we both moved and started breathing on our own.

What was this? Was this real? What is real? Was it some momentary interim between reality and unreality? Like being in some dream that is only happening in your imagination. Yet, living in this interim is living against the bare bone; sometimes a carnival, bidding farewell to the flesh; sometimes the deadly doldrums, being surrounded by water, thick, anesthetic and heavy, with no wind, movement or relief in sight. Life can be so fragmented; so delicate. An inaccurate word, an awkward glance, a misplaced gesture – and an otherwise workable day becomes transformed into a desire to leave this planet, this realm, once and for all. All people want – all they really want – is to be nurtured, and to forget the emotional pain and trauma of daily life. The pain is continuous. Anything that makes them forget, even for a moment, is sought after and coveted. Sex, shopping, drugs, all anesthetics.

I once had aspirations of being an artist and spent several years studying and practicing portraiture. It was a good excuse for looking at faces.

The study taught me how ephemeral beauty is. Take a homely person; slightly change the curve of the mouth, the width of the nose, or the angle of the cheek bones and an indescribable face of beauty is looking back at you.

My Uncle, Shmuel (Yiddish for Samuel) Izzy Kominsky, was affectionately known as the "Duke" by all who knew and loved him. He liked to think of himself as a prophet, a survivor and a superman, of sorts. After the war, when he immigrated here, he needed something to do. He could no longer hunt enemy quarry in the woods of Eastern Europe, so he followed it in a fashion by becoming an investigator.

Duke, may he rest in peace, loved a good cigar. It helped him think, he said, as he sat back, letting his thought drift out like the billows of smoke emanating from his aromatic tobacco leaves. "Sometimes we just have to go through the motions to get to the heart of things," he would say. "Sometimes it's important to keep yourself in motion. Why or where are just not important. But if you use your 'sechel' – the Yiddish word for head and wisdom-based intelligence," – he said as his finger was tapping his right temple, "you'll find the way that you must pass through in order to get to your goal. Remember," I remember him saying with the look of almost stars in his eyes, "a goal is never what you think it is." The way he said it, I knew never to ask what he meant. Something inside told me that it would spoil the moment, and that what he was talking about probably could not be explained. This was something that could only be experienced, never described. I only learned much later that all goals are merely stepping stones to the next, and that goals are endless.

Having been an involuntary participant in human migration during the Second World War, he became an avid student of human history and psychology. He used to say that human history could be summed up very simply: on one hand, the need for love and nurturing; on the other, pure, unadulterated greed. Unfortunately, the latter often supersedes the former. Ultimately, it has caused the movement of a person and whole peoples. It is the basis for history – for even greed can be traced to the need for love and nurturing.

I remember him telling me that "complicated theories miss the point. People feel alone, separate and afraid. When there is togetherness there is never a story to tell."

He frightened me one day as he was staring off into space while billowing great plumes of cigar smoke. "Our world has simply become divided into zones based on the combination of labor and raw materials. Our world is dying. Everyone knows it. Everyone sees it. Everyone hopes death will not touch him or her." In this way, he used to say, "everyone is literally insane; and, hoping that his insanity will not be disturbed by someone else's."

One day I asked him the most complicated and most intuitive question that came to my young mind: "Uncle Izzy, how did you survive?" He sat transfixed for several moments as if he were involuntarily thrust into the terrain and images that existed only in his cellular memory. Then he looked at me straight in the eyes as if he were holding me in a visual bear hug from which I could not escape. The he said quite directly and bluntly: "I told myself that I would survive."

That was it?! No complicated theorems, plans. No hairbreadth escapes.

"I told myself that I would survive, over and over. No matter what, I believed it. No matter what happened, I never stopped believing it."

He acquired the wisdom of involuntary experience and lived to talk about it in the words of a master. Even when I was young I knew this. At 5'4" it was hard to put him on a pedestal. His words of wisdom, however, make him a giant till this very day.

"So here are the two 'bookends' of human existence," he used to say – "the need for love and nurturing, and the fear of death. Nothing more complicated than this. All our little dramas. All our little escapades. Mostly, all of the day-to-day, boring routines are played out wanting the former and hopefully avoiding the latter."

"As hard as it is, boychick," – a common Yiddish pet name – "just try to be a loving person – regardless of the fear of being exposed and out of control."

"The secret of my success is that I learned that there is, and always was, a life outside of the bookends. Veiled; not hidden. Just out of the corner of the eye; behind a shadow. Something that you vaguely remember, but just cannot put your finger on... . I also learned something that I find shocking to this very day. That life is created from the inside out – and life happens from the outside in. Always."

Years later I thought about that. Who of us really knows ourselves? I know from the market place of my career, that the admonition of Socrates, to "Know Yourself" is often misinterpreted as an invitation to an endless, self-indulgent inquiry into an emotional abyss which settles nothing and leads nowhere.

Many who have gone before us have admonished us for not recognizing that we are – and always will be – children of G-d, that we are eternal beings, and that we have access to everything an abundant Universe always has to offer. We only need to go deep within to feel our source, our "I-ness." Simple enough. Still, we often forget even when each of us has had clear evidence in our lives. Hence, instead of writing our Love stories, we write our own dramas. This happens until we each decide to step out of the drama and let the goodness of the Universe exhibit itself through us. So, if the Creator were to collect the individual stories of all souls who have ever or will ever incarnate in this realm, the story would be the same: longing for love in the Garden of G-d.

Uncle Duke would always talk about things being "singularly" important or unimportant; much in the same way that Conan Doyle's character, Sherlock Holmes, would often speak of things being "singularly" important.

Still, with all his philosophizing, he also taught me to respect details. Dealing with life one moment at a time, and letting these moments flow together like pieces in a vast, designed overlay; a puzzle, already designed, waiting for the pieces to be inserted. This is why he always instructed me to "know how the puzzle is going to look when it is finished. Not just envision. But, know, absolutely, to the core of your being. That is the key to the whole game. If you get lost, and you will, and you should, you'll always be able to find your way back home. You can lose many things in your life, but you can never lose your home. I know this to be true. When I was half your age I lost everything. My family. My world. But, I learned how to always be home no matter where I was or what I was doing. This kept me alive when I thought everything was lost. I knew to the core of my being, that everything was alright and would be alright. And, it was."

To Uncle Duke, this World was an enormous Rube Goldberg contraption, complete with connecting fulcrums, levers, gears, clacking chickens laying eggs, popping balloons, and, of course, a perfect pinball ball-bearing inexorably rolling in its assigned channel on its way to its destination.

I used to think he was talking literally, and that I was supposed to direct my outcome by some kind of thought wizardry. I only realized much later, how much I did not realize then. Mystics, by and large, have all said this world is a dream. If so, whose dream is it? And, if the dreamer is dreaming it, and we are images in that dream, then we have no business in doing other than living the Dreamer's Dream. Sounds so simple and logical in a visionary way, doesn't it?

But, if this were the case, why didn't all the multitudes who spend their lives day-dreaming ever see something come to fruition? No. There was something he wasn't telling me. Something else. The glue of it all. The key. The power.

I used to think that Duke liked to talk cryptically on purpose. Now I realize that he just didn't have the words. When I sometimes had the courage to express a lack of understanding, he would look at me with his tender blue eyes and simply say "You will!" A pat on the head or a pinch on the cheek would routinely follow. This went on into my early 20s when Duke passed away. He knew it was important for me, and everyone for that matter, to feel my way on my own. But, he was always available, and was always watching from the background. I know he is still watching from a place that I cannot even fathom.

The most important discipline that Duke taught me was to rely on my hunches. Even as a therapist, this is critical. When you are awash in a client's ocean of raw emotions, when there are no boundaries or landmarks, it is the only thing that keeps both of us afloat.

Listening for hours upon hours to Duke's stories put me in the frame of mind to listen to stories. People like people who listen, I suppose, especially because they usually do not listen to themselves very well. Or, they do everything possible to not listen to the mind-voice that talks and talks and talks in their heads - and so they talk incessantly in order to get away from it. If someone else listens to them, it is evidence to them that they must have something important to say. Too often I have seen people, great and important people, not following their own best advice and losing for it. I have seen them turned into pawns by events set into motion by their own hands and devices.

I suppose, though, that these things are just the pictures they have made for themselves, as Duke would say. People sometimes set events in motion and then sit back in the wake of the inertia, bewailing their fate. It is often not the person or persons involved that dictate the result.

Contrary to Duke's philosophy, I did not have the faintest idea what this picture would look like at the end. But, I did have a clear picture on how I wanted it to look; so this was a start. In the meantime, it appeared that my days would continue to be filled with the loose ends of everyone else's lives and dramas.

VI

Kathryn and I braved the crowds on Tuesday afternoon, and went to the opening at the Hall of Antiquities.

The Hall is an exact replica of the Parthenon at Athens, with a few other replicas of the Acropolis thrown in for good measure. It was built on one of the higher elevations along Elmwood Avenue. It was only a few blocks from my Elliott Square Building.

Approaching the museum from the west, we came upon an enormous throng completely circling the museum. The museum itself covered an entire city block.

The excess line extended down two more blocks down to the Bryant Building. Police directed traffic for a circumference of six blocks. Apparently the controversy had really touched the nerve of the peoples' curiosity.

As we circled what the ancient Greeks called the Erechtheion, I got a long viewing of the Caryatids – six statues of women supporting the roof of the veranda-like structure.

After two and a-half hours we inched our way to the monumental museum entrance way. It was constructed in the Doric order, with Ionian columns flanking the central passageway. Metopes contained carvings of gods and giants, Lapiths and centaurs; figments of the Greek imagination - or, perhaps, Greek experience for all we really know. Perhaps actual events before the advent of history recorded it, or chose not to record it. At any rate, bits and pieces of mythology heralding the entrance into aisles of ornaments from ancient cultures.

As a young boy, my parents bought me the first installment of an encyclopedia being sold at a neighborhood supermarket. I read over and over again the entry on Aristotle, the great logician. When I got to the letter "R," however, logic took a back seat to something much more interesting. I read the word "reincarnation" and was fascinated by the prospect of having lived before this time. So began a lifelong interest in the subject; a passion for learning more about what had gone on before, and perhaps what would go on later. This is why I like to think of myself as an archeologist of the future.

In the same vein, I also developed a fascination for early ancient history. I mean anything up until the Greeks. After that, as far as I am concerned, the world has been in a repeat cycle of Roman empires, complete with personal and societal excess and self-immolation.

My theory is that these "ancient" people, like the Sumerians and other Mesopotamian cultures, Egyptians, and Hebrews, were closer in time to the beginning, and hence, closer to the true secrets of life. These secrets are now long lost in the depths of the memory of mankind, and possibly in artifacts not yet discovered. This theory is similar to the theory that children are more able and more willing to receive psychic transmissions, and that adults are more psychically adept in the early morning moments shortly after awakening. I always believed that these ancient people knew something not in our active consciousness, and I wanted to know what it was. I was hoping that I was now going to have the opportunity.

We came upon rows of ancient amulets. As we looked with interest, a staffer came over to explain that the amulets were protective devices commonly carried by both nobles and commoners. Inscriptions on the amulets were supposed to protect the wearer against disease and enemies, or cure some type of malady. Each amulet was supposed to link the wearer to the particular god which could help provide the relief requested. A system that would narrow the imagined space between we-limited beings and our superiors. She told us that the ones we were looking at now were Egyptian – Old Kingdom; about 4,700 years old. Very old indeed, I thought, but just an infant to what Ponti wanted to exhibit.

The staffer had a name tag, with the name "Antoinette" calligraphically emblazoned on it. I had seen her before on some of my excursions to the Hall, but had not spoken to her.

"Antoinette," I asked, "where is the 'good stuff,' if you know what I mean."

Her head turned right and left very quickly; a sort of involuntary attempt to make her escape. Her cheeks flushed enough to tell me she could not really speak freely. "The prehistory section is down the hall and to the right, if this is what you are referring to. I hope you enjoy the rest of the exhibit. I know that Mr. Klinger is strolling. As you know, Ferdinand Klinger is the acting director in Mr. Moon's absence. If you are looking for something specific, perhaps you could talk to him when you see him." With this, she left somewhat perfunctorily.

We continued walking. I wanted to see Ponti's true exhibit, and I knew I was going have to snoop in my own way.

I was looking hurriedly, but with focus. The prehistory section was very well stocked, but the information plates were very sparse and matter-of-fact. Nothing about the paranormal; just many identifications which indicated "use and age unknown." There was nothing about where they were discovered or from whom they may have been loaned.

Many of the objects had been cast from clay and adorned with unusual symbols. Some looked frightening, some appealing. Others were carved from bone. There was no description of what type of bone. And, there were some metallic-looking objects. Many were long and narrow as if they were projectiles of some sort, or used in some kind of ceremony. Others were round and open and resembled pots. This was amazing to me. The so-called Bronze Age was only several thousand years ago, and the invention of iron even much later. How in the world were metallic objects from heaven knows where, made and used, and by whom? If not from Earth, then from where and brought by whom?

Each of these also had various indecipherable markings on them. They resembled no known dialect or script of which I was aware. It all seemed so shamanic. In fact, it felt pre-shamanic in a sense. Suppose an early people was so learned, so connected with source energy, that its knowledge would be considered transcendental and its ways and practices absolutely miraculous. Only a gradual loss of knowledge would have even required the need for a class of healer or medicine person to keep some of the higher knowledge intact. But, what if over time, more and more of the knowledge was lost?

Surely the articles would be put through some scientific scrutiny to determine age, etc. But, why hadn't it been done already. How could they have remained hidden for so long? And, why now? Why were they being released now? Wouldn't it have been better just to let the status quo remain? Now these articles would be a source of hope; or at least, tremendous interest. They might even make the importance of the Dead Sea Scrolls pale in comparison. If nothing could be determined about the proper use or meaning, they would, indeed, lend themselves to sensational exhibits rivaling King Tut. Perhaps this is why the Board let them be exhibited. For eternity, the exhibition at the Hall of Antiquities would be the first exposure to the light of day, and the Hall's prominence would skyrocket ... forever. Unless... there was something unkosher about them.

Not only would Ponti's reputation be made or shattered, but the Hall's as well. Reporters filtered through the crowds, but photographic equipment was banned. This added to the frustration since the Hall had not yet included pictures in the official guidebook. Was it planned this way, or did something about the timing compel the Board to act fast?

This catalogue of questions could only quicken the mystery and the appeal to the public. In the mind of the Board, however, I am sure all the members felt that displaying the pieces they had viewed in a non-sensational way was better than not displaying them at all.

Speculations were openly expressed. It was impossible not to have a theory, whether you felt the articles were legitimate or not. Theories running amok by everyone. In an instant, everyone became an amateur archeologist. "What could this have been used for?" "Do you think it could make me powerful, wealthy, happy, etc.?" Not so different from the modern practice of wearing modern names patterned in hieroglyphics and portrayed in a cartouche!

The spiraling atmosphere of the "roman circus" started by the media frenzy only accelerated in the very area where the objects were openly displayed.

We continued walking from case to case. I didn't see anything that seemed to substantiate what Ponti had vaguely described. "Wait a second!" I thought, "Let's take a look at this!"

Before me in its own case lay a stone that I did not recognize. The description said it was a meteorite! It was gold flecked in the manner of lapis lazuli. The ancients used lapis lazuli to symbolize the starry universe. It was actually on a turnstyle so that both the top and the bottom could be viewed. "Why this piece?" I wondered. The top was rough and unfinished. The underside, however, was a different story.

On the finished side were wavy forms of script and design I had never before seen. I had seen many forms of ancient writing, but had never seen characters designed quite like these. The design had the beginnings of a Star of David in the center, in that there was an equilateral triangle pointing down and one was pointing up, and the points were almost touching! It made the figure of infinity or a stylized hourglass. If the triangles would merge, the interlocking triangles of the Star of David would have been evident. And, there was an identification plate associated with this item. It was discovered in the ruins in the open fields of Megiddo in Israel. Megiddo is the site of the rumored Armageddon.

Looking quickly at the explanation card, I did not see a date. I did see, however, a description, "date unknown" with no other explanation about the design or the writing. Why would this card have any description when the others did not?

As a meteorite, could it have been fashioned elsewhere, and have been brought here long ago; perhaps by an alien race? Or perhaps from a massive meteor explosion in our atmosphere?

"You know Kathryn, I would like to imagine that the people who caused this inscription to be struck - whoever they were - were closer to source knowledge; closer to the elements which exist outside of time."

"Yes," she said. "And they knew something that has been long lost, or hidden in our deep subconscious for a long time. Some kind of a missing link which was hidden. Perhaps it provides a link to perfect health or eternal life. Something we all sense we need, even if we do not consciously know the name or what it is. It's time all of this came out and saw the light of day. I feel this tingling just by being near it." She paused for a moment and then said, thoughtfully, "The infinity symbol is also a stylization of the heart; not the physical heart, but the spiritual heart. It is the source and font of unconditional love and timeless wisdom which transcends all of the day-to-day experiences that cover up what is really so important. It is the mother aspect of all creation."

There has been much written about the heart in both ancient and current literature. While it is ascribed to the principle of love, something still seems to be missing. If everyone knows that love stems from the heart, and if everyone is looking for love in some degree, why do people not live from the heart in the first place? Unless, the reference to living from the heart means something entirely different; something not associated with the human, physical heart at all. Something so apparent and so obvious that it is obscured from vision and association.

Kathryn is extremely well attuned to the female energies that are the creative force for all life on this planet, and the savage suppression of that force throughout recorded history. If she also felt some kind of a psychic link to this article, then it certainly deserved more attention.

Then we both looked at each other, as if to say that we both recognized that the inscription on the identification plate was only a partial one; and, that this definitely had something to do with Ponti. We both knew that he knew what the inscription was, and how the symbols fit in. He knew it was not a meaningless combination of lines and form. He knew it had real power behind it. Not only this. That it had real promise behind it. With this realization, we both felt lighter, as if gravity had lost some of its power.

Just then one of the "traffic" cops in the museum politely asked us if we wouldn't mind moving on to a different exhibit. We were holding up the works. I also think we were collecting a crowd around out conversation.

We started talking softly about how early cultures understood better than us the journey of the soul through time; how it occasionally is transported by means of the flesh until at last there would be no flesh and its test in this sphere would be over, and ... ."

These peoples, whoever and wherever they are, were nearer to the beginning and understood that we are all voyagers from distant times, having sailed into the present with hidden memories of all we have been and seen, and all that we will do and be. We are all sailors throughout time. Small items were often vehicles through which ancient peoples conveyed the ideas of spiritual progression for reentry and reformation in the world of time.

As we walked, we talked about the endless possibilities we would have today just knowing a portion of what the ancients had known. But, then I stopped. I remembered Ponti talking about the Aleph. We didn't see an Aleph א on the meteorite. Where was the Aleph א?

Maybe there was another piece we were supposed to see, but haven't seen yet.

I excused myself from Kathryn for a moment and coursed my way back to Antoinette.

"Antoinette," I said very softly, you know that Ponti and I were close friends. I know you have to be careful about what you say, but can anyone please tell me where the meteorite came from?"

Her cheeks flushed. She was not one to lie, but had been instructed, probably threatened, to be very circumspect. She looked at me and quickly said, "Carnahan," and walked away quickly.

Andrew Carnahan, from an oil-rich family, from one of his expeditions in northern Israel shortly towards the end of World War I. It was then known as Palestine, having been taken by the British during the war. Another result of the war was the collapse of the once powerful Ottoman Empire. If he did not keep a spectacular piece for his own private collection, he often loaned it to the major museums. Most notable was the British Museum in London.

The item reminded me of the heart scarab, perhaps the most important of ancient protective signs or charms. The heart scarab – an image of a beetle cut from a gem or fashioned in a precious metal and engraved with hieroglyphs or language signs on the underside – was mainly used for funerary purposes. The main purpose – why it was developed in the first place – we do not know. But, I remember learning that at some early date it was not only used to be carried on the breast of the deceased, but was someway associated with a certain special class of the living. A protection for the upper echelon.

The positioning of the triangles on the meteorite was intriguing. The Star of David has two intersecting triangles. In the meteorite, however, only their points were touching or almost touching. It was hard to tell. Was it a precursor, or a successor?

In the Kabbalah, the ancient Jewish mystical system, the center point on the stylized Tree of Life is known as Tifferet. It corresponds to the Heart. Not the human heart, but the spiritual heart, so-to-speak. The point of conjunction where physical and spiritual can intermingle, each into the other, and then go back into their own. The center point of the Star of David would also be a symbol for the conjunction known as Tifferet.

The Star of David symbolically consists of two equilateral triangles. The top triangle symbolizes heaven, and the bottom, earth. Also, male and female; both parts of the whole. The Heart center point formed by the intersection is the synthesis. The top triangle is also considered to be symbolic of the element of fire. The bottom triangle, symbolic of water. But now, in this meteorite, a separation? Could this mean a permanent conjunction of heaven and earth, so that now there was heaven on earth? If so, how to access it? Or, could it mean a permanent separation due to some kind of incompatibility, or some other reason? Or could it all have some connection with the very creation epic artistically, if not symbolically, described in Genesis.

Creation. The most intriguing word in our language. Something from nothing. An object from the ethers. The alchemist's quest. Heaven and Earth coming together in a visual display. Not magic. But, the miracle power of formation from the silence and stillness of the huge melting pot of possibilities, of which we are such a form. Huge vistas. Smaller and smaller arenas of display. How big or how small is your world? This is the question we ask ourselves every day, multitudes of times, based either on our desires or a reaction to the world around us. But what if – what if – it were all relative – personal and universal simultaneously – creation of worlds in the blink of an eye, the snap of the fingers, the pronunciation of a statement, invocation, incantation – what if?

The backdrop of history. Movement of persons and whole peoples. Great movements. Small movements. All relative; all related even though not seemingly so.

Megiddo and Armageddon. Synonymous with the mention of the end times in Revelations. A place of the gathering of troops of the forces of good and evil. A place to mark time or end time.

Andrew Carnahan. He died a short time ago. He lived the life of a pampered monarch, was heavy into collecting objets d'art, and had an interest in ancient cultures. He was very secretive and reclusive.

I caught up with Kathryn. We walked past articles from the time of our recorded history. They no longer held the same appeal, even though they were monumental examples of the skill of ancient artisans. We walked past a relief portrait of the Assyrian King Sargon

II, 723-722 B.C. (Excavations at Khorsabad); a case containing the third tablet (of seven) in the Babylonian series relating to the story of Creation (from the British Museum); a Sumerian prism naming the ten kings who ruled before the flood (from Kish, about 2,000 B.C. - Ashmolean Museum, Oxford); some very early Sumerian inscriptions employing a pictographic script (from excavations at Kish - near Babylon, around 3,300 B.C.) (no comparison to the symbols on the scarab, which were obviously much more advanced); past the eleventh tablet of the Assyrian version of the flood (excavation at Nineveh, about 650 B.C. - British Museum); a reconstruction of the temple - step tower, or ziggurat, as built by Ur-Nammu, King of Ur, about 2,100 B.C. - with platforms reconstructed in different colors (black, red, blue), and a temple at the top which was covered with silver, and terraces which were covered with bitumen and planted with trees. Finally, the Rosetta Stone, 3 feet 9 inches of Black basalt which opened the art, language and culture of ancient Egypt to the modern world. In addition, there were hundreds of scarabs, amulets, jars, plaster casts of heads, fragments from various palaces.

I knew the press was going to have a field day. Kathryn and I were tired. For a break we strolled through some medieval exhibits showing armor, armaments, tapestries, and costumes. It was much less crowded and gave us both a break from the shoving crowds.

Since this was the opening day of the much heralded exhibition, museum officials were on their best behavior. They strolled amongst the crowds playing host to "their" exhibit.

Aside from the prehistory exhibit, all lines converged on the "Throne Room." It contained a conglomeration of solid gold artifacts from Egyptian and Mesopotamian vaults. King Tut's was not among them. Pandemonium would surely have resulted given the pre-exhibit publicity the exhibit otherwise received.

Nothing in the exhibit programs even hinted about metaphysics, other than the first meteorite-scarab I saw. The glitter of the past is always a good way to corral people. Those in power know that monumental artifacts are a wonderful and effective way of keeping the masses in their place. It appeared that the critics and the behind-the-scenes players may have had finally had their day. They were reaping the benefit of Ponti's industry, without the controversy.

I caught a glimpse of Ferdinand Klinger, interim curator since Ponti's disappearance. Dressed in a double-breasted blue pin stripe suit, crimson foulard print tie, light blue shirt with white collar and collar pin, he graciously swayed and filtered through the crowd. His natural grey hair, even though combed back and thinning, completed the image of the cultured and well-groomed gentleman. He had mastered the art of appearing aristocratic. And, were he to even use the word, "aristocratic," it would certainly have been pronounced in the cultured British fashion.

"Mr. Klinger," I said inching my way to him. Ponti had introduced us on several occasions.

"Ah, Mr. Cushner," he said in his best clipped European manner and with a slight bow; his hands behind his back. His slightly paunchy face was aglow with surface fellowship, but underneath I sensed the furnace was burning bright. How he must have hated to have been subservient to Ponti Moon, a man 20 years his junior, with half the experience. That, however, was how the cards were dealt. Now his chance to make up for lost time had presented itself.

"I extend my condolences, Mr. Cushner. I know that Mr. Moon and you were good friends. I am sorry for your loss."

I was immediately startled and looked at him with a penetrating glare. He seemed to parry my glance with a glance of nonchalance which spoke volumes.

Kathryn and I looked at each other a little incredulously. How astounding and curious that he would have the gall and chutzpah to cavalierly suggest finality in a pending investigation where nothing was resolved. How like so many, I thought, who think they are simply above it all. His use of the word "condolence" was very telling.

I said nothing, but noted that he certainly seemed happy for his gain. He had emphasized the "your" in "your loss" a little bit too heavily. He was not feeling a loss at all. To him, this was a breakthrough.

Had I spoken, my response would have been unflattering, to say the least. I restrained myself and simply parried back by my omission. Sometimes it is better to follow the philosophy about running water and flow around the rocks instead of trying to flow through them. The old adage about the path of least resistance.

But, I couldn't avoid all queries. "I am curious, Mr. Klinger," I asked, "why are the identification cards in the prehistory exhibit so vague?"

"What do you mean?" he answered cautiously, if not snakily. He turned with animated expressiveness letting his right arm perform a 45 degree sweep. "The cards have as much information as we were at liberty to give, Mr. Cushner. You, of all people should know this."

"You know what I mean, Mr. Klinger. What about the emphasis Ponti wanted to express? The articles are here, but without some kind of explanation they are like a beautiful automobile without the keys. Nice to look at, but of no real use."

"Mr. Cushner, this is a museum of antiquities. Visual appeal is what we do. We leave the rest to the pragmatists who often have little use for what we do. As you know, funding for the arts is always uncertain. The ability to house an international exhibit is not only good for the community, but also for the entire industry. It allows us to provide concrete proof to the critics who are always arguing that hard-earned dollars should not be expended on aesthetics."

"That may be, but if you are concerned about the scope of your exhibit and its international impact, why not display not only the aesthetics, but the true transcendental aspects."

"Mr. Cushner, the opinions based on spiritualism, or what have you, are decidedly personal opinions. They may well be offensive to many who would otherwise enjoy what we have to exhibit. Our goal is to make the community welcome, not just a segment."

"But, what if there was truth to the rumor; that some of the articles actually had the power to go to other realms. Think of the boon to the entire world."

"Mr. Cushner, that is the realm of theology, not of art. The Board had an emergency meeting shortly after Mr. Moon's - eh- disappearance. It was unanimously decided that all reference to metaphysics, what-have-you, be stricken from the exhibit. I, as a paid employee of the museum, had to obey the decision. I'm sure you understand. Perhaps there will be an initial disappointment, but in the long run the Board feels that this decision will have the most beneficial effects."

"Well, I do not agree with you, Mr. Klinger. The vast majority of lookers here would not be here today, but for the sensational aspects of the exhibits. I must say, that it was ever-more sensational as a result of the news-spin placed on the artifacts by the 'news-hungry' reporters of whom you have just spoken. At best, you are going to have many disappointed, disgruntled patrons who may not want to brave the crowds next time. But, I do not want to argue with you about it. Ponti let me know that he left me a message of some sort, and I believe he left me a package as well. Are you aware of any package or envelope for me?" I asked knowing full well this "gentlemen" would not cooperate unless there was some distinct advantage for him.

"No, I'm afraid not, Mr. Cushner," he said with a tarnished smile. "Unfortunately, Ponti's unexpected– uh – departure, shall we say, left things in a bit of confusion. Should I come across any item segregated for you, I shall surely call you at once. If you will please excuse me, I must now attend to my official functions."

He gave me another slight bow and strolled away. His philosophy always had pointed more in the direction of the most expedient path to the goal. Expediency was certainly behind his statement that he would call me about any news. I knew he wouldn't and so did he. The impression he left was that if the Rosetta Stone fit into the breast pocket of his suit coat, he would already be trying to fence it.

Now I had to make a decision. What was I going to do? I might have seen what Ponti wanted me to see, but was not sure – and, I really did not even know whether Ponti was still alive. Timing, I knew, was very important. Neither too soon nor too late. Too soon and you force the clues and players to go underground. Too late, and they are underground. But, wait a second! I'm a therapist, not an investigator. I deal with the mind, not criminal investigations. What could I really do about this other than to leave it to the professionals? My investigations were always explorations of consciousness; not ones for real! This little tidbit woke me up more than a little bit.

I started to think. One thought led to another, as usual, much like the gathering of forces preparing to do battle. I sat down on a bench as Kathryn was waiting in a serpentine line destined for the ladies' room. My breath started to get long and deep, and I felt calm inside.

If any of those articles were legitimate and predated the historical era by thousands, hundreds of thousands, or even millions of years, they were from a time when the world was fresh and new. The complications of modern life did not exist. Communication with other realms was easy and constant. And thought. What about thought? It must have been pure? Can any of us in this era, at this time, imagine pure thought? Thought not adulterated by the past or the desires of the future; but just the momentary aliveness inherent in just being.

I wondered when the first thought occurred. What was it? All of these religious and spiritual objects from thousands of years ago, or just yesterday, all asking for the same thing: love and safety in a world that is unloving and unsafe. Who thought the first thought? How did it know that thought was permitted or even possible? What thought preceded all life forms? Is it still accessible? What is behind it?

Maybe that scarab holds a key or at least points in the right direction.

Curious, I thought, that the forms would have been in the shape of triangles. The equilateral triangle is a universal symbol of unity in a fixed form. Completion in a certain arena. Like a terrarium in a flower shop. Self-existing and self-perpetuating in a world of constant change. Like being present in the here and now, without past or the future.

Two triangles with their points touching can only mean some direction, perhaps some contact, I thought. Maybe a path. But, a breakthrough? No. The points have to intersect. What about the points almost touching? This was only the beginning, I thought. Perhaps, I thought, the point of contact is just the beginning.

I decided to walk back for one last look. As I made my way to the scarab case, I saw it was surrounded by museum attendants wearing surgical gloves and moving quickly, but trying to act innocuous, furtive and inconspicuous. They were removing the scarab from the case, without explanation to anyone asking.

Why do I keep getting that sense of tingling across my upper back? Is someone trying to communicate with me?

Then I realized that the positions of the triangles looked like a stylized form of our letter "I." It could also look like the letter "X," without the base line and top.

Socrates admonished each of us to "Know Thyself." The most profound question in all of philosophy and metaphysical inquiry is "Who Am I?" Suppose throughout all of linear history, this question has not changed, but has remained an ever present constant – as if the question once asked becomes the backdrop for all existence in this realm, recognized or not. All realization leads to and from it. It is the path of the prodigal son, Sir Gawain and the Holy Grail, every searching heart everywhere, throughout all time. And in it, in the "I," there is no time.

Pontius. It means "marine," or "from the sea." It can also be a derivation of "pons" which is Latin for bridge. Which sea? Perhaps a bridge across the vast ocean of ether which makes up the primal element of our universe. Perhaps he was trying to lay the foundation for something so fundamental and essential that he could not even make reference to it to anyone.

The perennial problem with writing, or speaking, is that try as we might, we cannot convey the actual experience using words. It does not stop thousands of trillions of words being used to try to lead to or explain an experience; but those who have had a transcendent experience usually acknowledge that words are absolutely inadequate to convey the feeling. Millions of quintillions of words have been written or spoken about enlightenment; yet, those who have had the experience attest to its happening instantaneously and otherwise being indescribable.

What is it that we want? Usually to keep everything that is good, release everything that is bad, and substitute it with something that is good. Ultimately, this is insanity. A universal law that we have all experienced is that once one thing - no matter how minor- changes, everything changes.

VII

There is a message on my answering machine from Mrs. Mellenstreet. I decided to call her back later; I need an hour or two to piece some things together. I went straight into my office and closed the door.

An old edition of National Geographic was open on my desk. It was open to an article on the sinking of the island of Santorini in the Mediterranean. As theory has it, the sinking of the island by volcanic eruption may have occurred at precisely the same time as the Red Sea parted for Moses. Scientists have speculated that the sinking caused a disequilibrium which caused the waters in that area of the world to drastically subside. Others speculate that the sinking occurred at a much earlier date and have linked the island to the mythic sinking of Atlantis. Many others think it was an act of G-d, or at least of true alchemy.

In this day and age, with all of our supposed advanced technology, why don't we know what happened, why and when? The answer is the same now as it always has been. There are forces outside of our range that operate on a vibrancy and frequency which we cannot even fathom. We, in a sense, live in a little fish bowl. We seek good and avoid what we determine is not good. We do our best to establish a status quo and keep it regardless of the stress and anxiety caused by trying to keep motion static. Yet, we do all of this in a tiny environment, completely oblivious to or intentionally avoiding the larger universe of which we are a part. Even if you have no interest at all in spirituality, and are a complete and unabridged materialist, even then, you must recognize the unimaginably immense size of our physical universe, and this must create a sense of awe and wonder.

At times like this, I felt that I owed it to myself to just bury myself behind the comfort of the written word – everything set in black and white, even with all of its limitations. It was all there. There was a beginning and an end, not an interminable "maybe" or "somewhere over the rainbow" interim. It is definitely not the Black Fire on White Fire with which the original Torah, the Five Books of Moses, were said to have been written; but, comforting in its encapsulation and its escape.

My thoughts drifted back to the triangles with points almost touching. This was not a situation where no explanation was necessary or possible. This was an article made by a hand; human or otherwise. Its meaning could be deciphered. I intended to do it. It denoted some kind of a connection. That much I knew. But of what? And then, to what effect?

My shoes were off and so was the telephone. The world had turned into a wonderful place. Quiet. Peaceful. A Japanese garden.

The human psyche is steeped in the desire for a magical power over the natural physical order. People want to be alchemists and create gold out of thin air. They want to walk on water. They want everyone to marvel at how special they are. Then they want to go home, have a good dinner, watch television, and go to sleep. Mostly, people just want. Wanting is endless.

What if Ponti wasn't missing. Maybe just hiding. As the phrase goes, maybe he was hiding in plain sight, or in a plain site; somewhere so obvious, on later reflection it would seem so silly to not have known.

After my reverie, I listened to the other messages on my answering machine. Mrs. Haverfield - Felicia Haverfield - called to cancel a 10:30 a.m. appointment tomorrow. She said it was about her son again. "Seems he has taken up with some cult or some such thing. She would explain later."

"Ah, yes, Mrs. Haverfield," I thought, as I smiled. Her father, Carl Bandolier made a fortune during the War buying and selling cars. He also had an underground stable of rubber tires; literally. They were in short supply and heavily rationed. He paid off the mayor, the city council members, the D.A., the Chief of Police, and the beat cops who patrolled the area. When you have that many people covered, you first wonder how he made any money at all. Apparently he did, and lots of it. When you are covering this many people they are all rooting for you as long as you continue to take care of them. And, he is reputed to have taken very good care of them. I suppose you could say that he was a very charitable man, in his own right. Anyway, you either danced to his tune or you had difficulty finding another source of wheels; simple as that. As his only daughter, Mrs. Haverfield took it all when the old swindler passed on to his reward. She put a large chunk of it into trust for her dear son who makes a spendthrift look like a penny pincher. He will never have to worry about paying the rent. Unfortunately, his mother is shouldering all the guilt for how her father made all of this money. In her own right, she is a very proper lady.

Next, was a message from Ponti's housekeeper. There was package addressed to me at his home! I almost bolted though the ceiling! She said that it had been opened during the police investigation and resealed after it was considered safe. I was free to pick it up if I chose. If I chose!!! I called back to say that I would be right over. My short reverie had calmed me for what was coming next, or what I hoped would be. An explanation, I hoped; not just more information.

VIII

Ponti lived simply, yet elegantly. A stylish home in a sequestered subdivision, but certainly not a regal palace. It was tastefully decorated, not brimming over with artifacts and art work. He regularly worked in his beautiful garden and took great delight in its natural abundance. Even the few Greek and Roman marble statues fit as if they were made just for this purpose.

His housekeeper met me at the door. Her look was somber, and she was obviously trying to keep a stiff upper lip. She kept Ponti's home like a dedicated second mother, and treated him with the loving attention and concern that comes from being a senior citizen and having no other family.

I knocked at the door and heard footsteps of someone who had undoubtedly been waiting for me.

Stella opened the door, and although usually circumspect with her feelings, seemed happy to see me. She was not holding anything, which indicated she wanted me to come in. She was normally very precise in her routines and did not like outside interferences. Although she did not wear a starched uniform, it would not have been out of place if she did. Still, behind the precise demeanor was the kind heart of someone who had never shared in the excess of life, and to whom precision had become a necessity of survival. Being invited into the house was out of character for her. Having been interrogated by the police would also have had a profound effect on someone indelibly tied to a schedule and dedicated to maintaining the peace and privacy of a sequestered life. Ponti may have had legal ownership, but this was her home, and it was her world. Without Ponti it was like her firstborn had been taken.

She sat down on the couch in the living room and I in a facing chair. I sat silently, waiting for her to say anything she needed to say. Instead, she reached over to a coffee table and picked up a small box and handed it to me. "Ponti wanted you to have this," she said with a far-away look.

"Do you know what it is?"

"No. I only know the police did not have any interest in it. I wanted to give it to you as quickly as I could. Maybe it will help you find Ponti."

"How do you know I'm looking for Ponti?"

She looked at me with pursed lips, in a slight upward angle. She cocked her head slightly to the right and said, "Of course you are looking for him, Michael."

I briefly nodded in acknowledgment. Well, now I was "for it" as the World War I combatants used to say as they bounded out of their trenches straight into the waiting machine guns of the enemy.

"Please tell me whatever you can, as soon as you can," she asked.

"I will Stella," and stood up to walk out. "I will show myself out," I said as I walked hurriedly to the door, wanting only to open the package.

I got into my car and drove to the parking lot of a nearby park. I looked around to see if anyone was following me. I didn't know if the package may have been planted and I was being spotted for some reason.

I parked and hurriedly opened the package. Inside was a note in Ponti's handwriting: "Michael, stillness becomes you." It was signed "P." There was wrapping paper in the box, which had been opened and unceremoniously stuffed back into the box. I shuffled through the paper carefully, and as I did, I heard a metal clang. I opened a creased portion of paper, and inside were two metal equilateral triangles. They were loose but had been attached to a piece of waxed paper. The paper still held their imprint. Two equilateral triangles with their points almost touching in the middle.

IX

The Creator of this reality loves drama. Why else would thoughts proliferate like budding amoebas in a vast sea of brine?

Dramas can be on many levels, simultaneously. Often, however, they are played out on that lower, visceral level which gives rise to the quickening; that congestion of flesh, emotion and propulsion. My clients may start on a higher sphere, but usually cascade to the lower in a matter of moments. Where else can you successfully avoid dealing with your problems, immerse yourself in the problem-arena of your constituents and become wealthy all at the same time?

Marriages in these arenas often take on interesting twists. Some marriages are more investment-oriented from the beginning. Enter Ms. Victoria Lake. She was the "cause" of "so much distress" to her estranged and "concerned" husband; or should I say, her wealthy and powerful husband, Jacob Lake.

He told me that Victoria was having dinner at the Algeria Club. The name had nothing to do with the country. Its owners, Al and Gerry, thought the name would lend a "Casablanca – Humphrey Bogart" mystique to the place. The palm plants and Boston ferns did add character and the 40s style furniture did add some charm that is missing from so many modern establishments. In any event, it turned out to be a good place for anyone living in the public eye, ranging from prima donnas to politicians, and all the image trendy wannabees.

Mr. Jake, as he was affectionately known, had employed every decent private investigator in the area from time-to-time. Victoria knew them all. He asked if I could do him this one "favor" and just let me know what I could see. I must have some hidden investigative talent, because once again I said I would – even though reluctantly. Victoria did not know me.

I had a good vantage point at the bar, ordered a gin and tonic, and kept my eyes and ears open. This was sort of exciting to me. G-d loves dramas, and he certainly shares the wealth.

Victoria's date was Timothy Bonticlaire. Unmarried, very ambitious, very political, with strong labor connections – a real business butterfly. Not the type to engage in a public affair with the still present wife of Jacob Lake – a wealthy real estate developer and money entrepreneur with a penchant for getting things done, and getting them done his way.

Victoria, however, was not a stay-at-home wife. She was on the city planning commission and an important vote was coming up. It was about an item in which Bonticlaire, and Lake, were very interested. It also received a lot of press play. So, while dinner together may have raised a few eyebrows, it didn't seem to cause a lot of undercurrent conversation. The potential conflict of interest probably never crossed anyone's mind; the intrigue and speculation was so much more palatable.

Obviously, this was the public side for business negotiations which had already taken place very privately. This was only an opportunity to put a pretty face on what could otherwise be a very complicated controversy.

Their table was close enough to the bar area that I could generally hear that they were talking business. He was trying to make the best pitch he could about how the best interests of the community were in total sync with his interests. She was playing "cat and mouse" with him. Because of her marriage to Jacob Lake, she was going to have to abstain from the vote, but everyone knew she held sway regardless of whether she was going to technically participate.

This didn't tab out to be just a jealous husband situation. There was a lot of money at stake with Ms. Victoria Lake. They knew it and she knew it too. Hardly a classical tryst, but a tryst just the same.

I thought back to the meteorite. I thought back to the triangles and the way they pointed to each other in some kind of mystic or spiritual way. This human triangular connection, however, was not of the same category of holiness. Each of the participants in this "triangle" fully realized each of their relative positions, powers and priorities. As in any business, separate they were valuable, but any combination with Victoria gave that team real power. This was why Jake was so concerned. Somebody was getting to his investment. While some marriages are created by something less than love, this one smacked of expediency all the way around. She married Jake to use his influence and now he was collecting interest. It appeared, however, that Bonticlaire was toying with the principal. And, Bonticlaire was not the only one. During this breach in their marital relationship, Victoria had collected quite a treasure trove of suitors, admirers, and "puppies" who attended to her every whim and need.

It is often said that the fear of death is the most potent and pervasive feeling we can experience. Others will quickly retort that the fear of life is that much more fear-inducing. Death is over. Life is prolonged. Yet, as many have experienced, the fear of something is usually more acute than the actual experience, if it even does occur. Fear as a feeling pushes and throbs, making its host a simultaneous slave to passion and a victim of restraint. You cannot move, but you are compelled to move in several directions at once, to accomplish – nothing; just for the sake of the movement.

The feelings of anxiety came upon me again. I did not know why, what, for whom, or from whom. But, I was feeling something. It was not anything about here. It was like I was looking into the future and the future was looking back at me. The feeling stopped me cold. I literally "lost" consciousness for a few moments as I was lost in this reverie. When I "awoke" the club hadn't changed; the conversation was still going on, and I had seen enough. I knew it was time to move, get out of my surroundings and walk off the anxiety – at least wait in my car and see when they came out.

I started thinking about Uncle Duke. He was from the old country and never truly emigrated to America in the cultural sense. He always sipped his espresso through a sugar cube. And, there was always a bag packed next to his bed just in case he had to make a quick run for it. Not a run because of any personal intrigues, but from an unexpected change in the political climate. I suppose you could say he was merely transplanted here. He didn't know from Freud or Western deductive reasoning. He did know what he saw and what he felt. The turmoil he had experienced in Europe was literally built into his very genes. He thought of America as just a temporary respite. Wealth and comfort make ordinary people turn their heads to that which would otherwise be reprehensible; but comfort – even temporary – allows them to easily suppress the incentive to resist or repel it. If America stayed clean during his life, so much the better; but, he did not have any illusions and the phrase "Never Again" was indelibly transcribed on his heart.

I never asked where he obtained his switchblade, since all-in-all it seemed so uncharacteristic. On the other hand, I just found it too uncomfortable to think that he had been in situations where he would have even wanted or needed one. If so, why not a gun?

The body of the knife was beautiful and elegant with a handle of midnight-black onyx emblazoned with a yellow Star of David. I think he may have considered himself a modern day sicarius - the ancient Israelite patriot of 2,000 years ago who carried a hidden dagger to quickly dispatch unsuspecting Roman soldiers. As a result of the Roman-enforced dispersion of the Jewish population of Israel, called the Diaspora, and the resulting continuous persecutions, he, in his own way, continued to wage war against Rome and its progeny. But, he always had hope and respect. His constant companion was a Book of Psalms. He knew them by heart, and would sing them under his breath regularly. When he did, light seemed to radiate from his eyes.

Some thought this made him a fatalist. Actually, he was anything but. He saw with clear, clean vision. He had no real wants or desires. He spoke and acted from a place of innocence and purity. In this way, he was somewhat of a saint. From his tortured early years, he knew how to divorce himself from what he was doing, so that he literally was not the "doer" of any activity in which he was involved. Hence, he "knew" how to be at the right place at the right time. The rest was not his business and he gave it no mind. He received his instructions from a different realm; a higher realm.

He had described similar situations he had been in over the years, while he was telling me to stay away from investigations and just enjoy a "white collar" life. "Be a mensch" – a good boy – he said. "Stay away from the connivers and the 'gunuffs' – the thieves. People like Victoria Lake, he would have said, were entirely predictable. They were also trouble, he told me more than once. "The men they attract are just dynamite" he would say. The woman is the blasting cap. If you have to deal with them at all, "stay close enough to get what you need for the client, but far enough away to avoid getting caught in the explosion. And, mark my words, there is always an explosion" he said. He was fond of relating the current to what he knew of mysticism or mythology. "Controllers or manipulators are a dime a dozen. They all wind up like Sisyphus of Greek mythology. Almost to the top of the mountain they constructed through design, manipulation and savagery, they step on a stone and roll to the bottom, alone, afraid and with nothing."

"These people are easy" he had told me. "They have made one pattern for themselves. They will carry into this affair what they have put into and taken out of every other affair, be it personal or business. A lot of baggage. The pattern is always the same; only the players have changed. Those who get caught in the little game are there solely for entertainment. They will be handed a fistful of IOUs from every other relationship and will be expected to make good. They will be drained in the process. In the end, whatever remains of them will be spit into the wind. Then they will dine at the banquet they constructed for themselves. This is just the way of the world. Stay aloof. Stay apart from it." The fact that this was coming to me with an Eastern European Yiddish accent made it, at once, out of character and totally believable.

Sometimes the accuracy of his images truly frightened me. He would speak these words while his eyes were off, far into the distance as if he were staring into a void of such magnetic potential where he ceased to be while he was speaking it.

He had a very basic and practical view of life. "Every living thing," he said, "wants love and will go to any extent to get it. They will go to an enormous extent to obtain this approval from another person; they will look everywhere and in everything, other than in the only place they should be looking; in themselves. Because they never look for it in the right place, they are frustrated, angry and hostile. Then a twinkle would illuminate his eye when he said, "I only wish the people today had the manners and the morals of the gangsters in 'The Maltese Falcon.' It would be such a kinder place." He loved the gangster movies from the 30s and 40s and often used them to press a point.

Anyway, I knew he was right. Some suppress or sublimate their desires better than others. Others express the non-fulfillment in anger, fear, control and manipulation. He felt that manipulation, self-absorption and seeking approval from others for self-centered, sociopathic behavior was becoming the hallmark of this civilization.

I once asked him why no one ever seems to find what it was he was talking about. He said very matter-of-factly, "Because they are afraid of staring at themselves in the mirror."

I asked him what he meant, because I really didn't have a problem looking in the mirror. And from the number of women in office buildings whom I have seen staring at themselves in elevator mirrors, I figured that a lot of other people didn't have problems with mirrors either.

"That not what I meant" he said matter-of-factly. "Listen; it's this way. People want something from other people that no one else can give them, even if they wanted to. That's the whole damn problem in this place! Even if the giver has the highest, most noble aspirations imaginable, one person cannot make another person feel loved. It is up to each of us to do this for ourselves. We each have the responsibility as well as the means. All you have to do is do it. That's all. I was born into a world that provided everything for my care. It was taken away from me in an instant and has never returned. I had to find other ways. This is what I am telling you."

Seemed simple enough. Duke hated philosophy. "Philosophy was made for the pretty people in their drawing rooms" he told me. "Philosophy has nothing to do with life. For that matter, either do psychology, religion, or any other practice that doesn't start from the beginning. What is the beginning? Lead someone to have a true spiritual experience; an experience of the totality of being. Everything in their lives from that point on will be surplus. Everything in their lives from that point on will flow. I do not mean that everyone has to be a monk or street-wise to have some smarts, but philosophy and most of all of the sciences are more about theory than experience. Theory has everything to do with intellectualizing. It has nothing to do with that which keeps you going against all odds; gives you insight when the mind is blank, and talks quietly to you when the world is screaming at a deafening volume. It is your Heart! That's where your life is! Connect with it, and you connect with the Universe."

He told me about the hard times he went through in Europe. I knew he knew what he was talking about. Anyone who could talk openly about the heart with his life experiences had to know what he was talking about.

So, the questions he would often ask, as if looking into the deep, dark past of Europe in particular, was .... Knowing this, why? Why do we let it continue in our lives and our world? Wouldn't it be so easy just to be a loving person – regardless of the fear of being exposed and out of control? Wouldn't it be so easy to simply accept death as a normal part of the human drama, while reflecting on the spiritual reality that everything is energy and energy never ceases to exist? Wouldn't it be so easy just to be!

Then, he would stop with a shrug. "I know all the "what ifs" and "shoulds" and "becauses." I have experienced them poignantly. They usually revolve around money. Ah!! Another creation between the bookends. What would this world be without even the consciousness of greed?

What if there is, and always was, a Life outside of the bookends. Veiled; not hidden. Just out of the corner of the eye; behind a shadow. Something that you vaguely remember, but just cannot put your finger on.

I have said this enough times to have made it a rule in my approach to understanding their world. If Creator were to collect the individual stories of all souls who have ever or will ever incarnate in this realm, the story would be the same: longing for love in the Garden of G-d. Each of us writes our own story of longing.

Sometimes I was in a light, carefree mood. Then came one of his "bombs." I knew the horses were out of the gate and the race had just begun. I was just going to ride with it till the end.

"Do you feel this concrete?" he asked me once when I was a young child. "Can you see the people who are walking on it this very moment?" I answered yes to both questions. I had no choice really. "What do you make of it?" he asked. "I don't make anything of it" I replied a little incredulously as I shrugged my shoulders. Heck, I think I was only 7 at the time. "Well, what do you feel about it?" he asked, emphasizing the work "feel." "I feel they're all in a hurry to get to work," I again replied shyly and skeptically. "Good!" he exclaimed. "Observe, put the facts together, and then let the feeling take hold. Then, just let go. Their patterns will tell you everything you want to know. People become programmed very easily. There are patterns everywhere. Just follow the patterns. Do not try to understand why they are doing what they are doing. And, don't interfere. That is for G-d and no one else. Remember this is His dream, not ours."

I had no idea about how he knew when or what G-d was dreaming. I only hoped G-d didn't have any nightmares. At 7 I knew this place was strange, if not outright dangerous. We didn't need any fuel for the fire.

Uncle Duke had that innate knowledge of why people do what they do, especially if love or money was concerned. And, as he told me, "Love or money is always involved. Everything you see in any relationship is nothing but a variation on a theme. It is as though G-d lives one life over and over in as many variations as infinity allows."

He would have made a good sabra, the Hebrew word for an Israeli born in Israel. Tough on the outside, with a warm heart inside. He started life as a quiet, shy boy whose only interest was studying the Torah and the Talmud. After his family was murdered in the Holocaust, and he managed to escape, he became a hunter of sorts. He liked to work behind the scenes. Slowly. Patiently. No muss. No fuss. A quick dispatch. Then it was done. If one of his quarries happened to be an officer, he considered it a good day's work. Yet, after all of this, I never heard one bitter word of hatred or condemnation. It was as though he had found the secret of releasing hatred as a means for his own survival.

I often try to picture what Uncle Duke would do in certain situations I'm faced with today, like Victoria Lake. But, as far as Victoria Lake and her men are concerned, I think I have already answered that.

Among other things, I knew that Bonticlaire, in some way or another, was very interested in an industrial revenue bond issue which was going to provide funding to completely refurbish the convention center along with a new, adjoining sports arena, hotel and multi-level mall. The center had been built at a time when housing statewide conventions was its only purpose. The purpose was largely agricultural. That had largely changed over the past 20 years. Large mineral deposits had also been located several miles outside of the developed area. The multinationals moved in, commerce grew thousands fold, and international prominence followed, along with the chance for major league baseball, football and basketball teams. A major convention was being planned a year and a half down the road.

Bonticlaire wanted it to be known by the proper people, and the general populace, that he was instrumental in getting the IRB issue to the launch pad. Getting the project passed by the city planning commission was, of course, out of his jurisdiction. His involvement with it would also put his burgeoning gubernatorial campaign on the "go" cycle. If the issue passed, and the construction work was undertaken, long-term jobs would be guaranteed and the city would take its place among the national trade centers. The issue could very well decide the next gubernatorial race.

Victoria figured into this because she had developed the reputation of being the pivotal "swing" vote of the 9-member commission. Now that she had a distinct conflict, the possibility loomed for a court proceeding in the event of a tie. The vote on whether to present the issue to the general voting electorate would be decided shortly by the commission. The fact that her communications with Bonticlaire were an obvious conflict of interest was otherwise irrelevant to her.

The commission was stereotypical in its makeup. Two conservative Republicans, two liberal Democrats, four middle-of-the-roaders (two Democrats and two Republicans) and Victoria. She flitted between the camps like a butterfly.

Jack Slate was even more conservative than the new Republicans who typically voted against major social projects. He was certainly not one to embrace even the more conservative Democratic ideals and programs. His young protégé, Neil Demeraugh had originally come from a ranching family, and was brought up on the Protestant work ethic. They saw the convention/ arena project as being unnecessary, and nothing more than a further step in the political careers of some self-serving Democrats – and, another opportunity for organized labor and organized crime to entrench themselves in the area. This would also bring into the area many unskilled laborers. It also raised the distinct possibility that these immigrant workers might not leave after the completion of the project.

Slate and Demeraugh consistently voted as a block. The two liberal Democrats, Griscomb and Ash, also voted as a block. The other four looked for the middle, which often coincided with their party. Victoria Lake, therefore, stood out as the prize. Tall, slender, long dark hair, and striking features, she was certainly desirable in any respect. Jake's connections helped her get elected to a four-year post on the commission. She surprised everyone, especially her husband, by exhibiting an informed and independent judgment in such a politically-charged atmosphere. She was good and knew it!

At 11:00 they each left the Algeria Club, got into their separate cars and drove off. She went straight back to her home, alone.

Jacob Lake might be satisfied to know that his wife was not fooling around, at least not with Bonticlaire at the present time – not that extramarital episodes meant anything at all to Jake. But, if Bonticlaire got his foot in the door, it could mean big trouble for Lake's real estate and construction businesses. Word had it that he was "arranging" a low bid on the convention center, should it be passed. If so, he would be given the arena as a prize. He was then free to name his price on the surrounding hotel contracts and infrastructure improvements that would follow the project. It would have the effect of building an entire addition to the city. Billions of dollars were potentially at stake.

If the center issue passed, and should Bonticlaire be handed the key to the Governor's mansion, in part because of the IRB matter, then he would surely have a truck-load of political favors to repay. Hence, the convention center contracts.

A modern version of "Showdown at the OK Corral" was brewing. This wasn't, however, Dodge City. Death didn't come quickly from a well-aimed bullet. It came slowly, after months and even years of slow economic strangulation, and resulting mental anguish and despair. When you were this big, and lost this much – as one of them was bound to do – bankruptcy was just a Band-Aid, and not a very big one at that.

The city might be a behemoth, but people like Jacob Lake and Timothy Bonticlaire aspired to capture and control it.

Jake was really from another era. In his mid-50s, his morals were strictly waterfront. His speech and cadence were typically gruff and gangsterish. Money was his game and money was the only game in town. Real estate and construction, and whatever else he did with his money, were merely watering holes for what I assumed were bigger clandestine business ventures. How do I know this? That is strictly confidential. I can say that he did come to see me, privately, when even he could not control his anxiety.

Timothy Bonticlaire was in his early 40s; refined, educated, calculating and covetous. Money was his game, but it had to have a genteel twist. Control of the masses was his opiate. Politics kept him high. Same mold as Lake, but with a different presentation.

Had the underlying similarity of their egos not have presented a magnetic repulsion, they could have made a very effective team. Many were grateful that a compromise between them seemed unlikely.

X

T.S. Eliot in "The Waste Land" viewed society as a place of the living dead. In his poetry, he described modern society as living "in rats' alley where the dead men lost their bones." Society, however, has always had a tendency to devour its constituents. Like a self-absorbed demonic beast, it chews them up, takes the best for itself, and indifferently disposes of the rest.

Mrs. Mellenstreet was once young and curvaceous. The lines were still there. Unfortunately, as a result of undue emotional stress, she could only now only be gently termed as being "worn." I felt for her. While a professional is advised against being overly sympathetic towards any client, there is no substitute for kindness and compassion in this world. She was very deserving. Many in her position project emotional neediness. She was more stoic.

From her description to me, Andrew Mellenstreet was a study in predictability. Accountant. 65 years old. Own hair and teeth. 6 feet. 195 pounds. Likes quiet night clubs where he can have a drink, open a file or two and be by himself. Faithful to his wife and his job as far as she knew. Their marriage had been over for so long, that but for the children she would have considered it a vague illusion. She was not one for medication and needed help for a life she knew was well behind her.

She was my Wednesday morning, 10:00 a.m. appointment. It got her out of the house, gave her someone to talk to, and gave her hope that things would get better. But now she was worried about her husband's frequent absences. Could he be having an affair? What was going on? She did not want to get involved with investigators or the "seamy" side of life and she had heard me talk about Uncle Duke enough to know I at least had some investigative connections in my background. She also knew that even if she asked her husband point blank he would give her some clipped, droll explanation that would not satisfy anything.

This would have to wait until later. Tonight I needed some exercise.

XI

It was dusk at the Essex Country Club when I pulled up in my car. The Sun's descent propelled rich hues of red and blue across the vast expanse of the evening sky. The golfers were finishing up and it was safe to jog around the golf course.

I used to run more than I do now, but I still love the feel of a breeze coursing against me as my heart is pumping in a long and deep cadence. The mind chatter stills and I have the pleasure of focusing on just one thing, or on nothing at all. Running can be a wonderful meditation or opiate.

The running course followed the perimeter of the country club golf course. It was a standard two miles around. I took it easy the first time. A comfortable pace. Slowly extending and feeling the stretch. Gentle, but determined. Feeling the internal heat and sweat, the grandeur and grace of motion.

The second time around felt natural. I felt strong. The crunch of the sandy soil felt good and sounded good beneath my feet. The constancy of the sound was also relaxing – almost like listening to the sound of waves lapping against the shore. It made me forget. Moments of no thought build up an expansiveness and exhilaration; a gratitude towards life and an all-embracing attitude.

I was nearing a particular stretch which actually goes outside and beyond the perimeter of the course and down a fairly steep hill to a lower elevation that eventually winds its way back up to the course. I went down lower and lower as I had done so many times before. At the lowest point of my descent, I was totally alone. No golfers. No runners. Complete quiet. The well-cultured Essex Country Club was high above me and off to my left. To my right was a drainage ditch, and beyond it a number of prefabricated buildings used by some construction firms. They were apparently uninhabited.

Water in the drainage ditch lapped against the concrete sides as if it were continuing on a predetermined journey.

Ahead of me, the view to the horizon was clear to infinity. At this time of the day, the sky was becoming a canvas for a "living" Maxfield Parrish painting; changing every second – an impressionist's delight. Unreal sky hues, shade after shade of rich blue, in gradual descent from an almost turquoise blue.

It was a quiet time and it felt good to be running alone.

After I completed a short stretch at the lowest elevation, I was nearing the steep incline to the left. The sudden contrasts on this course continue to offer a challenge notwithstanding the number of times I have been over it.

My stride began to extend as I anticipated the upward slope. Once you are used to a certain course, your body will almost automatically adjust to the anticipated challenge.

As I made the turn and started up the hill the country club grounds came into view. Then I noticed something so incongruous it made me slow down, and then stop. Legs were sticking out from underneath some shrubbery on the country club grounds. This was manicured shrubbery on well-kept grounds, not haphazard, unkempt vegetation in the middle of an urban waste land. The face and body were hidden so I couldn't tell if the person was merely resting or perhaps sleeping off a stupor. This area was not too far from downtown, but it was very unusual to be dealing with this kind of situation here. Security patrols from the country club would normally ward off an unwelcome intruder long before he got this close. I wasn't sure whether to get going again, but presuming it was just intoxication, I kept on my run.

A warm, caressing, almost intoxicating breeze was beginning to blow. It wrapped me inside it. It was like it had been lying in wait for me. It seemed to come out of nowhere.

This kind of breeze doesn't just blow against you. It embraces you. It literally takes your body. At this point, all sense of time leaves. There is only the run and the breeze.

Now I feel alive. I feel extended. I feel like a marathon runner. There is nothing more important right now than running. Running has become identical to breathing, and my pace has become as regular. In short, I feel grand. I want nothing more than to keep running.

The scene at the bushes had not changed on my next time around. I decided not to stop, thinking that security would find the person soon and take care of it.

On my last time around I was not so sure. Approaching the hill again, I saw another runner coming from the opposite direction. He, too, saw the body and we both stopped to investigate. The legs were still protruding from the bushes. It did not look like they had moved at all. We moved aside some low-lying branches of the bush. The body was motionless. Not a sound. Not a movement. Absolutely still.

His clothes were casual whites of obvious quality; certainly not the clothes of a gin mill patron. I give him a little nudge with my foot. No response. I put my hand by his nostrils. No breath. Nothing.

I just felt a shiver go up my spine and got goose bumps from top to bottom. It was forceful and direct. I knew he was not sleeping. Security was still not in the area, so I found the nearest 911 emergency phone which was just off the path and called the police. The other runner and I waited there to give our statements.

The police came and photographed the scene. The forensics people scoured the area. Luckily we had not traversed too much of the area. When the paramedics came, I watched them as they moved him onto the gurney. It was then I saw it. On his chest, in red blood, was the double triangle symbol in the same form as the meteorite. Each palm contained the same symbols. It was also on his forehead.

From what I could see, the person didn't show any signs of perspiration. No signs of any struggle. No other gashes, lacerations or gouges. He had a quiet, peaceful look on his face.

I felt like I was a 5 year old having just gotten home from seeing the movie "The Blob." Any young child growing up in the 50s will agree that at that time, this movie was one of the most terrifying and left indelible marks still remarkable decades later. I had enough courage then to look under my bed, but I didn't dare go near the heat vent. Tonight, I don't even want to look under my bed.

That night I had a dream. I was dancing again. The same ballroom. The same beautiful woman in the white dress. Then my field of vision centered on the man and his eyes. It is almost as if we are staring at each other. And in that instant I bolted awake.

There was something so familiar. A déjà vu, but also a type of homecoming.

The look in his eyes seemed so entrancing. I must have fallen back asleep because I remembered something I had been trying to remember for a very long time. I was so happy to have remembered it. I woke up. I immediately forgot what I had been so glad to remember just a split second before. I looked at the clock and saw that it was 4:30 a.m. I lied down and fell back to sleep. I started to dream.

Then I was soaring through a cloud. Suddenly the vision turned crystal clear. I was staring at the face of an exquisitely beautiful person, or entity. Hard to describe. I could not tell if the person were a man or a woman because it resembled both. Even still, there was something regal, holy and other-worldly about his/her presence. The gender did not matter. I was staring at the presence of real beauty.

Beauty, as I will call it, was seated on a high, bright white circular throne. It was a tall cylinder, maybe twenty feet tall. The central circular portion and front curve had been cored or removed from the top of the cylinder to three feet from the bottom to create a seating area for the Presence. It had a radiant smile on its face as it was looking into the distance, deep in thought. I had a faint recollection of the face. I looked at the form. "Why does he not look at me? Why does it not acknowledge or recognize me" I thought.

I woke at 6:00 a.m.

The phone rang at 8:00 a.m. An official voice with the name of Detective Pritchard was asking me to give a statement about last night. Official voices over the phone sound like muzak after a while; they pervade the atmosphere but you really don't want to pay attention to them. My response was equally as automatic as if I wasn't speaking. "I gave my statement last night. There is nothing else I can tell you."

Not to be dissuaded, he continued. "It's about the markings on the chest. We were told that you're into this sort of stuff," he said coolly. "Can you tell us anything about them?" What he said next really got my attention. "Yours was not the only call we received. There were some bystanders at the Club who claimed this fellow seemed to appear out of thin air. They all confirm that he didn't walk to the bushes, he simply appeared in them."

XII

I knew why Detective Pritchard wanted my second statement this morning. The unusual markings on the body present a challenge for any homicide detective who is used to dealing with a common range of possibilities. Even so, it would be very easy to just attribute this to a yet unknown cult, and leave it at that. Depending on the victim and his or her family connections, however, there could very well be pressure to solve the case. I suspected this was the case. And, for whatever reason, I had been "chosen" to be involved in this, at least to some degree.

I didn't have to go through the factual story. There wasn't much to tell, and the report was accurate. Because of the ongoing investigation, he couldn't tell me more of what the bystanders actually saw and reported, but it didn't appear there was more to say.

The crime scene yielded no information thus far. He wanted to know if I knew anything about the unusual markings on his chest and hands. I thought better of correlating the symbol to what I had seen at the Hall of Antiquities, and so said I did not.

"Ponti Moon and you were friends, weren't you?" He asked.

"Yes," I answered incredulously, wondering what the connection was going to be. "What has that got to do with anything?"

"We don't know right now. The fellow had no wallet on him and no identification. He did, however, have a ticket stub from the Hall of Antiquities dated the opening day of the new exhibit. Some of the newspaper reports intimated some unusual behavior at the exhibition. Now, this is compounded by the disappearance of Mr. Moon. To us, it would be foul play or death, if we find a body that is missing. This fellow's body seems not to have vanished into thin air, but to have come out of thin air. And the only footprints on the grounds around the body were yours and the other runner. None of the footprints match the victim's. I am not suggesting anything, because we already checked out your timetables and everything checks out. But, how did the body really get there? It either walked or was deposited. There are no other real possibilities, and neither of them can be verified."

"What about the bystanders?"

"I wish that was the case. Most of them were in the club house and had alcohol on their breath. For the others, I am not sure what optical illusions made it seem like one moment he was not there, and the next he was, but I cannot seriously entertain anything else about what they said. In fact, neither can they."

"You used the 911," Pritchard said analytically. "Did you see or hear anyone? See any cars drive off; any helicopters deposit the body and depart?"

Pritchard had the steely blue eyes of an ice man. He had to force his lips into kind of a constipated smile. He was calculated down to the movement of his little finger. Hard skin and a severe brush cut finished out the image of the regimented man, solid as a rock on the outside; chiseled into life, rather than born into it.

"What about being teleported?" I queried.

"Tele *what!*" he responded.

"Nothing. Just being sarcastic."

I left and went to the office. Before going inside I visited Petey to see what his take on all of this was. Believe it or not, sometimes Petey is the only person who makes any sense to me. He wasn't educated, but was more literate in the basic elements of life than most. He was always looking and listening. Very unusual. Very rare. He wasn't living in the fast-lane, nor was he a slug. He was just always there. Looking and Listening. He had no worries about what others thought. His unpretentiousness allowed him to be fully present. This allowed him to see more clearly than most.

"Hey, Missah Cushneh, how's da man, now? How is he?"

"Okay Petey. How's tricks?"

He gave me a wide-eyed toothless grin which he quickly filled with his cigar butt. Always a butt. Always mulch at one end. I sometimes wonder where he buys cigars with chewed ends.

"Oh, I'm doin' as good as I ahways am, Missah Cushneh."

"What news do you hear today Petey?"

"You should know that Missah Cushneh; youse and the otha guy was in de paper dis mornin."

"Oh, brother; I didn't watch the news and didn't know." This means reporters are going to be hounding me. Their needling can be worse than Pritchard's.

"What do you think, Petey? A good disguise job to mesh with the museum exhibit – or, some kind of cult killing. Or, maybe something to do with spirits," I said smiling.

"Hey Missah Cushneh, I don' know nottin' 'bout no spiwits. Anyhoos, thewes enough goons down hewe ahweady. Don' need no mowe, if ya know what I mean. Whoevew don' it, jus' twyin' to covah it up, dat's all. Like when I fust came down to this cowna. It was always the 'talians gainst the Iwish. If one of them made a hit they wanted to covew, they jus' painted it to look like the othew guy. Dat's all. No spiwits in this one. Naw, no cults neetheh. Maybe jus' twyin' to hang it on Misseh Moon because of his exhibit; I don't know. If they ahh, dat's a cheap twick, ain' it?"

"Have you been to the exhibit, Petey?"

"Naw, dat's not for me. I'll be at his funewal though, if they have one. To pay my last wespects, that is. He was a weel gent, he was," he said with downcast eyes.

"No arguments there, Petey. Keep your eyes and ears open on this murder, will you Petey. If my instincts are right, it's more than it seems at first sight. A lot more."

"Will do Missah Cushneh."

"Right, Petey. Thanks. I'll catch you later."

"You be good, Missah Cushneh: he said waiving his stogie in his half-gloved right hand. "Oh, Missah Cushneh, hewe's you papah. Since they named you and the othah guy in the stowey, it's on the house. You a cewebwity today."

I went to bed early that night. I guess I had been dreaming. It was one of those dreams where you feel like you're really there. An ectoplasmic dream. It can be tasted, smelled and touched. The dream becomes as real as anything you've ever known. In my mind, the basis for the old saying about a man dreaming he was a butterfly. Some have said that it might also have been a butterfly dreaming it was a man.

What we think is reality can change rapidly, and the limits of our consciousness can broaden involuntarily without warning or preparation. The sleep state does not know of the boundaries we observe when our eyes are open. Many have said that the waking state is merely the dream.

I remember it vividly. All the sensations and the thoughts. I was flying over some grassy knolls. I was actually flying; no airplane or anything like that. It seemed perfectly natural. Then I was flying over some highway. I knew it was some peripheral highway which circled a major metropolitan area. I didn't see any buildings, but I had a knowing that it was London. Someone was talking to me. A strange dialect, a strange cadence. I tried to answer and woke up doing so. I was on my back and realized that my head was actually lifted off the pillow. I woke Kathryn up in the process. She asked if I was alright. I nodded yes, smiled and told her she could go back to sleep.

I got out of my bed and milled around the bedroom. Something drew my attention to the box Ponti left me. I opened it and looked at the contents. "Silence becomes me." I took that as a compliment since I did not consider myself a boisterous or cantankerous person. The triangles were in the stylized "I" pattern again. Still as confused as before, I put the items down. Then something on the wrapping paper caught my attention. At first it looked like doodling, like someone had tried to get a ballpoint pen to start writing. Then I looked at it closely and it looked more like script. "It is script," I said to myself in amazement. It was small and hard to read, so I got out my magnifying glass. But, it was not in English. Ponti knew I was fluent in Hebrew, as was he. He left a calling card for me that he knew no one else would be able to read.

I traced the lines carefully and something began to take form. Letters I recognized. Then, a name. Moshe ben Rafael. To some he was a legendary mystic and an actual historical personality. To others he was purely fictional. He was reputed to have never died. The first historical siting of him was in Safed, Israel in 680 B.C.E. and the second in the area outside of Marseille, France in 925 C.E. In Hebrew timekeeping, B.C.E. stands for "Before the Common Era," or otherwise, B.C. in the Western World. C.E. stands for "Common Era" or otherwise known as A.D. in the Western World. He is said to have "retired" after the Marseille experience; away, but not away.

Moshe ben Rafael is reputed to still be among us. Both Safed and Marseille were centers of intense Jewish mysticism at the times he was there.

There is one manuscript attributed to him, and it is reputedly in his own hand. Like any mystical document, it has come under intense scrutiny with widely differing interpretations. Its exact title is *"The Light of Generations."* The accepted translation begins as follows: "Creation is reflected only by the light it radiates. G-d's first creation in this Realm was Light. Light contains the essence of all other creations than can be created. The movement of light creates sound. In this Seventh World, everything is light and sound. Time is nothing but the bending of the light channel. Light holds Sound in its womb, and this is the meaning of "In the Beginning." Light, Sound and Time create a sequence which insists that we disobey what we see. In this way, we remember who we are. One portrays as three, and three must be disregarded for the one. In stillness we hear the movement leading to the light of redemption. In redemption, time is extinguished. Points of no space can only rest on each other in utter stillness, for they are not in time and there is nothing between them but space, silence and the Presence of the Divine Emanation whose name I am not permitted to utter. All knowledge lies here, for it is the knowledge which cannot be known. I commit this to you, I Moshe ben Rafael, the son I Am of an Angel."

What did Ponti want to say to me about Moshe ben Rafael? "Silence and the Presence of the Divine Emanation?"

Next to his name there were other symbols. When I deciphered them, they spelled "pardes" the Hebrew word for "garden." Garden! Which garden? A real garden or a figurative garden? Pardes was also an acronym for the traditional four methods of study or translation of the Bible, the Five Books of Moses: literal, homily, allegory and mystical. But, maybe there was something buried in the garden behind Ponti's home. Then, a chill went up my spine. Garden could also mean the Garden of Eden. The place of all knowing before knowledge was known.

Triangles on the hand, between the eyes and on the heart. A sign. A meaning. A remembrance? I then remembered the Biblical injunction from the Old Testament that "You shall bind them for a sign." Observant Jews wear tefillin, otherwise known as phylacteries, on their foreheads and non-dominant hand and arm, during weekday prayer services. They are small, leather boxes containing parchment scrolls inscribed with verses from the Books of Exodus and Deuteronomy in the Bible. This is in accordance with Deuteronomy 6:8. This is the literal translation. This links them to some deeper past, deeper than history and far more profound than any physical representation.

But, if we know our connection to G-d, what else is there to remember? What is it? And, now at this point, who am I to ask? For G-d's sake, who Am I? I am being beckoned to move forward; how or when, I do not know.

Light has been an image and a symbol since time immemorial. The Bible is replete with images and the force of Light. Ankenaton, the Egyptian Pharaoh, attempted to transform Egyptian religion by instituting a religion based on the worship of one G-d. The one G-d was symbolized by the Sun. Today it is also the source for many wanderings, speculations and ruminations. Rafael Cushing in his "The Filaments of Light & Power" has this to say:

"Take a prism into a completely dark room. Allow light to enter, in a beam at precisely 33 degrees at 12:00 noon. In a deep state of meditation, you will feel the essence of the light penetrate you. It will be like you are reading a magnetic tape containing information."

Light, in the context of what I was seeking, was pure Light. Not ruminations about refracting this or bending that; not using the force, but being a vessel for the force. The mistake of modern society and science in particular, is the desire to "master" and use that for which we are intended to be used as vessels. In other words, we have taken G-d's dream and turned it into our fantasy and our laboratory. What other than ominous portents can come from this? And, how far can it go before the Master Puppeteer, so to speak, yanks on the chord to create order where there has been catastrophic chaos? Or maybe, all of this, just the way it is, was written into the script long ago, and is being played out in all its glory, with not one scintilla of disturbance or variation in the performance of a lifetime. Maybe it is supposed to be this way. What would Rube Goldberg have thought?

XIII

The next morning I got into the office at 8:30.

Mrs. Mellenstreet had already called. She matter-of-factly left a message that her husband would not be coming home directly from work. She thought he would be leaving at the usual time or 5:15. She wanted to know where he went.

How did I get myself into this one, I wondered?

I felt this was just a prelude to a bigger, more interesting story. I tried to justify it by thinking that any information would only be conducive to Mrs. Mellenstreet's treatment, but even this seemed like a hard sell.

It was not unusual for someone like Mr. Mellenstreet to be fooling around, if that was what he was doing. His life was otherwise staid, predictable and debt free.

The first time I met Mrs. Mellenstreet was at her home. For some reason, she couldn't get down to the office. Their home is in the Pine Hills section; all custom homes on acreage. The living room was very well done in Chinese décor, very well done. They have a showpiece coffee table which is a real work of art: gilt-edged with lapis lazuli.

I know I mentioned before that Mrs. Mellenstreet must have been very attractive during her youth. Unfortunately, the stresses of her social position had been wearing on her. Yet, even at her age, Mrs. Mellenstreet still had delicate and attractive features: a long narrow nose, slightly upturned; a gentle curve to her eyebrows, which accentuated her wide brown eyes, high cheekbones gave a good outline to her face. Her thick dark hair was cut in a pageboy. I am sure she, at one time, wanted to emulate a 1920's flapper!

She is the type who always supported her husband by assuming the position in society which was expected of her. All very segmented and meant to flow together, but often cascading into separate and discordant parts in a vast sea of unhappiness.

She was brought up to accept the duties of the wife, mother and social planner. Mr. Mellenstreet was the breadwinner only. Little sharing; little communication. The children long gone, the grandchildren visiting only every few years; the house an empty testament to a marriage in form only. Mr. Mellenstreet may very well be seeking new adventures as a last hurrah.

Mr. Mellenstreet's office was in the Pan-Oceanic Exposition Building which was in the midst of the financial district. Actually, not too far from my Elliott Square Building. The area was a mass of monumental and awe-inspiring buildings, devoted to the propagation of wealth and money. Whereas the mysteries of life once consumed the waking days of high-spirited individuals; now the acquisition and consumption of wealth has become an end in itself. These beautiful buildings were all marble and glass. Constructed for the World Exposition in 1901, they reflected a grace and grandeur completely missing from today's architecture.

New construction and refurbishing of old buildings was constantly in evidence in the vicinity. Construction cranes were as ordinary as mid-day lunch goers.

Cathedral Square separated the financial district from the Museum of Art and Hall of Antiquities by about a quarter of a mile.

At 4:50 I parked outside the Pan-Oceanic Building and went inside and strolled around the lobby.

The Pan-Oceanic building was a marvel for its time. One of a new breed of office buildings, it literally electrified the business world in 1901 when it installed electric light capability in each office. It heralded a new age for industrial age ethics. It was specially constructed as one of the jewels in the architectural splendors of the World Exposition of 1901. As if the building knew its special breeding, it retained an aura of exclusivity and bearing even when eclipsed by its more modern cousins. It seemed to know that it could never be overshadowed by rectangular boxes with window holes cut out. The modern versions seemed to know it too. It was almost as if their additional height was meant, not to overshadow, but rather to bow down to the glory of their predecessor.

The outside of the building was a light, slate grey color. It may have had fewer flourishes than many other opulent structures of its time, but had enough to give it the clean appearance of spartan dignity. The real grandeur was saved for the inside.

Three revolving doors, heavy glass surrounded by brass, guided the way from worn sidewalk concrete to a bygone era of grace elegantly packaged in marble and crystal.

The entire entry level floor was an enormous mosaic. A stylized floral design, perhaps Greek or Roman in origin, was surrounded by a crimson border. The designs were ornate and fanciful. I didn't recognize any of them. Perhaps this was the intent of the artist. The sense of mystery is preserved until something is identified. Until then, it is left up to the imagination, and in the imagination anything is possible. It fosters a tension that keeps your interest aroused.

The mosaic could have easily gone in some mythic medieval castle surrounded by heavy stone walls on which hung enormous tapestries depicting heraldic and heroic events.

Brass rails led to the mezzanine by way of a wide, ceremonial marble staircase. The walls were heavily veined marble of a lighter hue, leading three stories to the ceiling of this Grand Entrance. In the center hung an imperial chandelier surrounded by six other subservient chandeliers equally positioned across the expanse of the entrance hall, almost in the shape of a Star of David. In a way, the immortal beauty and ageless character of the building reminded me of the Hall of Antiquities.

During the day, the interior activity was bustling and the mood was full of life. Later in the day, when the work-a-day crowds had left, it resumed its aristocratic bearing. In fact, it was almost a sin to be nonobservant in this place of wonder, and possibly of worship. The Pan-Oceanic Building reflected the best in all of us. We needed to return the favor.

The building was constructed at a time when people got their air from the atmosphere; not from internal conduits which happened to pipe in air or any reasonable facsimile to the captive office workers. Even after the building was refurbished, the windows were left intact, allowing the user to actually open one.

Even the office doors at the Pan-Oceanic Building were made of a sturdy oak or maple, with opaque glass filling the top half. Door signs were still painted by commercial artists. Window sills were also solid wood, not aluminum.

Few buildings, if any, in the city retained the charm and elegance of the Pan-Oceanic Building; certainly not the new office building rectangles.

The Pan-Oceanic Building still spawned the image of wide-brimmed Fedora hats and smart-looking suits, with starched white shirts and carefully knotted ties. While I am sure that modern architects, engineers and energy conservationists consider the building a dinosaur, it is rich in history and alive in character. Spared from the wrecker's ball on several occasions, it was recently refurbished by some multinational. I was very grateful. There is a soft spot in my heart for buildings with soul and character – or anything for that matter – with old soul.

The elegance of the interior inspired a comeliness on the part of its regular patrons. All very civilized, genteel and well-bred.

I had heard from a few old-timers that in the 1920s, the city's planning commission had tentatively scheduled a subway run underneath Culver Street. Some digging and remodeling had begun. At one time, I was told, there were also subterranean walkways leading from the Pan-Oceanic Building and the nearby Bryant Building all the way over to the Hall of Antiquities, and beyond. This spurred my interest and I decided that I would try to find out more. I knew someone who knew someone who knew the chief engineer of the Pan-Oceanic Building. The engineer owed him a favor. Perhaps my contact would let me cash it in.

Andrew Mellenstreet came walking out of the elevator into the lobby when I was in mid-fantasy about times gone by. He exited the building, walked into the parking lot and got into his Volvo.

I followed him down High Street, and stayed a comfortable distance away from him on California Avenue. He turned up Grand Boulevard and made his way into the University.

He parked behind the library, got out, and went inside. He was unaware that I was following him. I stayed with him until the ancient history section; one of my old haunts in school. He picked out some books, settled into his cubicle, and stayed there until 8:30. I stayed in a cubicle some distance away where I could watch him without being noticed myself.

Without further ado, he stood up, put on his coat and hat, returned the books to a book cart, and left the library.

Before leaving the library, I took a quick picture of the books: "The Esoteric Rites of the High Priest;" "Funerary Incantations of the Ancient Egyptians;" "Esoteric Ceremonies from Prehistory;" "Prehistoric Civilizations in the Gobi;" "The Mystical Origins of the House of Israel" and, "The World Before Atlantis And Lemuria." Also general texts on "The Egyptian Book of The Dead" and also

"The Tibetan Book on Dying."

I was stunned. What in heaven's name was he doing with these books? I would come back to inspect them later. Now, I needed to follow him to see if he was going to offer up anything else unexpected tonight.

He drove onto one of the major arteries leading out of the university complex. After driving for about ten minutes he took an exit and parked in front of an outdoor newsstand. I parked a short distance away and waited for him to resume.

After paging through the newspaper under a street lamp, he got into his car and went for a leisurely drive along city streets. He seemed to be going nowhere in particular. Maybe he just needed time to think. Then he got back on the freeway and took it to the Pine Hills exit. I left him as he approached the gated entrance to his subdivision.

The late news had a live report from a seedy bar on Metal Avenue. Another random appearance in the city. The area was well-peopled that night, but no one saw the whole incident. No one, in fact, really saw anything, or so they said. No one wants to get involved in an investigation, especially in that part of town. It was as if the body simply appeared out of thin air. A double triangle with points touching was painted in blood on his palms, forehead and heart. The victim was alive, but suffering from total amnesia. When asked his name, he kept repeating "Osiris." Osiris is the Egyptian god of the dead and the underworld.

The name of the victim was later identified to be Geoffrey Haverfield, Mrs. Haverfield's son.

XIV

The next morning I went to the Haverfield mansion to extend my regrets and to offer whatever I could do to help.

I rang the door chime and waited several minutes for the maid to open the door. She was unsure whether I could come in and went to ask for instructions. Other family members could be seen filtering throughout the house. It must have been a good five minutes before she returned and gave me leave to enter.

It was a bright, sunny morning, but the sunshine stopped after the door closed. For good reason, this Tudor mansion had been transformed into a kind of mausoleum after the news of Geoffrey's appearance and his condition. While they were certainly happy he was alive, this last episode was the last in a lifelong series of sensational events surrounding Geoffrey's life. Mrs. Haverfield just couldn't take it anymore. Even though her son was alive, his amnesia made him even more of a stranger than he was before.

I was shown to a sitting room that had the appearance of being midnight inside. It had the feeling of being in a solar eclipse. I had to stand at the doorway for a few moments in order for my eyes to adjust to this new condition.

I could see a form inside the room and knew that Mrs. Haverfield was there, at least in body. Then I saw her, sitting upright in an easy chair. A plain glass and a half-empty bottle of Chivas Regal were on a coffee table to her left. For the moment, they were her best friends.

I walked over to her slowly, softly, not wanting to disturb the solemn atmosphere which permeated the room. It took a moment to get my voice synchronized with the quiet in the room, and so I had to subtly clear my throat several times when I tried to speak. "I am extremely sorry about this, Mrs. Haverfield. Thank G-d, he is still alive. If you permit it, when he regains consciousness I will try to talk to him and find out what happened. May I see him?" Her vacant eyes looked in my direction. After a few moments some life appeared as she looked at me imploringly. They had the look of a mother who would give anything just to have her little boy brought back to her. Since the treating physicians felt there was nothing more they could do with him yesterday, they sent him home. They knew that Mrs.

Haverfield would be in a position to provide full-time nursing care.

She then mentally slipped back to wherever she had been before I interrupted her. After that she neither acknowledged my request nor my presence. Her stare was downcast, as if she was looking at a microscopic dot on the carpet, and had become completely transfixed by it and focused upon it.

The housekeeper showed me upstairs to Geoffrey's bedroom. The door was slightly ajar. The nurse was occupied in studying the latest machinery which reflected his vital signs. The maid briefly told the nurse I had permission to be here for a short period. I thanked her, and the maid left. The nurse gave me a brief look as if to say, everything is stable now, leave well-enough alone. I nodded to her in acknowledgment and stood by the bed looking at his face.

He was lying on his back, under the covers. His eyes were closed. I got close to him to try to feel something. Obviously he could not talk to me. Maybe something about his physiology would reveal something. I placed my right hand over his face to feel his energy. Anything I could do. The nurse gave me a sharp look. I motioned, as if to say, there is no danger; please just give me a moment. I could feel a staccato rhythm radiating from him, uncomfortable and pulsing. He was on medication and this could have a lot to do with the energy pattern I was feeling.

"Has he said anything?" I asked the nurse.

"No. Just mumbles a lot. Every now and then a word. Something about I is, Ice, or Rice is. Nothing else I can make out. There are times when his lips move very quickly, but no sound comes out." I said nothing, but I thought there was a distinct possibility he could have been mentioning the ancient Egyptian deities, Isis and Osiris. Isis was regarded as the goddess of heaven, earth, the sea, and the unseen world below. At one point in Egyptian theology, Isis had a consort named Osiris.

"Are the marks still on him?" I asked.

"They were dark last night, but have been steadily fading. However, they were made, they are not permanent."

"Thank you."

As I was about to leave, she said, "He thinks he is somewhere else. I can see him carrying on conversations as if he were talking to someone else, somewhere else. He may be here, but he is definitely somewhere else. I have seen many patients on medication who become delusional. This one is different. Sometimes his conversation is actually coherent for a moment. This never happens with a medicated patient. There are no lucid moments until the medicine wears off."

"Do you have any idea where he thinks he is" I asked.

"No," she said directly. After a few moments of reflection, however, she added, "only that there seems to be a lot going on. Sometimes he seems agitated and uncomfortable." "There is one thing," she said with a concentrated glance in another direction. "When I was adjusting the curtains early this morning, a ray of sunlight peaked in and hit him square in the eyes. For a brief moment he smiled."

I spoke with Mrs. Haverfield's relations in the house; some cousins, aunts and uncles. No one knew much about Geoffrey's life. He was a spoiled rich child who was bored and dissatisfied with life. They did not know about cults with which he might have been associated, or in general, any cults or clubs at all. I couldn't even establish whether Geoffrey had a girl friend or anyone at all closer than a mere acquaintance.

I knew it was time for me to leave. I walked to the front door. The maid opened it for me. The sudden rush of bright morning sunshine assaulted me. I stepped onto the front steps while suffering from temporary blindness. I stopped, turned from the sun, and noticed that the maid was still in the doorway, with a longing look to be outside. She had that tired look on her face. "If not for the money" is how I read her expression. A hidden force field prevented her exit into the free world. Someone called her from within and the heavy wooden door with the cast iron lock slowly closed.

It wasn't too far out of the way to go back to Ponti's house and inspect his garden. I didn't know what I was looking for, so I was open to anything. Some little hint; just any trace of anything.

Stella showed me to the garden and I walked around. How peaceful it was. No breeze. Perfect stillness. I sat on a garden bench and just let my thoughts take me. After 20 minutes, I had not had any great thoughts or intuitions. I stood up to leave. Something bright caught my attention in a row of shrubs off to my right. The sun was shining on something metallic. I thought I would have a look. I looked at it cautiously; wanting to make sure it was not part of a little creature's home. I thought, "Wouldn't this be great if he hid a key to a safety deposit box which contained all of the secrets for which I was searching. But, it wasn't a key. It was a long, thin piece of metal, 6 inches long and 3/4 of an inch in width. On it was a word, "Ema," in Hebrew, pronounced Eema. Ema is Hebrew for mother. Now what in the world could this mean?

The Herald reported the name of the mysterious stranger in what had become known as the "Essex Country Club Incident" to be John Witheral. It also reported his address as the Lincoln Avenue Apartments on the east side of town.

Lincoln Avenue intersected a middle class part of town. Nice, clean garden apartments dotted both sides of the street. Small, neighborhood strip plazas looked like bookends on every corner. It was generally regarded as a nice place to live; nothing too expensive, nor trashy. Just clean and substantial; decent and well-kept.

John was 23 years old. No next of kin were reported, but there must have been some report to someone, somewhere. Otherwise, his name would not have been reported. No apparent means of employment. The article was short, matter of fact; nothing more than a filler. There had to have been some connection to someone somewhere, otherwise the investigation would have been treated as drug-induced occurrence and put to rest.

And then I decided to follow through, even though it frightened me very deeply. I found the apartment manager, Joe Humphrey, in the furnace room. He greeted me with a soot blackened hand. I gracefully declined the friendly introduction. Luckily, he talked to me without any coaxing. He really couldn't elucidate much. Witheral had only been there for a month and a-half. Seemed polite. No complaints about him. No wild parties. In fact, he didn't recall ever seeing any friends going into the apartment. From out of town; a small town in the forested mountains a few hundred miles east of here. He would have to check the apartment application to make sure, but recalled that the name seemed odd. Something about Caine or something like that.

Humphrey said that he took a chance on John. Usually didn't rent out to young kids. Most of the tenants were older and had been there for some time. Didn't want to rock the boat and bring in a new guy who was going to rock and roll the neighborhood, especially during the early morning hours. But, that didn't happen. He would have known anyway since his apartment was right across the way from John's.

I asked if I could get into the apartment to have a look around. He said that was out of the question. I took out my card and left it with him. "A shrink!" he said. I thought you were some kind of a private eye!" "It's a family matter" I said. I asked him to call me when the police finished their investigation, or when someone called to pick up his belongings. He sort of shrugged his shoulders, not committing one way or the other.

XV

The equilateral triangle is a universal symbol indicating psychic awareness, completion, groundedness and ascension. The duality of the triangles indicates the union of physical reality and the spiritual, or heaven and earth, and male and female. These are some of the common explanations behind the Star of David. They can also symbolize prosperity; and, for that matter, they can mean many things, all positive and beneficial depending on how the symbol is used by those who were employing or promoting it.

The meaning of a symbol can be very straightforward or mystical; how they are used can be quite another. The name "Nazi" -which was an acronym for the brutal National Socialist movement in Germany – is eerily similar to the Nasi, a class of religious ascetics mentioned in the Book of Numbers in the Old Testament. While the symbol may otherwise be clear and unblemished, the intention of the user can add a facet never intended.

In its primal state, a symbol may be clear, but life on the human plane is far from clear and always has a positive and a negative. Only on the human plane can symbols be used for positive or negative.

Symbols can only be truly effective when used for the good, for this is the only human portal leading to love. And love is the synthesis of the equilateral triangles, or so I have read. One, losing its distinctive identity, and fading into the other. The other doing the same, until there is only a synthesis.

Love. Everyone talks about it. Everyone seeks it. But does anyone really know what it is? How minimally it figures into our work-a-day world- and this limitation shows how limited and unsatisfying is the world we have come to know.

As has been said by the Masters, love is the only gateway in the human realm leading to eternity. Beyond human awareness and the duality of existence, the Star of David then opened a vista of unimaginable depth and magnitude.

Much has been written in the West about the Hindu concept of karma; the law of cause and effect. For instance, for centuries the swastika was an Indian sign of good luck until it was made notorious by the Nazis. The Nazis employed the symbol to commit a savagery almost unparalleled in the recorded history of the world.

It is said that karma is not waiting for future lives any longer. What has been sent out is coming back with increasing rapidity in this life. What has been sent out in this life is being realized in this life. Is it a new time approaching, or simply the vanishing of the delay between cause and effect? Is this the time which has been foretold, or are we seeing with clearer eyes?

I thought again about Moshe ben Rafael and the "Garden."

The cool night air was invigorating. I carried a sense of relief outside with me like a veil separating me from the pains and complexities of life in a cosmopolitan society. Stars illuminated the sky. Tiny pin pricks giving just a hint of insight into another world; a hint into eternity. Enticing and untouchable. Unquenchable temptation.

The cool, soft night air always made me feel like I'm on some sort of threshold. Ready for flight. A time for hope and peace. A time to say farewell.

XVI

The next morning I was back at the University library. Before I went to check out Mellenstreet's books, I went to the reference section. I was looking for anything having to do with organizations, past or present, having anything to do with the triangle. As expected, the research was enormous. In going through pictorials, however, I did not find anything dealing with the positioning with the two points together, or almost together.

I didn't know what I was looking for, but intuitively felt that I would not find much. Then, what was I doing on this search in the first place. It would have been apropos to discuss it with Mrs. Mellenstreet in my office, but to actually do the field work was another matter. There was so much I didn't know, but, the very topic of the books was so appealing that I didn't need much convincing to at least make an inquiry.

Well, what did I know about him? Not much. Mr. Mellenstreet might simply have an interest in ancient cultures. He never shared much with his wife; this too might have been a secret. Not something a staid accountant would otherwise share with a wife, especially one who was serving a role, as was he. If there was something more to it, I had no evidence of it, and didn't know what to look for in the books. As improbable as it seemed, suppose he was a member of a small occult group that had an interest in ancient culture; something akin to the modern Druids. Those who live in "hermetically sealed" containers, suppressing all emotion, sometimes or often need to find outlets that are completely incongruous to the image they otherwise project. This follows the universal principal that energy cannot be suppressed completely or eternally; and that which is being involuntarily repressed will find a way of expression. Even this, however, didn't mean there was anything untoward about what he was doing, even though repressed energy can be exposed in really off-balanced ways.

While I was here I decided to take a quick look at the books just to see if anything popped out. All of them were either erudite or esoteric source books on ancient cultures, religions, festivals and funerary rites and beliefs. Interestingly, the focus of the books was decidedly related to times before the dawn of recorded history.

Regardless of their historical dating, however, their purpose remained the same: how to prepare for death; how to quell the fear of death and, how to live beyond the physical death. They did this by trying to ensure the well-being of the deceased by what is considered "magical" means today. Our adherence to major religious rites today is not too far removed. The fear of death pervades society, culture and life in every respect. It fuels the "stay young" emphasis, and is the basis for everything from food, housing, and clothing to psychology and spirituality. The fear of the unknown permeates almost every waking moment from birth to the point of death. It also fuels the eternal desire for immortality. Life beyond the grave has also been the topic of speculation and preparation since time immemorial.

I recalled learning that the ancient masters believed that everything in the universe was alive and animated – sun, wind, water, tree, rocks – and made no sharp boundaries among states of being – human and animal, living and dead, human and divine. The entire universe was animated by the life force, whether or not it was evident to our senses. All of the cultures had their own method of describing the single substance of life, the one continuous source and spectrum of life, which existed from prior to the physical incarnation to after the physical death. All ancient cultures spoke of existence being far more broad than what we can witness with our senses. This was featured in the practice of alchemy.

While we think of alchemy today as the medieval practice of trying to transmute lead into gold, the ancient practice was not based at all on self-aggrandizement. The Talmud and the Book of Exodus relate how Bezalel knew the secrets of creating heaven and earth by means of the Hebrew alphabet and used them in creating the Tabernacle in the Desert. Hiram and the construction of King Solomon's Temple is another example. Moses is often considered a, if not the, major alchemist. These skilled beings were able to transmute the "normal" laws of nature and create "miracles" for their people. This was done in the spirit of integrity, truth and wholeness. G-d was in command and they were merely vessels for G-d's omnipotent power. The secrets were closely guarded for obvious reasons.

Alchemy. I knew that if I was going to approach this situation, it could not be done on the intellectual-therapeutic level. It was far beyond this. It would have to be on the experiential level. I did not have a clue as to how that was going to actually be done. I knew, however, that if I didn't, certain forces which were at work would only go unchecked. In some vague way which I didn't understand or really appreciate, I knew that I would have to go "somewhere else," to the realm beyond the five senses. How could I even begin to unravel what was going on without doing this. How would I go? Who would guide me? What if I got "lost" and couldn't come back? Uncle Duke may have told me that I could never lose home, but in this, I was focused enough to be really afraid. This was the stuff of true metaphysics, and there were no guides or guidebooks for what I needed to do. There was, however, a lot of fear, and an internal sense of not wanting to get in any deeper than I already was.

Then, maybe it was nothing more than people with good intentions or not, fooling with principles that they really couldn't control. Did I really want to get involved in this? It would be easy to just leave it to the so-called professionals. But, it was evident that they didn't have a clue either.

Since the earliest times there have been rumors of a group of nine people who literally hold the world together. Sometimes the group consists of multiples of people, who added up to the number 9. For instance, in the Yiddish culture of Eastern Europe there is the legend of the Lamed Vavniks. Lamed Vav is Hebrew for the number 36. If the numbers 3 & 6 are added together, they make 9. These people are reputedly so spiritually astute, and so removed from worldly pressures and temptations, that they literally became founts of pure spirituality and temples of the living G-d. The vibration they exude is so powerful that even the most manifest evil from negative thoughts and malevolent social and political machinery cannot overshadow them. In fact, it shrinks from them. Some are said to be several thousand years old, or older, having retained physical bodies for the purpose of interjecting themselves in society when necessary, but otherwise being able to disappear at will. They were men and women who each had a crystal clear consciousness and were the living embodiment of pure Love. They remain in a constant state of meditation but can converse with those with whom contact is made. They were either the answer, or at least bright lights on the vague, foggy path. Were they even available if I needed to find them, or was this a solitary mission that I would have to take on my own? It has been said that many of them did not even know they were members in such lofty company. Contact with them, however, did not need to be physical. There could be a mental connection with them in much the same way as one holds a mental conversation with one's self. Maybe all self-talk is not as private as we might think!

Ponti's message that "silence becomes me" was beginning to take on a new light. Moshe ben Rafael's cryptic message that "in stillness we hear the movement leading to the light of redemption ... In redemption, time is extinguished" was a beginning to give me some direction. Silence. Stillness. Beyond thought. Before thought. From conscious to subconscious to....

At that moment I knew it was better not to call Mrs. Mellenstreet and tell her about what I found at the library. Between the disbelief and possible histrionics, nothing would be accomplished.

This evening there had been a slight drizzle. It stopped about 8 o'clock. I felt edgy from being inside; edgy from being involved in situations which were decidedly beyond my control, experience and comfort level. I didn't have a handle on what I was doing or where I was going and did not have any real expectation that I would. I had no one I could discuss this with. Kathryn would worry incessantly if I brought it up. So, in that focused ruminating, the walls just seemed to be coming together. Trying to figure something out often leads to circuiting in an ever smaller circuit, and finally to exhaustion. The internal ruminating was saying quite clearly not to get further involved than I already was.

Trying to relax just made me feel better for a while. But, there was something else. Like I needed to leave. To go somewhere. For some reason which I did not understand, but just knew, from a deep, unconscious place, there was something that I needed to do, and somewhere in the deep recesses, I knew what I needed to do. The more I did not heed it, the more I felt like I was being squeezed out and needed to leave before the walls crushed me. So, I decided to take a walk outside.

The Nigerian and Ecuadoran consulates were hopping tonight. Long lines of limos lined both sides of Andover Street. The chauffeurs, in their stereotypical blue uniforms and caps are conversing in small groups or rubbing down their cars with polishing cloths. In their own way they exhibit the same "clubby" atmosphere as their bosses.

I walked a few blocks over to Beethoven Street and gradually got to Main. It really didn't matter where I was walking though, each street seems to be like the last. Each street has that "nowhere" feel to it; like I am traversing a nowhere space in a vacuum zone. But, it is not the streets. Of this I am sure. It is me!

I walk and walk, paying no attention to the direction. The direction is irrelevant.

The walk was doing me some good. The jitters have left. In their place is a type of acceptance; just accepting whatever is and not passing judgment. It does me good. Instead the feeling of relaxation which is eclipsed by nervous tension, I feel more like a presence that just happens to be passing through with no aim in sight, other than to pass.

I happened into an older downtown neighborhood. I began to pass crumbling brick buildings. Old men are sitting in places where old men have sat before them. Generation after generation, sitting; just sitting inside of themselves. Staring blindly, not blinking, staring into windows, whether shaded, latticed or bare – whether involved, concerned or removed – they remain patients in a common waiting room. Mothers, sitting on cement doorsteps of identical row houses, block after block, surrounded by broods of children; children being weaned on asphalt.

The population of the future; actually more like participants in some "brave, new world" being revealed in the surrounding sparsely clad, but omnipresent, office buildings.

I walk past a site where buses load and unload. It is structured as a large circle. A line queues at the turnabout where ends and beginnings occur with regularity. I walk past restaurants, banks, bars; over the worn tiles of Cathedral Square. Past the doors of commercial enterprise. Doors on loosened hinges clatter on the sides of vacant buildings. And, all about, is the feint, fetid smell of stale air....

Passing doorways, I can pick up bits and pieces of conversations. But, it seems that each conversation begins only to wane and diminish. All about me are moving pedestrians, walking with downcast eyes; gazing prostrate upon the pavement. Eyes that refuse to meet the eyes of anyone who cares to engage them; even to speak of any pleasantry. This is the city, speaking to itself in the language of the dispossessed.

A wind from the lake is softly blowing; caressing my hair. Wrapping me in a gentle embrace. The kind of feeling that takes me away and transports me to a different time and place, conjuring visions of times past and future hopes, as if I am not really where I am.

The lines of streetlights seem to begin and end everywhere and nowhere. Their lines are symmetrical – perfectly even and exact; balanced and symphonic in design – without beginning or end; forever here and there. No statement. A chord once sung which reverberates forever, without conclusion. No resolution.

Right now I feel at just the same stalemate; neither moving forward nor back. Bizarre happenings. No leads or explanations.

Here I am. Maybe G-d is talking to me and I am just not listening; just not able to listen. In case, the Infinite Presence is speaking to me, I say to myself, again, Here I Am. Maybe it will hear me. But, then, there is nothing...

Present on a momentary street. The fog is now rolling in. It shrouds and consumes. I can see nothing. Touch nothing. In the fog there is no thing, but a mysterious presence – I am like a blind man in a dream.

At this time there are no newspapermen to relate hoarse and guttural litanies of the day's events. The flower vendors have also departed.

The stark realities of the night lay still against the backdrop of hand-fashioned cement; the cold designs of our time.

I am walking slowly, ponderously, not really paying attention. So many things seem to be just somewhere – here in the interim between some beginning or ending, or end and beginning; inveterate. I feel as though I am balancing on a sill, not sure if I am going to fall. Perched; immobile, as though I have come back from a daily wandering empty-mouthed, and with my eyesight haunted.

The stores are closed. Now only temptresses portrayed on cardboard signs woo strangers to peer into liquor store windows. The green light of the Turf Exchange Hotel strobes, "Vacancies, Vacancies, Vacancies."

The feeling of emptiness is so vast that wind could pass through without opposition.

I have come upon a stout, short church spire. It seems to be shouldering this dense and heavy sky. A con man sways into my path, gives me his song and dance, and asks, "What's the word, Man?" I reply, "No word, man; no word" and continue walking. Night walking with night eyes.

And in this void, I realize, I have found the Silence. And I rejoice.

Duke, may he rest in peace, would have visions. The dividing line between his imagination and life blurred to the point where they merged as much as possible in this realm. He would be wide awake and yet be miles away, years away, in some other situation; in some other existence. I'm not sure he really knew where Present time was, or really cared for that matter. It was a safety device he devised to get through what he needed to get through so long ago.

I was 7 years old the first time I saw a packed suitcase next to his bed. I will always remember this. I thought he was going away on vacation. The suitcase had become such a fixture in his room and life, that he didn't know what I was talking about. I do not think he even saw it anymore. It was just there, like breath in the body. He was simply not going to get caught off-guard.

He got into investigating because the business was as flexible and as non-committal as he was. Yet, he did build up loyal clientele over the years who liked his "soft-shoe" yet regal and dignified approach to life, and found him to be an able and trustworthy investigator. He never walked out of the house without a well-pressed suit, tie and an impeccably clean and brushed Fedora.

He was born in Russia. What family had not been wiped out by Cossacks or the Soviets would soon be by the Nazis. Whether Czarist or early Soviet, the government privately sanctioned the Cossacks to keep order in the rural regions, and gave them free reign to do it. Early on, during the Cossack raids, he hid in the wheat fields and watched. He spent his life watching. He felt that his life here on earth was merely transitory, a momentary stop-over, a connecting point leading to the real or better destination. Operating on this basis, he rarely saw any reason for much ado or aggravation about the irritations in life. This changed when the Nazis came.

We never talked philosophy. He refused. He didn't believe in it. He believed in living more than any person I have ever met. Decisive and loving, he packed a wallop of vibrancy in his 5'4" frame. Wavy black hair and smiling brown eyes. He never lost his accent.

In the transitory world in which he traveled, the women loved him because he loved each and every one of them. Every now and again I would hear about Stella Kaprinski who was affectionately called Mashenka. Very pretty. My mother hoped for something permanent between them, which never happened. I don't know what became of Stella.

I once asked him about her. He got this dreamlike look in his eyes. "Did you ever listen to a beautiful piece by the composer Saint Saens, called 'The Swan'? Many people think it was written to express the grace of a swan. In one sense, it may have been. But, I think it was much more. I think Saint Saens was deeply in love when he wrote it. I think he wrote it to his love, and also as a tribute to all women. He saw something that went beyond a personality. His was a tribute - not just to a beautiful icon – but to all and everyone."

"You know there is a very dangerous fiction in this world," he continued. There is the notion that it is a man's world and that women are subordinate in every way. This is not my experience. It is just the opposite."

"A woman has a creative motive force inherent in her that a man can never have. It is just not programmed in. Out of this grace comes the initiating power that propels men to act in this little drama we call life. Instead of recognizing it, we condemn it. People have a habit of condemning that which literally gives them life. Think of all the condemnations strewn at G-d-almighty all day and every day! It is the same. Life here could not exist without the female. How then could we not regard the female as holy? Our little part in the creation drama – being what it is – important, but still playing a part in a drama which has very little to do with us – other than to recognize divinity and honor it."

My mother was his cousin. She would have him at the house as often as she could. My father just didn't like him. Secretly, I think he worried that I would get caught by the glamour of investigating. I think they both despaired that I would follow in Duke's footsteps. My father told me that if I ever did he would disown me.

Since Uncle Duke had no children – that he would readily acknowledge – he treated me like a son. Whenever we were together he would give me some of his pearls of wisdom. When I was five years old, he insisted on at least taking me to lunch on Saturday afternoons. He introduced me to the first bookie I ever met in the old Italian neighborhood. I didn't know it at the time. It was only years later that I realized why the raceway gentleman was slipping little pieces of paper up his tie or into an empty Bering cigar tube. This was a good introduction for me to start working in the family business where I really encountered some colorful characters.

I know he knew that he could have changed if he had wanted. But, he didn't want to. He could have married, had a family, and done the rest. He would have been a terrific husband and father. I'm not even sure that the way he lived was so non-committal. He just exhibited a different commitment to life than is usually accepted. He embraced life more fully than most. Let's say his concept of life was more diffuse and ambient than what was otherwise acceptable in the myopic focus of expectation-oriented society.

There was a type of home-spun foreign charm about him. He could have been anyone's uncle or cousin from overseas, coming to look for long-lost relations. He always dressed with dignity, didn't spend money he didn't have, and ate sensibly. When the pixie twinkle lit up in his eyes, he took on a magical persona, and anything was possible.

All this leads to what I said before. He told me this so many times that I can see his face muscles moving as the words flow out of his mouth: "Know where you want to get before you even begin. That way, if you ever feel that you've lost your way you'll find home eventually." And he said, again, "You can never lose your home. The time it takes to get there is irrelevant. The turns and steps you take along the way are irrelevant." Then he would look at me, eyes blazing into mine, and finger pointing, – and he would lean very close to my face and say – "Deep in your heart you know where home lies. Look for it every day, and you'll find it. Sometimes, it will find you! But – and here is the trick – don't look too hard. Just keep it in mind, like you are looking for it out of the corner of your eye. And" ... he said again with a twinkle in his eye, "don't try too hard. Effort only spoils it."

As much disturbance and distress as he went through in his life, I think of him most when I am sitting alone, in room comforted by soft light. While he was not one for a nostalgic sense of pathos, he would have understood his image as being perfectly normal in the glow of the soft light pictured in genre art.

He would never exemplify just what "home" meant. All he said was that he couldn't explain it, but that I would know. This was awfully frightening, especially for a small child. The sense of overpowering fear and anxiety you experience when you are introduced to the outside world is difficult enough to take. Sometimes the only real game plan to survive is to literally put on your blinders. Now this guy is talking to me about finding my home, when I'm scared to death because I'm alone, afraid and I don't know what the heck he is talking about. But, I learned.

He would have been the first to tell me this triangle business was all a red herring. It meant nothing, as symbols only mean what you attribute to them. They have no power in and of themselves. Look for the expression of something, and forget about the symbol. It is the experience of it, not the theory that carries the power.

"The world is a thinking world because there is nothing easier to do, and nothing more helpful - or dangerous," he would say. But, he would always remind me that "thinking cannot give you the experience. Without the experience, the event is hollow and meaningless – food only for the palates of pundits waiting to charge admission for the privilege of hearing their empty wisdom. Why do you think intellectuals and pundits are a dime-a-dozen, and why thinking vocations are considered so attractive? Sometimes the line between savant and idiot savant is very narrow he would tell me. Believe me, if the world honored the lives of those rich in truly honorable, noble and enriching life experiences, this would be a different place. And, I do not mean stupid experiences. I am not talking about taking drugs or having unlimited sex. Not those self-indulgent experiences for the self-absorbed. I mean the experiences that raise the human condition to something more than the duality which is human; the chronic cycle of highs and lows; the un-G-dly self-deprecation and the belief that there is no hope. I have seen too much suffering and abuse in my life. I have also seen grandeur and nobility. Remember that the saints and masters were all built within the same framework that everyone else has. They are not to be venerated as something separate, but studied as light bearers on a path we should all be encouraged to take."

"The piano," he continued "has 88 keys. How long has it had 88 keys? Hundreds of years. The same framework used by Mozart, Beethoven and Chopin is available to us. Never, ever look upon these people as special. They are only special because, in certain respects, they broke free. That is the point of the experience. To break free. How did they break free? They let themselves go! In some kind of faith and trust that I cannot explain, they just let go. That is all. They didn't give up. The just became who they really were. When you break free, you know only love. My little boychick, be free!" Then there would be a loving look into my eyes and an affectionate pinch of much of my face.

"If G-d Almighty carved out "I Am G-d" in a rock in letters of fire, how many people's lives would change. Hardly any. Many would dispute it. For most, it would be a respite only. A few might say they felt redeemed, saved or enlightened, and then continue with their day wanting some things and avoiding others. No different. So, it is not the event; it must be the actual experience of enlightenment. If it were any different every archeologist with any major discovery would be a saint.

We go through countless moments, read thousands of books, think trillions of thoughts, and to what end: to try to experience a single moment that is being written about, and which cannot be truly expressed, except in the unapproachable abstract. These lead to more thoughts, desires and, often, despair. It is only at those times – those rare times – where we experience a moment of no thought, and thereby know what we have been looking for all along: the feeling of liberation which comes when we bypass controlling thought. That is the experience of freedom.

To Uncle Duke, the vision was the reality. The vision was the reality that had not yet become concrete. He had a three dimensional imagination: fathoming the clues, fitting together the pieces of the puzzle bit by bit; slowly and methodically painting a masterpiece – only to tell me, that it was once and always his intuition that solved the mystery. The methodical work just gave him the means of presentation.

I thank Uncle Duke for being candid about his visions. Otherwise, I might not have the courage to express mine.

Uncle Duke, living his own avante garde lifestyle, in his own aloof way; living life to the fullest. Taking the juxtapositions of life, the love, hate, majesty, degradation, boredom, and inflamed passion and living out his days in – I suppose all I can say – one massive meshing of emotions that affected and delighted everyone who had the good fortune to meet him. It was said of him that one either loved him or one didn't know him. I was devastated when he went away. While some spiritual avatars may be intentionally aloof, Duke was very present and would not have had it any other way. His studious, protected life had ended abruptly while still a child. Now he carried his studiousness into his observations of life and experience.

So much time is spent in "half-baked" and "luke warm" relationships. Or, they can be so meteoric that they are over as soon as they begin. Too much time, but not enough time to do something fully. Here, but not really here. Time and space, filled by this or that for short periods of time; the politics of living, and of loving. When someone like Uncle Duke leaves, the crater is mammoth.

I was breathing deeper, feeling better. The walk has done me good.

I started to laugh. To myself. A little chuckle. I remembered a story. A funny story. There was many a time in grade school when we had to write essays about our weekend. I was very young. I wrote a stunning essay about how my father and I had spent time over the weekend playing catch and having a really good time. But then we had to stop abruptly because my father had "diarea!" My teacher was kind enough to correct the spelling. Ah, the integrity of youth!

But, it was good to remember this. Laughter always brings peace, and a little space brings in breath. We cannot be the vessels of life if we stay small. The circuit of life in small beings stays small and controlled. Humor should be both the cause and the reward of getting big. Joy is the cause and the reward of being happy. So much Freedom can be gained by just a smile; a smile for no reason at all.

Looking at the situation with these eyes, I knew there was little likelihood that I would find anything of value by looking for an organization or a cult. Sometimes you have to look away from something you are looking at in order to see it. Like Uncle Duke said about looking out of the corner of your eye. Now I knew I was truly in uncharted territory, and all the studying and reading, and experience, had only led me to this point.

When I realized that I had gone a few miles down Main Street, I decided to turn back. The evening cacophony of racing engines, horns, bass-driven music, loud and excited conversations, had thankfully subsided into a more subliminal drone. The fog was letting up and the streetlights were beginning to lose their shrouded appearance. In the distance, however, they still appeared as stars; appealing, but untouchable. Slight relief from the cacophonous, clashing events of the normal waking day. Hardly contrapuntal.

The walk may have inspired a dream I had that night. It also seemed "real." I was walking somewhere, except that I wasn't me. I mean I knew it was me, but the person looked much different. I was having a lot of difficulty walking because a strong wind was keeping me from walking where I wanted to go. Then I remember running. I was being chased. In a basement. Cold. Dark. Damp. Subterranean. Can't remember by whom or why I was afraid. Wanted to scream, but couldn't. Kept trying, but no sound would come out of my throat. Voice just wouldn't work. Something about a basement. Terror-stricken. I awoke with a sudden shock; Wide-eyed and breathing rapidly. My heart was pumping so rapidly, I knew that I would probably be up for the rest of the night. It was 2:00 in the morning, and I just resigned myself to lie in bed. Kathryn was sleeping soundly. I was glad I had not awakened her. Watching her in stillness and peace apparently brought a sense of quietude. I fell into a deep sleep.

It was late. I was lost. I happened upon this house with the lights on. I knocked on the door. I heard, "come in" and entered. Then I saw myself standing in front of a man who was sitting at a desk. I could feel something being lifted from my body. I felt lighter. I reflexively looked up. I knew it was night outside, but there was a steady stream of natural, brilliant light flowing through an aperture in the ceiling of the room I was in.

I was about to bolt from the room but something kept me there; not really against my will, but because of an intuition. I stopped, and after several moments realized that I wasn't breathing. The man at the desk looked serene. A shock of wavy white hair rested comfortably on his pale but luminescent skin. His eyes told me that he had something to tell me, and that he could be trusted. He just sat there as though he was waiting for the best moment to speak to me.

Time seemed to stand still, like we were in a photograph; but the photograph was animated and we were moving and, at least silently, communicating. Then, as if the right moment had been reached, the man in the chair said, kindly, but assertively, "My friend, when light comes to you, it is best to receive it."

I stood there, dumbfounded wondering why I didn't run when I had the chance – not that anything was holding me back now.

He knew I was puzzled, so he continued: "I used to be like you, until I decided I didn't want to be anymore. It is all a choice, you know. When you are able to receive it without resistance, you will not remember who you were, and you will forever bless, with each breath, who you are."

"Who are you?" I asked, shaking my head with bewilderment, so grateful that I was able to speak and speak up for myself.

"Why, I am an M.D." answered the man.

"A doctor?" I said incredulously.

"My friend, I am an M.D. That is, I am a Master of DeLights!"

At this, I almost fainted. I wanted to bolt out of the nearest door, but when I looked around there weren't any. I felt the stiff shiver of panic throughout my being. The primordial sense of ultimate danger with no hope of escape; no one to call, no rescue possible.

He sat there looking at me as if he would neither try to compel me to stay nor help me leave. It was as if he were in some space, some magic space, and at peace with – whatever. He did not react at all, neither to comfort me nor to appear to hurt me. The man behind the desk just kept looking at me, with kind, open eyes.

I was completely aghast. Where was I? Where could I go?

"My young friend. The door is open if you would like to leave." Off to the side, a passageway opened. But, to where? It was dark.

I could see he meant it. At first, I thought it might be preferable to leave, to just run away; but, maybe there was something I was supposed to see here.

"What is a Master of DeLights?" I asked as I shivered through the asking.

"When we are done, I think you will know" he replied in a quiet, almost perfunctory way; the way you reply when there are no words to use to even begin to explain.

A chair appeared in front of me. I sat down right underneath the Light aperture in the ceiling above. I felt the light around me begin to pulsate and vibrate. It felt strange, but good. The man said that he wanted to ask me one question.

"Alright" I said.

"Who are you?" asked the man.

"My name is Michael."

"And behind this, who are you?"

"What do you mean? I just told you. My name is Michael."

Yes, but other than being a name, who are you?"

"I don't get your question"

Are you a rock?"

"No, I am a person." A soft glow began to make what I was looking at just a little bit fuzzy.

"Now you get my direction. And besides being a person, who are you?" The Light was starting to ebb and flow around me, in a kind of wavy energy dance. I knew that if I were awake I would be really frightened, but knowing that I was not awake, gave me a license to really enjoy it. It was so satisfying to experience. The touch of the light against my skin made it tingle. "What is this?" he asked.

"You will understand, my young friend, as we continue our little exploration."

I began to recognize that each time I heartfully answered a question, I felt different; I felt lighter. Like something was released in the expression; the honest expression.

As the questions went on, I went from a person, to a human being, to a singer, an actor, an artist; baseball player; musician; caregiver, until finally I ran out of categories. "What do I do now? I thought as he continued to ask me who I was. I thought, well, since this is a dream, I might as well play a little. Maybe I would remember this. Maybe I wouldn't.

"Who are you?" he asked with great equanimity.

"I am a universe."

"Who are you?"

"I am a grain of sand."

"Who are you?"

"I am every G-d of mythology."

"Who are you?"

"I am a shaman."

"Who are you?"

"I am an alchemist."

"Who are you?"

Seeing that this could and would go on forever, I decided to cut to the chase. I knew where he was going, so I decided to just go there.

"I am a star child, a light being ... a light ... until ... I was both nothing ... and everything. And, as I felt lighter, I would laugh at each question, until I was laughing with abandon. Was this all a joke?

With each question and answer, the light was changing color in a dizzying display of effervescent projections. And then ... the light stopped. Silence. Perfect Silence. Comfortable. With my eyes closed, I lost all sense of myself. I had become the Silence.

"Here are your directions you have been waiting for my friend," and he handed me a map with instructions. I looked at it, studied it, and for the first time in a long time, felt secure, aware, self-confident and certain. I opened my eyes and was delighted to finally know where I was going. I really wanted to go home.

I stood up. For the first time in a very long time, I felt a sense of wholeness and completion. I did not even remember what it was to feel a sense of wonder. Now my sense of wonder attached to everything as I looked about this beautiful room. As I did so, the room expanded. In an instant it transformed into a huge, pantheon-shaped circular domed room. It was white marble. Smooth and cool to the touch, yet warm and welcoming to the senses. The man had the same sense of kindness and compassion in his eyes as he looked at me and gave me a little smile. I smiled at him in return. Then the room disappeared, and there was ... nothing.

I awoke feeling alive and wonderful, with a big smile on my face. But, what about the map?

The instructions! The map! Oh, my G-d!! What about the map? I knew I knew it all just a moment ago. Now what was it? Where is it?

I will take a walk after work tonight.

XVII

Everyone is looking for answers. What is the meaning of life? What is the meaning of today? They look for the answers in relationships, in money and possessions, and any other material object that has personal meaning.

In one sense, whether in my counseling or in this new endeavor, I have been left with the odds and ends of events; little tidbits, where the substance was either gone or is hidden. Emotion. Feelings. Thoughts. Mellenstreet and the ancient world; Witheral, Haverfield and triangles; Moon, missing and presumed dead, meteorite exhibit. The stuff of legends, debate, drama, and sometimes, death.

I remember when Mrs. Mellenstreet told me, somewhat ruefully, that because of her husband's strict observance of routine, there were many sides of him she knew she had never touched, nor would be able to touch. I remember she remorsefully stated that "I have tried. Long ago I would yearn for some great meeting with this man, like in the romantic novels. You know, a husband suddenly discovering that he has completely avoided the one person in the world who loves him dearly, with a following scene of tenderness and a promise for a new future. Those days are long ago and I no longer even suspect a possibility of that happening." Mellenstreet had needed a beautiful wife for show and tell; she needed financial security, although I do believe she also loved him. They struck a bargain long ago. The mettle of that bargain, however, has worn very thin.

"Lately his aloofness has changed. Now, it is preoccupation; with what or why I just do not know. He seems focused, in another world. His indifference to me has now grown to complete avoidance. He seems annoyed to have any contact with me at all. I assumed that it was another woman. You have not discovered any evidence to lead me to believe that he is having an affair. What you have told me about his going to the library and reading these unusual books is very difficult for me to believe; and a bit humorous as well. Incongruity does not even begin to fill the description," she added with the only brightness I had seen on her face in a long while.

"Mrs. Mellenstreet, maybe it's time to get a professional involved in this. You know, a professional investigator. This is not my life and not my line. I've been happy to try to cooperate, but I am really at a loss as to what to do," I said hoping she would let me go; and even if she wasn't I was planning to distance myself. But, then, what if some symmetry of events or synchronicity involved Ponti's disappearance as well? Then I stopped. What? Why? What could be the connection? Then I knew that I couldn't exit even if I wanted to. But, why would I even think this, I wondered, and stopped. Was I getting so possessed by the Ponti investigation that I was losing all sense of proportion?

"As you know, Mr. Cushner, my husband has always been a very precise man in business, and in his personal life. He reserves his free time at home for reading his trade journals on accounting. I haven't even seen him pick up a novel in decades, and he has never exhibited any interest in religion or spirituality. Something as unscientific and unprovable as an interest in pagan rituals and holidays is completely contrary to his whole belief system or his limited field of interest that it is laughable" as she started to laugh heartily again. It was good to see her laugh. This helped smooth out the lines in her very lovely face, and remove the concrete pallor from her demeanor.

It actually made me laugh too! When we regained ourselves, she said with a much more lighthearted tone than before: "These topics have never interested him before, and I simply can't see why they would interest him now. There has been nothing traumatic in his life that would put him over the deep end if that is what you are thinking. And he is much too old for a mid-life crisis." She stopped for a moment, became reflective, and said with a sigh, "everything has been going on as it has been for years. It is our inertia; our system. Good or bad, it is what he has, what we have, and what we have had for many years. I have no reasonable expectations for anything more. We were never truly married in the broader meaning of the term; and we will probably never divorce. My husband is hardly the charismatic type. "In fact," she said with a smirk and a little laugh, "he is also a very poor tipper in restaurants – much to my embarrassment. Even with our distant relationship, I cannot see why he would feel uncomfortable about reading these books at home other than, this is just none of my business. I guess I just do not understand and was hoping you could help me."

"Well, on a professional level, I certainly can." There are methods. On any other level, I am not so sure. People, by and large, only like to deal with what they can see and touch. They prefer not to extend their reality to any broader concept, even if, as some have said, that ultimate reality is broader than we could ever imagine.

XVIII

The night air really opened up my senses tonight. A soft wind is coming from the direction of the lake. It is slowly wafting and caressing my hair. The kind of wind that can take you away from where you are and transport you back in time, instantaneously. Not merely a wind, but a channel for memory, traveling between time and space; a conduit between the past and the future, and now going right through me. The wind spiriting the soul, so airy in and of itself, and so easily moved – memory of events decades before, recalled in the most minute detail as if happening now. Memory of the place and time where something happened, where a feeling was felt, what feeling was felt, or desire realized – where a particular song was heard – these things – these sometimes trivial reactions to the stimuli of an earlier age; these stay imprinted forever.

The only element that has a stronger effect on me is light. Certain shades of light will mentally transport me somewhere else so fast that I am literally there. It is almost as if I am riding in the pulse and wave of a light beam; timeless, rich in elemental life; and focused on the only true focus: the immediate richness of being alive.

Moments out of time – moments which can actually be re-experienced just through a mental connection. At moments like this, logic fails to give a clear direction, for it is blind to all that which exists out of its environment. And everything exists out of its environment for illusions exist only in the land of make-believe as do....... Give the problem to the vapors. Let the proper path come misting in like a fog which, although clouding the vision, unchains and excites the senses to go beyond the present dimension.

City of dreams. City of charm. Tonight, on such an unseasonably warm night, the spirits are surely out walking amongst the bar goers looking for a quick hit; easy bait for which to latch on; with lonely widows and widowers staring out of open windows as the soft breeze takes them back to happier times; with laborers half-sleeping in easy chairs with a beer in one hand and a desire in the other; with all the searchers standing on street corners and waiting for their connections; with new couples walking tentatively arm-in-arm to night clubs and movies and dreaming the dreams of lovers to be; with the haggard masses of white and blue collar workers living in anticipation of yet another day of unremitting pressure; of television impresarios and all those who paint the face; and with all those who have said their grace after the moment of sundown.

And then, if you listen closely, very closely, there are sounds in the light, as if the light were impregnated with music. Maybe it is just my imagination; maybe it is over-sensitive hearing, but at different times of the day, the sound in the light takes on a new vibration, a new color. The best times are sunrise and sunset. The music is the sound of hymns singing glory. In this glory, there is true happiness and peace, for it is permanent even in the transitory light. It promises return, forever. If you let them, the sounds leave an imprint which becomes cellular to the extent that you have a permanent smile.

This time of ritual death when darkness has conquered the light, and Puck and Pan come prancing – why do we wait for the time of death to seek the joy of life? We are the rainmakers in our lives. We are the High Priests and Priestesses of each of our own life religions. Why do we persist in living in the shallow, in the middle, – not in the middle way of moderation, but in the shadow; in the interim, the meantime – being nowhere, all of the time; in a cylinder with no entrance and no exit. Perhaps we shall retain the knowledge and the spirit of yesterday tomorrow.

City of Lights. City of Hopes. City of possibilities. City of situations.

The lights in the distance far below twinkled Twinkle Twinkle little star, I wonder how you really are.

City of conjunctions. City of illusion. City of fantasy. City of division. City of unrequited love and hope. City where is bred the breath and life of despair. City of perpetual separation and loneliness. City of desire.

Even though I had been out walking in the City, I realized that I was just walking in a sense of silence. Then I remembered Ponti's cryptic message: "Silence becomes you." Now I was beginning to understand. He was not suggesting a compliment; he was suggesting a method. Quiet. Silence. Becoming. But, how? Where? When?

Sometimes I wonder if all the troubles in the world are not the result of people talking too much, but of talking at all. And this coming from a therapist!

I have spent long periods completely alone, and felt more unified by the experience. Talking can be very fragmenting and divisive. The attempt, anyway, with a certain sense of verve added to the words, only increases the sense of separation and division which people normally feel anyway. Communication in silence can be "singularly" unifying and satisfying.

Silence has been a method practiced in spiritual centers since time immemorial. It promotes harmony by not using words which so often promote disharmony and division. How many billions of people have been murdered as a result of perceived differences caused by the promotion of written doctrines of different religions and the misunderstood presumptions and prescriptions arising from them?

XIX

I learned from the coroner that one of the items tucked away in John Witheral's shoe was Andrew Mellenstreet's private business number. Mr. Haverfield also had Mr. Mellenstreet's business card in his shirt pocket. I also learned that Mr. Mellenstreet had been checked out by the police and was clean, at least on the surface.

I walked through the garden behind Ponti's house several times. I didn't see any clues. No arrows pointing. No "X" marking the spot. No facsimiles of triangles. I thought something might be buried there, but where would I even begin? Could he have taken something from the museum? And the marker that I found before, with the word "Ema" on it; what did it really mean?

It turned out that Mr. Haverfield was in Mellenstreet's office to pick up an income tax return prepared for his mother who was a client. Witheral, it turns out, was a very distant relation who was in town looking for a job. My instincts told me that Mellenstreet was still a key. The irony was that it was his wife who connected me to the case, and his money which would be paying my fees.

I did hear an interesting tidbit from Mrs. Haverfield – who still had her sources – that a Detective Bowlin let slip that white collar crime and the Department of Justice were working jointly regarding real estate scammers plaguing the area. Jacob Lake and Timothy Bonticlaire came to mind.

Back at my home. The late afternoon sun was pouring through my sliding glass doors. I settled back in my easy chair feeling a little isolated and dispossessed. I stared out the window for a long time. Evening began settling in with flashing hues of reds and blues. The evening sky was giving off the appearance of electricity, the verve of creation, piercing what had been a cloudless sky. Parhelia. The final burst of color before the drapery of night and the awakening of the other world.

I felt like the brunt of the "Triangle Murder" - as it was now being called - was resting squarely on my shoulders. I now knew how those Caryatids at the Hall of Antiquities must have felt.

I needed to humor myself to get out of this funk.

XX

The telephone rang. Mrs. Mellenstreet was on the phone.

"I am a bit perturbed, Mr. Cushner, but not surprised. My husband is entertaining clients tonight. I always go along when he entertains clients. Tonight, however, he has not even extended the invitation. He stated that he will probably go back to the office after dinner. That is highly out of character for him." Her voice had as much pain and anxiety as bitterness in it. At times like this, making a complete sentence is even a tremendous challenge. She was the rejected woman; the entity now became the non-entity.

"I'm sorry that it is turning out this way for you Mrs. Mellenstreet. Should we wait for our next Wednesday appointment, or would you like to come in sooner?"

"I'm not sure. I'm too upset to talk about it."

"I have a 2:00 o'clock open today. How will that do?"

"Fine. I will be there."

At 2:00 o'clock we started our session. She preferred to spend a good deal of the session with eyes closed. This helped her focus away from the demanding irritation that was consuming her; at least a little bit. Today it did not seem to work as well. She was no longer herself, so to speak. She was literally imprisoned by the mass of raw, repressed emotion that was literally eating her alive.

"You know Mrs. Mellenstreet, even if we find out where he is going, and what he is doing, this will not change a thing. You're a volcano waiting to explode. We've got to get you released before you are truly the victim of this whole episode."

"How do you propose to do this?" she asked.

"We are just going to have to find a way to open you up so that what is compressed will just release and leave."

"Haven't we tried everything?'

"We've talked. Some days we seem to be making progress. Others, I feel we've just been scratching the surface. Let me ask you. How do you feel right now?"

"Like you said, an explosion that wants to explode, but isn't being allowed. Even if I were allowed, what would I do? I am certainly not about ready to have a crying hissy-fit in your presence" she said with hands and arms flailing. After a pause ... "I respect you too much for that."

"That's what I'm here for. Let me ask you this – where do you feel "it," whatever "it" is?

"In my throat and here," as she pointed at the bottom of my breastbone.

"Good. What does it feel like?"

"Tight. Rigid. Like I am using all of my force and will power to keep it where it is, so I can maybe disregard it, dissolve it, or maybe it will get better and go away."

"Let's play a game. It's a laughing game. If all else fails, at least we'll get you laughing. Are you game?"

"Some humor would be very good," she said directly.

"Laughter seemed to help you before," I said.

"Good. Then let's just pretend that whatever you are feeling is something, and you and this something are going to meet, so to speak. And to get close enough to speak, if there are any roadblocks, you are going to laugh your way through them."

"Am I really paying you for this?" she asked.

"Bear with me. I think this could be helpful. OK?"

"I've trusted you this far!" she said.

"Good. Just close your eyes. Let's pretend that you can see this as an image that looks comical, and that you can actually get close to this thing, no matter how it feels. That is what I want you to do right now. Start getting close to it, in your mind. Just make believe that you can do it."

"That's just what I don't want it to do. Why are you making me get closer to the pain? I don't like pain!".... Am I supposed to see myself going there in my throat and chest?"

"If you can. Remember, put a funny face on it as best you can. If you feel any pain, I want you to laugh until the pain subsides. Then, get closer, and start laughing again if you feel any pain. Let laughter be the method we use right now for pain management. Pretend that you're feeling your way to this presence, as if, by magic. As you get closer, the feeling of this something may magnify. If it does, just let it. I know that is contrary to everything you know or have been taught, but just let it magnify as much as it wants."

"But, this hurts!"

"Why aren't you laughing?" I asked directly and abruptly.

She started laughing. First, contrived and fake with no zip in it whatsoever. Then I started to laugh a little as if to lead her; make her feel it is okay. Then the symmetry began to happen. We both started laughing loudly and naturally. I could tell it had been a long time since the concept of authentic humor had entered her life. I knew it would be good for her to have it as a remedy.

"Okay. Now make pretend you are moving away. Just for a moment – but in doing so you are still allowing this something to be whatever it wants to be and to feel anyway it wants to feel."

I just sat and watched her for a minute. The tightness in her brow was beginning to subside, a little. Her breathing was beginning to get a little more regular. Deeper. Less shallow.

"How do you feel now?"

"A little better; but I'm shaking a little bit. This is a new experience."

"Good, one last time. Let's get right up to it, as close as you can get. Make it cute, really, really funny. "Let's start laughing again. How are you doing? Do you need to back off again?"

"No, I am actually doing alright. The pain has really just gone away"

"Good. Now, let's move into this something, as far into it as you can go. Feel it. What does it feel like?"

"Like tar. Black. Hard. Impenetrable, but there's no pain."

"Good. Stay with it. Just be with it. Don't try to change it. Just let it be whatever it wants to be. As you stay with, just keep your laughter going."

"It doesn't feel as resistant anymore, but it's still a little uncomfortable."

"Good. Does it have a feeling? Any contours?"

"Just like this black hole. Once I fall into it, I'll be gone forever."

"How does that make you feel?"

"Afraid" she answered.

"OK. Stay with it and laugh out the fear as best you can."

"OK. I am"

"How does it feel now?'

"Thick, but tingly.

"Let's pretend again. Let's pretend that you are here and are completely safe and that I am here to protect you. Now, let's pretend that you can go into this thing, and explore it, and that you can come back here, safe and sound."

"If you say so.

"I do. Now, with a big, rich smile on your face – make the Cheshire cat's smile look like a minnow."

"OK" she said as she slightly adjusted herself.

"Remember the first time you were getting into a swimming pool. You had two choices. You could slowly get in, and maybe feel the excruciating cold of the water, or you could just jump in."

"I'm in."

"That's my girl! Feel the energy of it. Feel the essence of it. Just feel it and let it express itself to you."

"It's like ... It's like it just wanted to be recognized. It's just... like ... nothing. It's going away."

"Stay with it."

"Straight Aces!" she said.

"What?!" I exclaimed at this out-of-place disclosure.

"He often likes to entertain clients at "Straight Aces." There is good jazz there. Good jazz is something my husband really enjoys. Up until now, I would have said it was one of the few pleasures he would permit in his life."

"I know the place, on Court Street. I'll get over there tonight and report back to you tomorrow."

Straight Aces started out as a cellar joint during Prohibition. Its reputation for providing good booze and good music has never waned. While it would no longer be considered a "cellar joint," its plain brick walls attest to its "rustic" beginnings. It never went top-heavy on decor anyway.

About 40 4-seater tables lined up in front of the bandstand area. The proximity among the tables helped create an air of collective intoxication when the crowd was really enjoying the music. Didn't really seem like quite the place for the likes of Andrew Mellenstreet, but I suppose we all have to have our outlets. Anyway, if you wanted more privacy, two rows of booths lined the walls.

The relative darkness added to the intimacy you felt when you were comfortable, felt relaxed, enjoyed your company and those around you; had a little alcohol buzz and, most of all, felt right in tune with the music. I usually happened here once a month. Never noticed Andrew Mellenstreet here before.

A newcomer was playing tonight. Rufus Melody LaFontaine. Wow! What a moniker! Preliminary reports were that he was developing a reputation for playing a real "sly" sax. Sly in the sense that sax music will usually hit a man in the heart and the head, where it stirs up feelings of romance. As for women, I am told, it seems to hit them, well, a little bit lower. I am told it is equally as stirring. People said he could lead the crowd into a real cloud of blue with a silver lining.

At half past eight, Andrew Mellenstreet was seated with two other men in their late fifties or early sixties. He still had his business suit on; they were wearing sport jackets, and slacks. Their shirts were open at the neck, and they weren't wearing any ties.

Mr. Mellenstreet had a briefcase with him. He put it in on the small circular table, opened it, and took out a file. I could not hear him, but could see he was talking with his serious accountant face. His mannerisms, the way he carefully lifted each sheet of paper in the file, talked of serious and undivided attention.

After talking for about ten minutes, he put the file away. Then he took out a map! Then I remembered my dream. A map! I was going to move heaven and earth to see it. I stood up as if I were walking to the men's room in order to get the best glance I could. I could see a point highlighted by magic marker, but could not get close enough to see it before he put it away.

Rufus Melody LaFontaine was introduced. Young, but very confident. Polished, but genteel. Adventurous with the sax, but educated and astute.

The set started. It was very penetrating. Very enjoyable. LaFontaine finished a long number. The place was really charged. Everyone felt great.

Mellenstreet and company got up and left.

I called Mrs. Mellenstreet and asked her to stay up after her husband went to sleep, and to do something she had never done before: invade the sanctity of his business briefcase.

XXI

Headline news on the radio announced that the City Planning Commission had voted to put the industrial revenue bond issue to the people. A special election was two months away, and the general election was six months down the road. Political campaigns were in full swing, heading for the stretch, and political claims and counterclaims were flying high and wide.

Mrs. Mellenstreet dutifully, and I am sure, joyfully went through her husband's briefcase after he went to sleep. Fortunately, it was not locked. He, no doubt, presumed that the sanctity of his property would never be violated in his home. She told me that "Crystal Lake" was handwritten on the map in a rural area about 100 to 150 miles south of the city. No nearby towns. Just a rural route 51.

I decided to pay Crystal Lake a visit, but I had no idea what I was going to do when I got there. The feeling of not knowing what I was doing or why I was doing it was now getting routine and "normal." Funny how the surreal can get habitually normal very quickly!

I got into the general vicinity about 3:00 in the afternoon. No signs announced Crystal Lake, but by the tall, stone fences with jagged glass cemented on top, and the "No Trespassing" signs, I presumed that all the land in the area was very private. If so, my next question was, "who owned it?" I decided to keep on driving to see what else was in the area. It was very heavily wooded; very pristine. The map did not indicate any small towns nearby.

I continued on Route 51. Now it was nothing more than a two-lane dirt road. I cleared the top of a hill and came upon a small town below me. No reference to it on the map. As I cleared the "Main Street," I saw a sign announcing the name of this metropolis: "Pink's Cane – Population 360 – Formerly Winthorp." This stung me for a moment because it registered that John Witheral had moved to the city from a small town named Winthorp. We could find no trace of Winthorp on any map. "But, what is Pink's Cane! " I thought.

On the surface, Pink's Cane was a quaint little town with a drug store, gas station, a vintage Western Auto store and an F.W.

Woolworths. I figured the general store/ drug store had a soda bar inside so I decided to go inside and get some refreshment, and maybe some information.

The drug store was duly announced by an historic Rexall sign; and, as I suspected, a genuine soda bar was in full operation along an entire side of the store. You know you are drinking a little bit of history when fresh ice cream goes into a stainless steel cup and is whirred into a chilled perfection in an authentic green porcelain mixer. I half expected some "bobby soxers" to waltz through the front door wearing raccoon coats.

I sat down at the bar and ordered a root beer shake. It had been a long time since I had an ice cold root beer shake which was guaranteed to be so cold that you'd have a splitting headache by the second sip.

"Can you tell me the turnoff for Crystal Lake?" I asked the boy at the counter. He gave me a sort of queer, uncomfortable look and shrugged his shoulders. When you are an obvious stranger in a small town, there are a limited number of topics you can talk about without crossing the dividing line into "busy body," "meddler," or "real estate developer."

"I really don't know what you mean. The owner might be able to help you." He was young enough that he hadn't perfected the gentle art of fibbing yet. Too much blood shot into his cheeks as he was feeding me his little fib.

A few minutes later a grey-haired bespectacled, distinguished looking gentleman sat down beside me. With him was an old-timer, an ancient man with sleeve covers over a neatly pressed shirt, crisp bowtie, and gold-rimmed glasses with hexagon-shaped lenses. His very appearance served both as a testament to the progression of time and a pinpoint in the preservation of time. The old-timer said "I hear you are looking for Crystal Lake" he said in a crisp tone, with precise diction. His well-preserved looks and his mannerisms made me wonder about the health benefits of living in a very small town.

"Yes sir I am," I replied, being particularly careful to call him "sir." I was supposed to meet some friends there and seem to have missed the turnoff."

"That so" he said with an almost New England clipped directness, giving me a querulous look, and all the while looking me straight in the eyes. Here was a man who had no fear in digging for the truth, and making you uncomfortable enough to reveal it. I realized quite profoundly that now I was going to be on the opposite side of the inquiry. I was usually the one asking the questions and getting answers. For a time, this was going to change.

"Yes" I replied again, as innocently as I could, shrugging my shoulders, and making sure the blood wasn't rushing to my cheeks – and all the while knowing I, too, had not perfected the art of fibbing – and only wanted to get out of there while I could.

"I haven't been to Crystal Lake in years, – decades," he said, staring upward, almost dream-like. "When I was a little boy, that was the best swimming in the area. Maybe it still is, but nobody goes there or can go there anymore. Back in the 20s some tycoon named Carnahan bought it lock, stock and barrel. Turned it private and fenced off the area. Actually tried to prosecute some of us old-timers for trying to sneak in. Wanted the privacy I guess. Anyway, people stayed away from it. That's ok though. I was always sort of scared of the place. Rumored to contain an old Indian graveyard. Don't really know that to be a fact, or whether it's just another rumor started over a late-night campfire. But, to me, the place always had sort of an eerie presence at night time. Who did you say you were going to meet?"

"Uh ... uh, a friend from work has a friend with someone who owns land around here."

"That so," he said with eyes owl-like and piercing. The quality of his eyeglass lenses made his blue eyes appear very clear in detail and color, and penetrating in direction.

"Carnahan, ..." I thought to myself. "Could it be the same one they told me about before at the Hall? I wondered."

"I heard that old Carnahan died a short time ago" he continued. "Wouldn't be surprised if he was buried there" he said sarcastically. "We lost touch with that place a long time ago, almost as if it were on another planet. You know that these towns are divided by a lot of hilly terrain. Each town really exists on its own, especially during the winter."

"Do you know which access road leads from Route 51 to the lake?"

"Well, a long time ago there was a stone archway. Had some buck antlers on top. That used to be the entranceway. Don't know if it's still there. ... . Say, has old-man Carnahan sold the property to one of your friends or something?"

"Something like that, I guess. All in the family, you know."

"That name is a real name out of the past for me" he said, his eyes suddenly glazed, and sort of dreamy and far away. "When Carnahan locked us out, we used to imagine the wildest goings-on there. Ghosts. Women. You know, those sorts of boyish fantasies. Every once in a while though, you would hear somebody say that they heard chanting. Chanting! Lots of torches could be seen from a distance. Like some sort of a procession. Sometimes, a scream or a howl. Who really knows?!" he said airily, with a dry smile on his face. "I don't think there's any truth to it at all. There's really nothing else I can tell you."

"I appreciate the information" I said, not feeling entirely comfortable with what I had been given, or the attitudes with which the information had been presented. As I was taking some money out of my jeans to pay for the shake, I noticed the counter boy giving the old-timer a sort of telepathic look. I pretended to disregard it.

"Say, how did you get the name Pink's Cane?" I asked.

"My friend," he said disingenuously, that is a long story and left for another time." He patted me the shoulder - as if to say - "It's time for you to leave." He and his short-sleeved friend turned and walked away.

As I was walking toward the wrinkled, swinging screen-paneled wood doors, I could feel three sets of eyes focused on me. Not a word was spoken. Complete silence except for the sound of my footsteps on the worn, creaky wooden floor. I stopped, suddenly remembering that this town had some connection with John Witheral. I turned and asked, "Isn't this the town where John Witheral came from?" thinking back to that conversation I had heard about with Detective Bowlin.

They sat in silence. Small-towners weary of outsiders and especially old-timers, can make a religion of silence. Never ones to fill empty space, they would let their opponents hang themselves.

They looked at each other. The old-timer's eyes became wide and intense as he gave a quick stare to the counter boy; much more sedate and controlled when he momentarily looked back in my direction. "Yes, John used to live in these parts. Not much family here anymore, though, other than his elderly parents. Most dead a long time ago. He used to pass through periodically; stay with friends. Nice boy. Very sorry to have heard of his misfortune." He looked at me very keenly and asked, "Who did you say were the names of your friends?" "Johnson," I said picking a name out of a hat. "That so!" was his reply. Obviously, that was all the old-timer was going to say, as if it were a prepared speech.

I knew that more had happened here than anyone cared to talk about, or would talk about. And, I was an outsider. Word about a stranger and a snooper gets around real fast in a town like this. Anyway, the old school clock overhead showed it was 4:00 already. I had best be on my way to try to find the entrance to the lake … if I still wanted to go there.

I felt very uncomfortable about having given the information that I might be headed to the lake. Too rural, too wooded here. Anything could happen here and go undetected … forever.

As I was walking through the door, having thanked them for the information, the old-timer callout to me. "Sir?" When the pressure in a conversation let's up, if there is a next question, it can be a real doozy.

"Yes," I replied.

"You're from the city" he said pointedly, stating it rather than asking.

"Yes, Why?"

"Did you know Ponti Moon, the museum person?"

I was sort of startled by the question. "Yes, I do; very well" I replied. Now my interest quickened. "Why?"

"Nothing; just a question. He was here a few weeks ago looking for the lake. I heard he has been missing. Poor man" he said antiseptically.

XXII

I got back to Route 51, drove about a quarter of a mile past the gate they described. It still had the buck antlers cemented to the center archway, which the old-timer had mentioned. I parked my car in a thick grove where I could camouflage it.

I walked back to the gateway. The entrance was blocked by heavy wrought-iron bars, chained and padlocked. The gate had a stultified, medieval appearance. The six-foot high stone wall extended in both directions as far as I could see. Shattered glass had been cemented along the top. "After this," I thought, "a No Trespassing sign would have been superfluous and meaningless."

Figuring that I would be spending the night, I came equipped with a heavy sweater and jacket, along with food and blankets in the car. Wrapping a heavy blanket around my arms, I took a running jump over the wall. "So far, so good" I thought.

A single-lane road coursed from the gate. I assumed it led directly to the lake. Instead of staying on the road, where I was entirely visible, I walked into the forest just off the shoulder. I could walk undetected here at the same time as being able to see everything that might happen along the road.

Sunlight was filtering through the thick growth. Every once in a while a refraction caught me squarely in the eyes, blinding me.

As I walked farther and farther away from the gateway, I began feeling a strange sensation; almost an eeriness. My search, which began as a discovery and an adventure, now felt real, and dangerous. It also felt involuntary. Not being trained for this, and not otherwise having the disposition for it, it was almost like I was being drawn inward against my will. The fact that I was trespassing didn't help the situation. The wall separated me from the rest of the world, and the feeling of separation is always a cause for fear. The road to the lake was pulling me closer and closer into its vortex.

The trees were just beginning to change color. A metallic blue sky was overhead, with tufts of clouds floating by. A glorious time of the year. A soft breeze was blowing.

Almost an hour into my walk, I heard motors behind me. I stopped and remained motionless in the trees as they went by. Four cars with three men each. Mellenstreet was driving one. More cars were coming every few minutes. This was becoming a procession.

A shimmering reflection appeared in the distance. I could now see the lake about 50 yards ahead of me. Sun's evening rays were beginning to bear down on the ancient water. I could hear a soft lapping against the shoreline in the distance. There was moisture in the air. I was getting very close.

Crystal Lake, as its name suggests, is clear, sparkling, unpolluted, and all the rest of the adjectives for pure, evergreen, unspoiled and tranquil. It is truly heavenly. Pristine. A backdrop of verdant green hills was off in the distance.

The horizon here was not composed of manmade mountains of glass and steel. It was a resplendent lake surrounded by rich pine forests and rolling hills. The soothing aroma of long-needle pines drifted easily in the air.

From my vantage point, I could see the cars grouped at the end of the road. Next to them, a dirt circle with a diameter of a few hundred feet had been cleared and graded.

It was steadily getting darker, but I could see men milling inside the circle, conversing and socializing. They were congratulating someone. He looked familiar, but I wasn't sure if I recognized him. I was beginning to wonder if there were guards back at the gate and if anyone had seen me park my car. What about the old timer and the counter boy? What if they told somebody I was coming here? I wondered how into the thick of it I really was.

I looked behind me and to the right. I saw the outlines of several structures off in the distance. Intuitively, I felt something telling me I needed to get out of the vicinity of the circle ceremony for the time being. Thinking that it was Uncle Duke looking out for me, I said "Thank you Uncle Duke!"

Night was now quickly descending. The world was becoming more isolated; more encapsulated. A new world was revealing itself.

I saw the outline of a path which seemed to lead in the direction of one of the structures. It was covered by fallen leaves which still retained the moisture of a recent rain. I could walk on them without detection.

Lights from the first structure lured me closer. The door was open and an old woman was outside picking vegetables and herbs from a garden. She was 70ish. Tall. Too slender for her frame. Almost emaciated. Sunken cheekbones. Dark, stringy hair; greasy, not recently washed. Her makeup was almost a caricature, in that her lipstick extended over the natural lines of her lips, and her rouge looked like two circles on her cheeks. Just how you would anticipate an isolated, rural crone to look like. She was muttering something to herself, and started to hum. Her voice was not beautiful, and added to her worn, threadbare appearance. She gave me the willies.

She spoke to her plants, but in an odd way. Not out of a compassionate manner; more off-balance. She seemed jittery and hyper.

It was time to try to find my way to the other structure, or to at least find a safe spot for the night. As the Sun continued to sink below the horizon, wide rays of crystalline light covered the water, like a blanket of light; at first transparent; but gradually becoming brilliant in intensity. Like a candle which is nearing the final throes of self-immolation; casting its balance in a final glorious spectacle of light.

The evening sky was giving off the appearance of electricity. Parhelic. The final burst of color before the onslaught of night and the awakening of the other world.

Clouds then began collecting. Thick. Like starched hospital sheets covering the world, absorbing the color like cotton swabs in an operating room. The world was beginning to have a packaged effect.

The lights of day subsided quickly here, and the shroud of night absorbed the sky.

The Sun sank below the world. The transition was complete. As the clouds parted, tiny pin pricks in the night sky revealed the lights of other worlds, far in the distance; a glimpse of eternity. These lights, together, formed a semi-circle of gold and silver light across a cobalt blue sky. The universe had taken on the appearance of lapis lazuli, that precious stone which the ancients thought symbolized heaven because of its rich, deep blue color, speckled with gold. Here at Crystal Lake we were as much a part of that universe as any other particle that served to make up the shimmering whole.

A huge moon rose. When the clouds parted, the moon was clear and bright; its continents clearly demarcated. A brilliant halo surrounded it.

To add more color to the scene and my uneasiness, the woman began to hum louder, and then to howl like a wolf. But for shape-shifting, she had otherwise taken on the persona of a forest dweller. Her howl then developed and settled into a monosyllabic drone. I was beginning to feel like I was in a walled sanatorium. And, why was she not with the male congregants? Why was she here in the first place?

If this was the Carnahan estate, no wonder he went to such lengths to keep it very private.

Sundown apparently had some meaning for the male congregants as well, as far as I could tell. Huge torches were lit around the circle literally spotlighting the area. I could make my way back there in this darkness. There was more than one reason for it. I could feel the evening chill, but as I made my way back to the circle, all of the men were stark naked in a circle, surrounded by torches. They single-filed to the lake and each went in without deliberation. After coming out and drying themselves off, they dressed in long, flowing white-hooded robes. The robes extended from head to foot. The style was uniform for each person.

White robes in the night can be austere and haunting. Soft chanting added to the aura of otherworldliness. Something was being carried into the circle. It was a tower or platform of some sort and was placed in the center as far as I could tell. My vantage point was slightly higher than the crowd, which was beginning to get dense with people.

Then someone in a white robe and purple hood stepped forward and onto the platform. The hood covered his and each congregant's face in the manner of the Franciscans.

A scene began to unfold. Dancing and gyrations. Concentric circles were formed. Whirling independently. Wildness. Circles of dancers within circles. Between 75 and 100 people by my estimate. The chanting continued.

On the direction of the one on the platform, large concentric circles were formed, one around the other, and all turning counterclockwise around the platform. Moving slowly. Moving deliberately. Moving meditatively. Then upon direction, every other circle started turning in the opposite direction. Turning and turning. Slowly. Like a spiral in a suspended position. Patiently. Recitation of prayers in a language foreign to me. Then the circling stopped. Each congregant kneeled. En masse, heads to the ground. Backs bent in prayer and submission.

The emergence of the moon seemed to signal emergence and revelation, for when it rose the purple hooded one directed the tides of congregants to arise. Again, concentric circles, every other one turning in an opposite direction.

Gradually the circles began to grow closer together, and tighter. Like the spring of a watch being wound, tighter and tighter. But, as the mass was gathering in an even tighter concentration, one person appeared to be splintering off from the group. Eventually this person was expelled from the mass, like the natural forces of nature expelling a nebula in the act of solar birth and creation. He turned, and walked to the base of the altar. His movements were very slow and self-conscious, as if he were drugged and trying too hard to control himself. Step-by-step he moved, on the seven steps to the altar table.

Just then ... a hand was on my shoulder. The shock kept me from screaming, and frozen in form. A soft, feminine voice spoke to me in my left ear: "You should not be here. You need to leave with me before it is too late." As I gradually turned my head, I came to see the crone looking at me and smiling. Somehow, she did not seem as wild and preposterous as when I first saw her. "Move very slowly and carefully, so as not to attract any attention. The ceremony is about to go into silence." I intuitively knew she knew what she was talking about, and I listened to her.

As I started to move away from my vantage point, I caught a quick glimpse of the chosen one on the altar. He had disrobed. I saw him for only a moment, and the resemblance to the counter boy at the drug store was very striking.

The woman and I slowly backed away from the procession. I could not help turning around. The chosen one on the altar was being prepared by several people. He was shaved from the head down. It looked like mascara was being applied to his eyes. Then his body was rubbed with oils, and from the aroma filtering through the air, unguents which packed quite a delivery.

We turned away and she led me to her cottage.

She looked at me very carefully and then started a monologue to which I was an involuntary bystander. "I did my tarot cards today and knew someone not invited was going to be here and that I should relate my story to him. You are here on a kind of mission, but it is more dangerous than you can even imagine. As you can imagine, there have not been many trespassers here who have had the ability to leave. I do not know why you are here, but you need to leave while you can. There are goings on here that are not of this world."

I was stupefied. Why in the world was I doing this in the first place? If anyone in my life needed his head examined, it was certainly me!

She could see I was numb and let me collect myself. We walked to her garden which was far enough away from the gathering. When speech had returned to me, I asked. "Who are you?"

In the same way that she spoke without inhibition to the plants, she spoke to me. "My name is Daphne. Mr. Carnahan and I became acquainted in 1923 and I have been here since. His Will allowed me to remain here for the rest of my days. The Trustees maintain my home and provide basic necessities. My needs are few now, with my garden. I do not leave the grounds. I would no longer know what to do in the outside world. This has become my world."

"What is this place?

"Mr. Carnahan called it the 'omphalos,' the ancient Greek word for navel; the navel of the world, so to speak. It was not always such as this, though. It was filled with joy and gaiety in the early years; parties, nature walks, picnics and good breathing air! It was only after Mr. Carnahan's health began to decline that he became interested in, shall we say ... life after death."

"Baird" she continued, "was what you would call an internationalist, or an international citizen of the world. He called the world his home, and everything in it became a potential object of possession and acquisition. He lived to buy, to possess, to own. He longed for the opportunity to acquire the world's greatest treasures, for that purpose alone. I think he derived some little pleasure and fulfillment from the art. He felt that the initials of his name, "B.C." symbolized his right to unearth the treasures of the past and know their secrets. He derived fulfillment to see the envy it engendered among those he had beaten to the prize. Several deals relating to the purchase of antiquities were left unfinished when he died."

She paused, as if in a private dream, and continued. "After the First World War, the world turned on a different axis. Now the "little people" as Baird called them, could buy on credit. Not that they could ever hope to be in his league, but he anticipated living the life of a titled feudal lord surrounded by serfs who did his bidding. Baird felt like his exclusive world was being attacked. He then went about his business of collecting pieces of the past with even more passion. He felt that collecting objets d'Art, for their uniqueness and value, was the only way of keeping the breach between the emerging middle class and himself. Only the Depression would allow him the ability to reassume the exclusivity he had enjoyed before the first war."

"Was he looking for anything in particular in the ancient art he purchased," I asked.

"Yes." Then a moment of silence. "He was always searching for eternal life. He never wanted this life to end. He felt that with the privileges he enjoyed in this life he had found the formula for happiness in life. He wanted it to go on for eternity. A person named Andrew Mellenstreet became privy to many of his secrets."

"Secrets," I said with a little alarm. "You mean he actually knew something?!" I said softly, but with wide-eyed emphasis. I left Mr. Mellenstreet out of the conversation for now.

She avoided the question, at first. "He seemed to travel between air currents, so-to-speak. Money and privilege will sometimes do this. Even with the Great War going, he had special permission to conduct digs in Israel. He chose Israel because he felt that he knew that the secret of secrets had been with the royal line of the House of David, and he wanted it. In the late teens and early 20s of this century, before I knew him, he organized an archeological dig in northern Israel, at the ancient site of Megiddo. He was obsessed with Armageddon and the end days, because they would also mean his end. He endeavored to change it if he could, at least to ensure his survival if all others faded away. Many important articles were recovered which have been stored away and have never been disclosed to anyone. Some, however, have somehow surfaced in museums. I overheard the Trustees talking about one that was in the recent exhibition at a place called the Hall of Antiquities. Are you aware of this place?"

"I am" I said as I nodded with the certainty of a person in the know. Then, feeling a little more cavalier, I asked, "The double triangle?"

"Yes. That is it" she added with discomforting sigh, fearing she had gone much farther than she should have with a complete stranger.

"Did he ever say anything about it?"

"Not to me. Mellenstreet had become a confidante, of sorts – to the extent he really divulged anything to anyone. Probably also to his other close associate. His name was Roger, but everyone called him Ranger. He earned several medals for bravery in the First War. Baird was somehow able to arrange his discharge before the end of the war in order to come work for him."

"Can I speak with Roger?"

"He committed suicide shortly after Mr. Carnahan's death."

"What about this Mellenstreet? How did he meet Mr. Carnahan?"

"Taxes. Like most ultra-wealthy people, Mr. Carnahan was an incredibly secretive person. Mellenstreet was hired to do what was necessary to pay homage to the government. Mellenstreet was also involved in the probate and the valuation of this incredible estate. As such, he became privy to many articles and much information of which he had not previously known. Many of them will undoubtedly remain secret and sequestered. Much of this he got from Ranger. Mellenstreet is still working on dealing with the valuation of priceless ancient artifacts, some of which may have been purchased or acquired from, let us say, shadowy sources."

I said nothing. What could I say? I could express incredulity, but I knew full well that the congregation was involved in that ancient practice of propitiating unseen forces by offering human life.

"By then," she continued, "I had been here almost four decades. I found a place for myself, and made myself invisible, so to speak. It was certainly not all negative and bad. It only started getting more pronounced shortly before Mr. Carnahan's passing. But, you need to leave right now. It is not safe for you here."

"Is it safe for you to help me?"

"The cards showed me that I would be of service, and so this is what I am to do."

"Do you know Ponti Moon?"

"Yes. He has been here many times." She paused for a moment. Power is a strange thing" she said looking distantly. "I have seen it happen over and over again – often with Baird's associates, and finally with him. One thinks one is accumulating power, while the forces of power – whatever they may be – are simply using the person – like electricity through a light bulb. The bulb – if it could think – might believe that it is all-powerful. Look at what it is channeling! Look at how bright and brilliant it is! But, then what? The bulb is used up, thrown away – and that is that!"

She continued. "I was never privy to the secrets, such as they were. Baird knew I had my own interests, and they had more to do with the beauty and love so evident in the natural world. He honored this and is a great man for it. But, just by being here, I came to know a thing or two. One thing I do know" she said, "is that Andrew Mellenstreet has come upon some knowledge – whatever it may be.

"The funny thing is," she continued, "is that the power is whatever it is. The way it runs through and affects those who channel it, is quite another thing. Ego has a strange and often dramatic impact on how we use the gifts given to us. I am afraid that power in the hands of this person is not such a pretty thing."

"What is this power?" I asked.

"I can only tell you what I heard, and this may sound incredible, but here it is. I have heard it intimated that he is able to materialize in other times for short periods. He seeks to install himself as a new kind of priest-king or G-d in these other times. And, in coming back to this time, he seeks to use the esoteric knowledge only known to the ancients and long since lost. It would make him a kind of multi-dimensional G-d, or," she hesitated, "demon." "But like any mammal that lives in water, he must come up for air frequently. So, he cannot remain in the other time indefinitely. His body is a body of this time. It is too dense for the thinner atmosphere where his alter ego resides. I do not know when he will go, or when he will return when he does. I doubt he has that knowledge either. I do know his absence has grown longer and longer."

"What is it he really knows, anyway? Isn't power just power," I asked. The story was so compelling that I did not even think to ask if it was true, or to consciously decide whether she was even credible. Just another facet of this incredible journey I was on.

"That is a question for someone other than me. And, what he knows would not be a concern if there were not the potential for misuse. I have heard that he has the actual ability to physically transport himself to another time if he so desires. Or, he can spiritually transport his spirit to a past life, leaving his dormant body here. The form is still able to function for a time because it is not totally devoid of spirit."

Reacquiring my sense of consciousness of a here and now, I looked at her aghast. My eyes and mouth were wide open. What she told me was so incredible, but, I believed her.

Crystal Lake – a choice place for an altar devoted to an ancient rite. At Crystal Lake, out of time, one could attempt to return to a time when other gods were with the human race. Perhaps they still are.

XXIII

It's a lovely fall morning. Cool. A wonderful freshness in the air. Sparrows dashing here and there looking for food.

I had been overlooking a field of wild flowers in the late autumn and literally got lost in it. My head shook involuntarily when I "awoke." I thought I had been fully awake, but then realized that I had been "somewhere else" for Heaven knows how long, and I had been without thought while I was "away." No thought whatsoever. How liberating it felt. How free. Just a moment like this made me realize how oppressive the thinking mind is. When I came to I was looking at some beautiful orange wild flowers. Poppies, perhaps? I didn't realize I was looking at them until I "awoke." They reminded me of the story of the devotee who received enlightenment by looking at the Buddha slowly turning a wild flower between his thumb and index finger. The message was, "No Thought Is Enlightenment. No thought is freedom." I will forever more call these beautiful, orange flowers, "Buddha Flowers."

I waited for several hours as the car processional inside the compound, made its way outside. I needed to talk to Daphne, the crone, about what was going on. She told me where to find the keys to the three padlocks securing the gate. I went to her cottage and found her somewhat restless and antsy. From the look on her face I could tell that my appearance was expected.

Given the lack of visitors and communication and no one to talk to, she must have treated every opportunity as if it would be her last. Thus, she spoke with an enthusiasm and gratitude at just having the opportunity to speak. She seemed to go on endlessly about her life, and then she stopped and became silent.

"What is it?" I asked.

Then he became more personal about who she was.

"I was born and raised in the South" she said, solemn-eyed, and with her head down– lost in reveries of time long past. "We moved quite often. My father was an Evangelical preacher and believed you had to be mobile to spread the Word. My mother was a Christian Scientist who instilled in me a love of the mystery which is this world. So, you could say my entire youth was spent in prayer in make-shift churches or revival tents. It might seem out-of-character for who I am today, but it was exciting to a young girl who had her own sense of wanderlust."

"When I left home," she said a little bit more matter-of-fact, "I traded churches for speakeasies, and ethereal medicine for Canadian whiskey. I never forgot, however, the power of prayer. It literally saved my life more than once."

"Baird and I met in a glamorous club. I was dressed to the 9s; just flapping the night and my life away. He had on an elegant tux and top hat, and was carrying a gold-crowned cane in white-gloved hands. He looked so perfect he could have been a caricature! He had just returned from one of his expeditions. We were introduced, spoke for several hours, and that was that. We were never really apart except when he went treasure hunting in foreign lands."

"Over the years, when my life settled down, I was drawn more and more to the spirituality that was so much a part of my youth. Being here, on the estate, I had no real opportunities to get involved in church life. And, it became clear early on, from my little contact with the folks in the small towns around here, that they really didn't want to have much to do with me."

Baird may have been a dyed-in-the-wool materialist, but it was this sense of spirituality that really connected us. In fact, he was so extreme into collecting material wealth, it was this other sense that really saved him."

"For a short while we experimented with seances and the like, but they really were not for us. Along the way, I met many talented spiritualists who taught me another side of the same spirituality I learned growing up. Some called it metaphysics and tried to put a modern face on it, but, as I have learned, spirit is spirit, whatever you call it. I also became quite adept at reading Tarot cards. Something about the pictures really spoke to me – literally. I could look at them and just, sort of, engage in conversations. Maybe I was just lonely and needed friends. I don't know– it all seems real to me."

"That is when I decided that I wanted to be called Daphne. My given name was Dorothy. Something in me felt drawn to the ancient Oracles at Delphi, in ancient Greece. This is how I felt connected. My parents are long deceased. What little family we had are disbursed to only Heaven knows where. So, in my seclusion, the stars in the sky became my family and friends, and nature became my confidante. I know it sounds silly and egotistical. Really, what is in a name? Why not take on a new one?"

"My life was very complete in some respects, but wanting in others. I know everyone has the same complaint. I no longer have to worry about finances, so most people would naturally assume that I have no worries at all. I wish it were all that simple. But, all-in-all, I have lived a very happy and satisfied life.

Then she paused and seemed to engage in an inward conversation only she could hear. Then, without even noticing my presence, she started speaking again, very softly and whimsically.

"It started as such a beautiful experiment" she said with measured enthusiasm and a far-away look. "An experiment in experiencing the eternal life of the living G-d. It was not supposed to have become so – sensationalized. I fear what will happen next as the new hierarchy starts trying to protect its power. Mr. Carnahan would not have liked this at all!" Apparently there was much, much more here than a secluded estate formerly inhabited by a gentrified billionaire and his mate. But, she was saying no more and it was not my place to ask – at least at this moment.

We looked at each other in silence. Then, with strained emphasis in her face, she asked, "Did you hear?"

"I have been here all night. I have not heard anything."

"The report is that he is now alive. He appeared out of nowhere. Dazed. Confused, but alive. And not talking."

"Who is he?" I asked.

"John Witheral. Experiments in life after death and teleportation. John Witheral has returned from the dead" she said with downcast eyes and a sullen voice.

"So he has not said anything to anyone?"

"Not that anyone has said."

"Is that why Mr. Carnahan chose such a secluded place?" it was time for me to ask. She looked at me, then with downcast eyes, she skipped into another silent reverie.

I said nothing for several minutes. On the other hand, I did not pretend ignorance. In the short time I knew her, I knew it would have been superfluous. "Are you safe here? What will become of you?" I asked.

"The Trustees know that I am not a hazard, and that I have nowhere else to go. They have made it clear that I am welcome here for as long as I choose. I am not concerned about that. What I'm concerned about is what this place is being used for, and the atmosphere that is being created here. Even with Baird's incredible ego, there used to be real love here. Now, it's a new religion with a big secret."

"Are they planning to go public with what they know?"

"I hear the tidbits. They do not generally let me in on anything, thank Heavens. I just want to be left alone and live out the rest of my life in peace. I don't want to be surrounded by these sensationalists."

"What do the Trustees have to say about it?"

"Who do you think organizes the outings?"

"What about children? Beneficiaries?"

"I am it. Mr. Carnahan and I never married. He had no siblings or disavowed distant relations long ago. He always honored our relationship, as did I."

"Why are you here in this little cottage? What's going in the large estate?"

"It became apparent that my presence was not necessarily wanted there after Mr. Carnahan died. The Trustees had other uses for it, uses which require secrecy. "

"This almost feels like we are witnessing a repeat of the Frankenstein epic."

"Except, this is not a movie!"

"Are these all middle aged men who are going through mid-life crises?"

"Something much more sinister I am afraid. I spread my tarot cards every morning. When I asked about the estate property, the Death card kept coming up repeatedly. Keep in mind that the symbolism of the death card is not what you think it is. In the deck, it represents the end of one cycle and the beginning of the next. It is not necessarily an ending in the void of black silence. The transition into the rebirth, however, can sometimes be difficult."

"Tell me what you know about Ponti Moon."

"The last I saw of Mr. Moon was the night he was here with Sebastian Ponticello."

"The oil magnate?"

"The same."

"Did Ponti go through this – whatever – process?"

"Not that I know of. But, it doesn't mean he wasn't 'processed,' if you know what I mean."

"So, this all had something to do with the exhibit, didn't it? He was going to expose something that powerful forces did not want to be exposed. Piecing together many conversations, there was something about the true existence of the legendary god-man that lives in a state of perfect harmony, forever, and the means to attain this state. He was going to show the spirit of Jerusalem as it was spread over the entire globe, and herald the return of the fabled lost cities of the Gobi Desert in his own effort to stop this internecine warfare and bloodshed. He was going to show "Israel," not as a county, but as our reality. Do you know where he is?"

"I am not sure where he isn't right now."

"What could they have done with him?"

"As a spirit, we are everywhere, all the time. We only identify with the body because we are trained to do so. Once the mind transcends this identification, and literally sees itself beyond body, and even beyond mind, there is nowhere it cannot be at any time."

Now I was fascinated. Now I realized why I felt I was destined to be here. How I was going to explain this to Kathryn was another story. But, I pondered that if Daphne really understood this, then all my ruminations about consciousness might come into fruition. "How do you know this?"

"It has been part of my training since I was a small child."

"But, is it possible for this to have happened against his will?"

"That I do not know. You will have to find out for yourself."

"How is that possible?"

"In the realm of spirit, there is nothing impossible. In the realm of matter, everything seems impossible unless it has been done before. In between mystery and the knowing, is fear. There is also the real danger that once gone, you may not come back. The true hold on this life is so tenuous and illusory, that once more in the soul's natural surroundings, you may choose not to come back, or be so confused that you may be unable to come back."

"This sounds like alchemy on the grandest of scales. How does this happen?"

"It is both very easy in theory, and very difficult in practice. Now, let me ask you a question."

"Alright."

"What does love mean to you?" she asked as she gazed into my eyes. Feeling a little self-conscious, I put my head down as I thought. "You do not have to tell me, but I want you to go deeply into it. And be very honest with yourself. It could be a matter of life and death. There is only one reason I ask. If you go, it is the only thing that can help you. It is the only thing that can save you. Do you think dark thoughts? Do you dwell on things you would never reveal to another human being? Even if you never disclose them, they are still there. They are like demons eating away at you. Whether you think you are hiding them, or not, they are still there, affecting you, afflicting you and everything you say, think and do. This is why I ask. You cannot take this residue into the pure light of the sun and not expect to be unaffected. In other words, you will be trapped by your own thoughts."

I looked up, a bit incredulous; not really able to understand the real import of what she was telling me. As a person whose livelihood depends on thought, and the relationship between thoughts we willingly harbor and those we avoid, I found this to be really incredible and incongruous. How in the world – How in this world – was it possible to go through life without negative thoughts? Didn't all the saints and masters have them at one time or another? She could see me sinking into self-inquiry.

"You, more than others, know how small the arena is that we exist in; and you know that what we think is real is not even a speck in the totality of what is. All I am saying is that the totality of what and who you are must expand, and with that the darkness fades away. The darkness only comes in small spaces. What is left is love."

I said nothing.

"Does anyone know what true love is?" she asked ruefully. "I thought I did when I became involved with Mr. Carnahan, but that wasn't love. It was a very advantageous relationship for a while that really turned into a very long prison sentence. We all think we know what love is, but we all find out, sooner or later, that it has nothing to do with the romantic love of romance novels. It is something so much more. It has true, enduring substance. I only learned this after Mr. Carnahan's passing, when I reflected on who I was and how I fit in to this universe. Only after a long, and sometimes very painful, self-examination, did I actually start to love myself in a way that I never would have understood before. In fact, it is the stuff of life that I cannot even really begin to describe. You will need to find out what I am talking about. If you do or can continue on this little adventure, your life and your soul depend on it."

Startled, I asked "Daphne, why are you telling me all of this?"

"I drew a tarot spread for you this morning. I spread 9 cards on the table. All the cards lead up to, explain and support the card of resolution. The card of resolution for you was The Fool."

"Well, that doesn't sound very flattering."

"The Fool is generally depicted as stepping off of a cliff into thin air – and not falling. Do you know why? He doesn't know he should fall. He doesn't even know he can fall. He is walking with perfect trust, confidence and faith. Faith. Faith in the Source of All That Is, of which we are just part. But, as I learned only too recently, it is not the faith spoken of in so many religious circles. Faith is something different. The only way I can describe it is to paint a picture for you in your mind. Let's say that you are some eternal being, not the limited person with trials, tribulations and troubles. In this totality what room is there for anything to limit, distress, or trouble you? It is that you are so huge and vast that these seeming troubles do not even register. They become as pointless as a single piece of dust on the ground that you walk over and do not even acknowledge. It is as though they do not even exist. All beings on the Wheel of Life start from and eventually return to this simple state of perfection. With it all things are possible."

"Why did you ask me about love then?"

"Because, as I think you will come to find out, this life – this reality we think is so real – is nothing more than a movie of sorts. The Source of All That Is creates the creation and then experiences it through us. A handy system, don't you think?"

"This sounds very esoteric to me; almost cultish."

"Well, think of it as you will. But there are so many theories on living a successful, prosperous, abundant life. There is as much lust in metaphysics and religion as there is in lustful sex. Wanting.

Wanting. Always wanting. But, what is really going on behind the scenes? Magic! Magic on levels that we cannot even dream of," she said as she began to gesticulate with her hands. "Reality so high that reality becomes undifferentiated, so to speak." She said this in a dream-like way that almost reminded me of Duke.

"How do you know this? Have you ever experienced this?"

"Yes – to an extent; enough to know that there is so much more here than we can see and feel. I have tried. Heaven knows, I have tried. Every method known under the sun, and then some. I just live on that faith I told you about, based on those who have gone before me and have related their experiences." This seemed to put her in an almost mournful, depressed state – as if she knew that time was running out and the one thing that propelled her – the experience of a lifetime, or lifetimes, had not been hers.

"Love is what propels him. Love is the only thing he knows, and in this state, he sees only perfection everywhere, in everything."

"Who are you talking about?"

"The Creator... and the Fool"

"How do you know this?" Even though I was becoming more enraptured in the topic, it was still more fantasy and hypothesis. Did she really know what she was talking about, or was it just more mumbo jumbo?

"I know this," she said resolutely, "because there have been quiet moments, from time to time, where my mind just drifted, with no destination in mind – until I awoke, as if from a state. I may have been 'here' so to speak, but I was very, very far away. The way I went there, I do not know. What I experienced, for brief, fleeting moments, I will never forget. The feeling was of such intense love that I felt every cell in my being vibrating in a way that the person Daphne could never have experienced. But then, it was over so quickly, as if that was all I could take. And I knew that I had reached a state where the essence of all that is was radiating without interference. This is how I know" she said with the almost mystic look of a saint.

When I thought back to my experience with the Buddha Flowers this morning, I knew I had been given this experience so that I could understand hers. The experience also legitimated everything else she was saying to me. I did not know how I experienced what I did this morning, but I knew that it was real – or as real as anything could be here. I wasn't quite sure what to make of this being a movie, and all. It only added credence to the standard that this light show of reality is just a play of light and shadows, that there is no differentiation between anything, and that we – and all of us – are one. Yes, in these brief moments of reverie, it all made sense and was very believable.

For several minutes there was just silence. But then, what did this have to do with Ponti?

As if wanting to get a firm hold on what I had to do, I asked "But, how is this possible; loving everyone, all the time? In this world?! It seems absolutely impossible. Most aspects of counseling are dedicated to helping people function in an unsafe and unpredictable world. If this concept of unconditional love is the connection with the divine, no wonder the experience is so far removed from so many."

"That's why I asked you the question. You will have to find the answer. And, as we are told, this answer will set you free; free from the heartaches, the jealousies, the hatred, the fear. Freedom. That is what it is really, and only, about."

"But you're not free," I said. From what you've told me – pardon me if I'm blunt – you're telling me your life has passed you by and it's too late for a new start."

"I'm far from perfect, I know, and I do not mean to use myself as the only example. Regardless of how my life has prospered or not, there are still certain things which come with age and experience, and this is one of them."

"From a practical perspective, how do I, how does anybody, love everyone and everything all the time? Most people spend their entire lives reacting to what happens to them, and then talking and ruminating about it endlessly. Hence, my clientele."

"That is the challenge reflected by all the other cards in the tarot deck" she said. They all ask and answer the same question: humans cry out in despair and misery about how alone and abandoned they feel; how frightened they are; how much they want to come home. The answer is – and this is also an answer which comes with age, and sometimes near the transition – you know in your heart of hearts that you never left. You are home. You need only turn around." We all spend our lives looking away, searching for the Holy Grail. Turn towards, and you will find yourself literally holding what you seek.

It is another irony I have learned.

"Home" struck a chord. How like Uncle Duke where the point of everything is to get back to the home you never left. "But, it sounds like the prodigal son."

"One and the same. Remember, there is no longer the need for a murder investigation for John Witheral. This cannot happen in an imperfect world."

"So, in a state of perfection, there is only love."

"Yes."

"Let me look at your hands" she said. I turned my hands, palm up, for inspection. She did not say anything, but kept nodding. Finally, she looked at me and said, "You know more than you think."

"What do you mean?"

"Just remember what I said about love.

Kathryn was out doing errands. I sat at the kitchen table just letting my mind wander. In a day-dreamy moment, I happened to look at my left palm and studied the lines as a palmist would look at it. I do not know palmistry but am interested in the science. In tracing the lines, I noticed that a triangle was formed in the middle of my palm. I looked at my right palm, and noticed the same. If I put them together, I thought, I would either have a Star of David, or possibly the Infinity Triangle, formed by the points touching each other.

I traced the outline. I then got up and found a safety pin and sterilized it. I lightly put pin pricks around the outline of the lines, thus accentuating the triangles. I then traced over the outlines with a felt-tipped pen in the color of a beautiful blue – almost in the color of cerulean blue – a kind of replica of the Chilzon blue the ancient Hebrews made from a shell fish, and used in holy garments. It was made from a fish which is believed to be extinct. Not knowing what I was doing or why, I placed my hands together. At first nothing happened, but I stayed with it, hoping that patience would produce a result.

After a time my head bobbed. I must have fallen asleep for a moment, with no recollection that I was even tired. For a split second I had the scratchy feeling of something under my feet. It felt like hot sand.

I decided to take a bath. I wanted to soak and relax. The water was steaming hot. Very soothing. I did not doze, but relaxed to a very deep state. My thoughts subsided to the point where I simply looked at the water. No particular reason. No particular interest. But, a very satisfying focus. The focus then led to a reverie. Reverie to silence. Silence to a moment where I was awake, but not really awake. I shook my head to fully wake up as I realized I was still in the water.

Then I was trying to remember what I had been thinking about, because apparently it was very interesting. All I remember is that I was very happy, and felt very free. That broad sense of spaciousness which accepts everything without labels of good or bad, right or wrong, and feeling a great sense of peace and love.

How is that possible I thought. How can one be that advanced, that aloof, that strong, to have transcended judgment and criticism? How can one surpass the tendency to get dragged into the negative emotions one feels around him, or are even being directed against him? Apparently I had experienced this state of being for a short moment. I didn't really remember it, but recalled that I was experiencing something like it. For a moment, I was traveling elsewhere, and my whole being was there.

I wanted to see Daphne again. I needed her herbal concoction to relax.

XXIV

There was something I was missing. I was trying to find someone who I didn't know was really lost. I was also trying to learn about the demise of someone who was no longer dead. I was trying to pinpoint the methods of time transportation which appeared to use methodology from another time to transport from the here and now to the here and now of some other time somewhere else. No wonder people like to put on blinders and go about their daily business. There is too much going on. Specialists tell us that while we only use 10% of our true brain capacity, that we also filter out more than 90% of what is actually coming into our attention. Kabbalists also tell us that we are always surrounded by discarnate spirits. They also say that if we actually saw who or what was surrounding us, we would literally go mad. This is another example that ignorance is bliss!

In Kabbalah, the Jewish system of mysticism, it is said that the world was created when the Creator contracted the Light. Who but the Creator could have contracted the primordial Light? This allowed form to exist where before there was only undifferentiated oneness. The goal of the esoteric practice is to reverse the system of light contraction as much as possible. However, from ancient times comes the admonition that delving in these areas must be done carefully and with expert and saintly guidance. This leads to a startling question: What is, Who is and Where is? If now is now here, but there are other heres where nows are, where is the real now? And, why me? Why am I involved in this metaphysical mystery and conundrum?

Frankly, it just made me mentally jumbled. I dropped it all and went to bed. I started thinking about something really funny and started laughing. It calmed me and I dozed off.

The events of the day will sometimes appear in the dreams at night. The nice thing about a dream is that everything manifests immediately – and the incongruous appears as natural as breathing. We are led to believe that in the waking state things take time to accomplish, if they are accomplished at all. Not so in the sleep state where with each passing thought there is a spontaneous manifestation and connection, even if they make no sense. In dreams, one learns to be very careful of what one is thinking, because the immediate manifestation of thought carries a significant responsibility. There is also an awesome sense of release, and freedom from the normal restraints of the waking world. It is also said that the membrane between the waking and sleeping states can be very thin, if any at all.

I am in good health, but in my dream I am feeling that I am going into a death transition. It is just a knowing. I am lying here, relaxed with my eyes closed. I am waiting to be lifted out of my body. But, nothing happens. I am becoming impatient. The impatience leads to agitation then to anger and unrest and real frustration. My heart is pounding. Can't I even die properly! I let it pound. Louder and louder. Then I start to listen a little more closely. I never realized before what a rhythmic sound the beating heart makes. What a comforting feeling. What a sense of well-being.

Gradually, a feeling comes over me. I have never experienced it to this degree.

The vigilance has slipped away. Then, I feel this deep sense of love. It is the only way to describe it. I am outside of myself and looking at me and beyond me. The furnishings where I am staying are not very appealing; yet, they are majestic. I see the faces of some people who are so difficult to deal with that even the mention of their names causes severe anxiety. I see them trying to attack me with words; saying things to hurt me; yet, I feel such deep love for them. I am seeing them, but not them. I am seeing something in them of which they are completely unaware. Otherwise, they would not be acting the way they are. I see all the machinations I go through every day in order to feel safe, to feel loved, and see how pointless they are. On a screen I see the movie of my life. How much effort has gone into that which could have been done with merely a thought? How much worrying has been expended on that which has never been written and would never come into being? How perfect and graceful is my life? What a blessing I am to myself and everyone around me. How soothing it is to receive forgiveness for those I have hurt. How full and complete I feel. Everyone looks alike, even with their differences of appearance.

Yet, I know that even this is incomplete. The feeling of completion is but a stair step for something more. Even though I always acknowledge the goal of freedom, I am viewing it from arm's length. I have responsibilities and obligations. I want a comfortable life. I want and want and want, and in this wanting, I have become a veritable prisoner of my own desires.

I feel this tension, as if I am standing on a precipice over a deep chasm, with no safety net. I do what I have never done before. I let go. And in this falling I feel a grace and liberation which cannot be translated into words. I now understand the meaning and sanctity behind the tarot card known as The Fool. In a world of set designs which insist on allegiance and bondage, The Fool offers the sword to cut through the Gordian knot.

I know that I am falling, but feel the thrill of descent. I do not know enough to be frightened. I am in love. My body does not kick as it falls.

Then the falling stops. I am in a beautiful environment; brilliant light making all images that I see radiant in brilliant reflection. I come upon a tall, thin cylindrical structure. Even before coming close, I could feel its magnitude and majesty. It is pure white; a marble-like substance. There are some geometric designs on the outside. They seem faintly familiar, and an inner voice tells me I will read these later.

A vertical section of the cylinder, from the top to three feet from the bottom has been cored out and removed so that an occupant can sit inside. There is a man seated inside. He is dressed in a finely woven white wrap; toga-like. It is loose-fitting and flowing. I stare at his face. He is very handsome with almost a feminine beauty to him. He is fair-skinned, with a well-trimmed dark beard. He is deep in thought. He turns in my direction.

"Hello Ponti" I said. "Hello Michael," he returned.

The single column became double and I sit down. The toga I am wearing feels more comfortable than anything I have ever worn in this life. It is smooth and silky, but not made from fabric. I look at it closely, and see that it is made from very fine threads of light interwoven in intrinsic detail. And I know something else.

I am not sleeping.

I am feeling light and agile. I look at my palms and each have Stars of David emblazoned in gold and radiating. The symbol of heaven and earth, culminating at the heart. A large star radiates from my heart. I am no longer bound by natural laws. I can fly, travel to universes or feel the still point of G-dliness vibrating in my Being.

The scarab at the exhibit was a precursor. The points almost touching eventually had to lead to something. And what they led to was ... nothing, which is the essence of everything. Staring at the space in between the points led to a feeling of wholeness, completeness, and transcendence. A conjunction and transcendence, all at the same time. Only then could the forces be truly understood as not being forces at all; but representations of reality in a realm in which they were transcended. And in this, anything was possible.

Could this now be used for healing on a grand scale? I am going back through my life, with the light in hand, and feel the burdens lifting away. I touch those who have affected me, and those whom I have affected, and all bear the mark of the living light. We each look each other in our gleaming eyes, no longer aware of what was once a barrier between us.

But, with thought comes feeling – deep feeling on a cellular level. And what of history; the holocausts which occurred and are occurring to this day. What of the mass suffering and the mass dementia which perpetuates it? How can the meeting in a pure place alleviate the cellular trauma embedded in both the victim's and the perpetrator's psyche, and hence, in existence for perpetuity? Would the mere reversal of roles – if such were ordained – alleviate the distress meted out on a global scale? No, of course not. This would only perpetuate the situation.

By and large, people have been looking for strange gods. Generations of aberrations have mutated into an acceptable mix of poisoned normalcy. They all seemed to be crowding around me. Their existence is only justified if I acknowledge them. How like people they are. Even toxic illusions long for acceptance and approval.

What is it about me that even attracts them? I wonder. Then I feel this throbbing in my solar plexus area. Some need or want, unfulfilled, and thereby a clarion calls to the untempered byproducts of the ages. I become still, silent. My mind becomes quieter and still. I let the feeling flood over me, and it is gone. The thought forms vaporize with the feelings. I feel like I am becoming more of myself.

Ponti and I began to communicate silently. This was more natural than speaking, for words betray the moment and the message. Likewise, it is only when the feelings leave me that I feel liberated. Humans have permitted themselves to become living repositories of thoughts and feelings, as if they were meant to be libraries, remembering for all time, the happening of events and reactions. It is this that has made existence on earth a prison cell, no matter the economic station or other benefits of title or privilege. And so, as if a file were being erased from top to bottom, memories fade, feelings leave and the fresh, clean air of presence bathes me in its welcome. I do not know where I am or what is going on. For the first time in my life, I feel like I am truly home.

I know there is the choice: to exit reality, body and all and fade into the bliss of this that I have been allowed to enter. But, I can also go back from where I came. I know this, although it is already becoming more and more vague.

Like a tape unreeling, I am going farther and farther into a light which is shining with more density and brightness than is humanly possible to endure. I am nourished by it, no longer being just a human. This light is my family, my origin, my homecoming. It would speak of love if it had a voice. It would represent freedom, if it were at all symbolic. It is neither. It is what it is, and promises or pretends nothing more, nor less. It seems to say that I can follow suit, by just letting go, more and more and more. I offer no resistance.

I know there is a choice to be made. Who am I to make it? What power is left in this mind?

I feel joy in being. There is no regard to having or seeking, for I am everything and have everything. Yet, as if an internal monitor was repeating in a monotone refrain, I must choose. But, I no longer understand, why or what.

There is free will, in a sense, in this realm. Free will within certain boundaries; certain choices. Not ultimate choices. We are what we are, in this regard.

What do I know about love? What have I ever known of love? In those quiet, solitary moments, with my soul bared and my heart pounding – this was not love; but supplication. In my encounters, where did the purity go when desire eclipsed all else? So, what do I know about love? Only that which I have glimpsed from afar, with even less certainty and understanding than in this vibrant light. But, if this light would speak of love, and this light is of me, perhaps I am being too hard on myself and understand more than I think. Perhaps what is unknown is merely waiting to be discovered or uncovered. This is easy enough to do. We are told, "Be still and wait." And so, my movement leads to a rich pause where I feel bathed in the amniotic fluid of the living universe. And I wait. All is Silence. In Silence is more than I ever imagined. More than I could ever explain, even if new words or colors were invented just to describe it.

The waiting becomes excruciating. Waiting. Waiting for what? So now I see how tricky and sly the mind is. From where did this thought come, and to whom is it directed? Now I see. And I just let it go. And wait.

But, now, I feel exuberance, exhilaration.

There is no need to explore the mysteries of the world's wonders. There is the experience of a mystery that is far greater than any adventure which could ever be imagined. But this too, is a product of the mind as I think about it. And, I just let it go.

We are taught to always look outside of ourselves for answers. We are often treated, and treat ourselves for that matter, as unwashed, ignorant and undeserving. From the earliest age, we are taught that only a wiser and more learned person can help us; can save us. Even in religion, the font of spirituality in society, it is always coming from the outside – from the book to the inside, to do something. All the great Masters who have walked this Earth, and, I believe, walk it still, have taught us otherwise. The wisdom lies within, all else is, at best, an expression. Often, it is unnecessary or surplus.

As the armor plates of emotional protection fade away, this sense of deep appreciation, satisfaction and joy fills me. I feel nothing but an intense tingling. Joy personified.

How many times have I said "No" out of wisdom? How often have I acted at all out of wisdom? How is it even possible to act out of wisdom when so much is disagreeable? How bountiful in beauty is the world we accept?

Choice. If, after all else, we are love visualized as light, then what choice is there? How much misery is caused by resisting this basic, primal, inherent nature? Ultimately, what choice is there?

What elaborate mental and emotional programs we have constructed to avoid the ultimate, or to make it impossible to reach it even with wanting? Thousands of lifetimes may be necessary to undo the tangled web we have woven. Oh, and what distress we accept as commonplace. The voyage to the heart of the inside is also marked with electric signs throbbing with the warning of the Fear of Death if we come too close.

Why are there no images here? I am alone. Where is the cylinder? Where is Ponti? Perhaps there is no one else. Perhaps I am inventing all of this, including myself. To whom is this thought? Who Am I?

I could feel a heart-swell in wonder as light in different forms began parading. Then, an enormous bridge of light of varied colors – a rainbow bridge – appears. This would be my causeway to wherever the intention directed.

XXV

Professor Ezra Suberstein at the University was professor emeritus in the anthropology department. It was rumored that he fiddled with a Ouija board, and considered metaphysics as real as any other acknowledged reality. I wish I had located him sooner. His major opus was a treatise entitled "The Treatment of Minorities in Civilization." It was an enormous tome looking at the treatment of captured peoples and subdued cultures over the course of time.

His office was located in the older section of the administration building, built in the 1920s and hardly refurbished since that time. Books covered every conceivable area of the office except where necessary to sit. His seating area was actually carved out of the space left from several tall piles of books. Two bright blue eyes, a bald pinkish head, and a shock of white hair surrounding the sides, greeted me as I walked into the office. An ordinary wooden desk and chair were pushed against the wall. Bookcases set in the wall started about three feet above the desk. The room was overflowing with books, magazines, and plenty of dust. He added to the appearance of antiquity in the office.

"Good afternoon, Mr. Cushner," he said politely. He remained seated at his desk, smiled, and gave me a short bow with his head. He motioned for me to use a tall pile of magazines as a chair which I did.

"So you have some questions about ancient symbology. I am not sure I can answer them. Perhaps I can give you an answer, but you would have to believe it without independent verification. The extent of our recorded history has yielded little else than the most irrelevant aspects of ancient history. So much of the visceral, and so little of the exquisite buoyancy which actually fueled these civilizations. The buildings, the art, all important; but only a subtext. It is the ancient mind, the ancient consciousness that is nowhere recorded. It was forbidden to record the true oral traditions. With the passing of those who truly knew the traditions, went any real hope of understanding, or replicating their spiritual exercises. These exercises were dedicated to their understanding of the divine impetus in this world. Modern man considers the spirit a mere caprice, if he considers it at all. If something has no direct, tangible benefit, and does not equate to the acquisition of wealth, it is considered pointless at best."

There are some people who tell you things and you believe them without further thought. Intuitively I felt that he was one such person. His life in pursuit of knowledge and wisdom had yielded many results, including a reputation for speaking the terse and unbridled truth, albeit with both metaphysical and intellectual overtones.

"You know Mr. Cushner," he said with a crisp, trained European accent, "I am not an American by birth. I was born in what became known as Palestine after the demise of the Ottoman Empire. To this day, I look at the Turks and marvel at their powers of administration, gained through thousands of years and several empires. But, one thing of which I am certain, is that what they did was the result of knowledge acquired, not traits endemic to them."

He paused for a moment, searching for the right words. "While you and I may share the same heritage, in general, your personal history is marked by the celebration of Thanksgiving and the governmental recognition of laissez faire. My history is marked by the footsteps of Noah, Abraham and Jesus the Christ. It is also steeped in the spiritual basis behind Hebrew. While Sanskrit may be the spiritual language of the East, Hebrew is the spiritual language of the West. Hebrew is the basis for all exoteric or esoteric religious traditions in the West. Naturally, there are different perspectives in a newer culture which was born in the so-called "Age of Enlightenment;" albeit man-made enlightenment. I do believe, however, that the Middle Eastern cultures, and particularly the one from the land of my birth, were formed and nourished by extra-human sources; sources which helped to shape and mold the human psyche at a very early date. Not the space people, the Extraterrestrials I believe they are called. All life comes from the same source. Why bother with another form? No I am talking about higher spiritual sources; sources, without which there would be no humanity today; just animals in human form – living to eat and satisfy their passionate desires; sources which go up the chain – so to speak – to the creator source. I believe there were many who spoke directly to the Creator-Source with the same ease as we are conversing today."

This was so far beyond my experience, but from my recent transits, I was able to believe this. I could hear him put into words what I had suspected or fantasized about for a very long time. Maybe, just maybe, he could provide the key.

"But, just as there are degrees now, there were then as well. We know that many of the Middle Eastern cultures were able to communicate with spirit forms which have inhabited the earth plane since time immemorial. Do not ask me how I know this, but just accept it – at least for the moment. While they were disassociated from the earth plane, some were far removed from the likes of Metatron, reputedly second only to the source of all. These spirits could be vain and fickle; sometimes useful. Having no physical form, they would attempt to live vicariously through the humans with whom they were connected. They are, of course, still among us today, but go unacknowledged during this period of scientific inquiry and emphasis. In other words, their existence is based on our recognition."

"From what you have told me about Mr. Mellenstreet and the Carnahan ceremony, apparently there is some attempt to contact them again, although, perhaps, unwittingly. While they might think they are doing otherwise, just remember this. While different forms are imbued with certain characteristics, intelligence and power, they are just another creation. In other words, Mr. Cushner, do not waste your time on preliminary contacts; always go to the Source. No doubt, the Carnahan revelers thought they were doing just that. They were wrong."

I sat there, not knowing what to say. I think the professor took it as a sign that I either wanted to argue with him, or didn't know what to say. Since he has probably played out the same scene on many occasions, he proceeded to speak, unabated.

"Please," he continued, "I do not mean to belittle you or your culture. That is not my intent at all. It is all really very simple. You have seen my book, perhaps?" referring to "The Treatment of Minorities." I wrote it as a detailed and studious tome. It can all be summed up in a word: Greed! Greed is the basis for human history. Those in power want something from those out of power. They will take it by any means available. It is nothing new and has been played out from time immemorial. Unfortunately it played out in cultures seemingly much more spiritual than our own – but it happened all the same."

"Listen to what I have to say from a different perspective, an older mind, an older soul. You cannot listen to what I have to say with modern ears. It just will not work. It may strike a note of fancy and curiosity - but you will miss the whole flavor."

I knew he was warmed up and primed. Now, I did not dare interrupt him.

"Think in terms of a society where there was no division between worship of the creative power and every aspect of daily life. Spirituality filled and sustained everything. By and large, people simply saw themselves as living in a dream; and not their dream, but the Creator living through them in the Creator's dream. While the role of priests as intermediaries is a primary focus today, the fact is that these truly administrative roles started much later, long after the advent of the society, and led to the representation of the pantheon of gods representing different aspects of the divine." And then he caught my attention. "In many of these cultures, the triangle was a symbol of the presence of the Divine."

"What is a symbol?" he asked rhetorically. Technically, it is nothing. If a triangle were to hit you in the head, it would hurt only because it was a foreign object striking you. There is otherwise no inherent power in it. A symbol is nothing more than the idea which is associated with it."

I took a sketch of the meteorite scarab out of my briefcase and asked him what he thought about it. For a moment he seemed stunned, almost to the point where he was not breathing, like he remembered something that had been forgotten long ago. The blood seemed to fade from his cheeks. Then he became very absorbed. Then, as if something very touching had struck him, he looked up with a twinkle in his eyes and a slight smile on his face. "I think I understand," he said.

"What does it mean?" I asked impatiently.

"I interpret it by the effect it has on me. As I look at it, it seems to speak to me. It speaks of stillness, one-pointed concentration, yet expansiveness. This is what it is saying to me: 'Be still and know.' In other words, it is an invitation. It asks you to come deep within the forest of what you think you know, beyond the fear of what you do not know, and to knowingly dwell with the Divine. This is what is says to me. To me, this is the entire message behind the Torah, the Five Books of Moses. G-d not only asks, but instructs us to quiet the mind, and through the quiet to be absorbed in the whole vastness"

"How can you be sure?"

"As I said before, I cannot. I can only tell you the effect it has on me."

After a pause, he continued. "The Jewish system of mysticism, the Kabbalah, is replete with methods, details, mental and spiritual labyrinths and esoteric associations. Lifetimes can be spent in fathoming its mysteries. But, let me suggest something to you: there really is no mystery. It is all very simple. I can make the entire system clear to you in one example. Clench your fist. Make it tight. Even tighter. How do you feel? Tense. Irritable. Jumpy. Nervous. You are constrained, edgy and as such, are naturally protective because you feel exposed. Fearful. Out of control. This is as if to say, I am tense and feel weak, nervous and afraid. Afraid of what? The unknown, for you can see from your surroundings that you are not in jeopardy; certainly not from me," he said with a little laugh. "But, the unknown is sending you into torrents of speculations. You are saying this, 'I am afraid that if I am attacked right now, I cannot defend myself, and I will not survive.' "Am I right?" He took my silence for recognition. Now, let your fist relax, just a little. A little more breath is coming into your being. Now, a little more. You are breathing deeper in the chest. The beginnings of a smile are coming onto your face. Now, let go completely. Feel your breath go deep down into your abdomen. Acknowledge the sense of safety and satisfaction you feel. You feel at one with the world, and as such, one with G-d. Energy is circuiting within you without opposition. All is well. The Kabbalah is nothing more, nor less, than simply feeling one with G-d. This allows you to go about your business in a frame of mind where G-dly things are attracted to you; life is joyful and you willingly and joyfully embrace life. Now keep this frame of reference in mind when we talk about your amulet. Whenever discussing ancient works, it is more important to recognize what is not there, than to analyze what is.

I knew I was not going to get in a word "edge-wise" so-to-speak, so decided not even to try.

"Now, think about this," he continued. "Two triangles, one atop the other, not really touching. A slight space in between. Figurative. The lower triangle: Perhaps a representation of the base line between the knees, with the apex above the genitals into the lower abdominal area. The upper, with the base line between the shoulders, leading to a point in the upper abdominal area. The space in between: the navel or umbilicus. The entry into this world from somewhere else. Creation. Also, a figurative form of the letter "I." Indeed, the letter "I" is not particular to English only. This form has been in use for millennia. The form could be looked at as a stylized "I." "I" being the self, that which is of and with the Creator always. Devotees of the eastern arts talk of this as being self-realized."

After a long pause, he hesitated, almost spoke, and hesitated again. The slight smile came over his face again. He cleared his throat, as if to speak clearly of something very important. A smile of connection and acknowledgment. He nodded his head briefly and said, "There is something else. The form suggests a third triangle in the middle of the other two. There are never just two. The third is silent or hidden, if you will. The third contains the motive force, the intelligence and the germination plan for the other two, in the same way a seed of a tree contains the blueprint for the entire tree. This motive force cannot be seen, but is felt in every aspect of the form. Without it, there would be no tree, no form, no anything."

"So, you mean, the third triangle is ..." and I hesitated, not being able to say it.

"Yes. The third triangle is G-d!"

"How does one use the two triangles to get to the third?"

"That question, my young friend, has been asked more times than 'what is the meaning of life?' If I knew, the better part of my life would not have been spent in trying to prove theories, but in experiencing oneness with the Divine."

XXVI

Heathrow Airport in London had changed little since I saw it ten years ago.

I took a bus to Victoria Station and caught the Blue Line to Earl's Court. Earl's Court Road still had the same conglomeration of small shops, with some new glitter from the discos. The same tobacconist near the tube station, the same proliferation of Italian and Pakistani restaurants and delis. The unmistakable character of a lower middle class neighborhood on the verge of being discovered by the renovation trendies.

London was where I had my first encounter with a new land; a different way of life – almost an airiness that unleashed my imagination and my life.

London was my conduit, my channel into a new world. It was that unknown which helped me locate a finer sense of self. I saw its cobalt blue sky along the Victoria Embankment. I reached into its misty night sky, and for the first time – away from my certain way of life – I felt the unadulterated touch of my soul.

The River Thames launched Sir Francis Drake, Blackbeard and Nelson. It was home to the Tower of London and to mist which sparked the likes of Oscar Wilde and Jack the Ripper – those who could capture the splendor of every moment, and those who could take it, with equal precision.

Until you are a foreigner in a new land, you cannot expect to know home. Until you are in a new land, you will not even know what you are looking for – you may not even know that you are looking. As Uncle Duke used to say, the only way to get to where you want to be is to go through a way where you are not. It is only then that the soul is unchained, having lost its familiarity of place and time.

Michael Danton's secretary insisted that Mr. Danton was booked for the entire month. After that he was going on holiday for another month. I explained who I was, why I was calling, and what I needed to know. Mr. Carnahan had been a long-time client. When I advised him that I was investigating some artifacts that had been purchased by Mr. Carnahan, which Mr. Danton had brokered through several of his clients, I was given an appointment for 10 a.m. the next morning. In all of this, I would have thought it odd that Mr. Danton was a celebrated psychic and occultist, but then, again, this was England. But, this too, fitted the stereotypical juxtaposition where the outward bearing of "stiff upper lip" often creates a psychological suppression of emotions which exudes in odd and surprising ways. Why shouldn't a psychic be involved in marketing priceless archeological artifacts?

Arriving early, I spent 15 minutes under the scrutinizing glare of his appointment secretary. I presented my identification and letter of introduction signed by Daphne, as "curator of the Carnahan Estate and agent to the Executor of the Carnahan probate." It was official enough to work. Daphne and I had discussed fabricating a letter of introduction by Mr. Mellenstreet, but we knew that he had been to England on several occasions in order to establish valuations for many of the artifacts in the Estate. Mr. Mellenstreet and Mr. Danton had certainly met on several occasions. It was best not to test the association.

At precisely 10 a.m., the double doors to Mr. Danton's chambers opened. A middle-aged gentlemanly person, finely dressed in a silver-blue herringbone jacket and trim-fitting wool slacks looked at me, smiled and ushered me in.

I sat in a leather chair with good back support; he behind a rosewood desk. I noticed there was a back door along the wall behind him. He pushed the record button on his cassette recorder. His fingers then came together at the fingertips, forming a triangle, and partially concealing his face from the nose to the chin. He placed himself in an aura of concentration, but performed it in such a stiff and ritualistic manner, as to be the result of practice rather than sincerity. That done, he said clearly and crisply, "How may I help you Mr. Cushner?"

Hoping to avoid an obtuse beginning, I said, "The Carnahan Estate has become linked to some bizarre happenings as a result of certain artifacts which it acquired long ago. I've come to see what information I can find which will help insulate the estate if the story becomes bigger."

"Are you working together with Mr. Mellenstreet?" he asked plainly.

"Mr. Mellenstreet has ... shall we say ... other things that are capturing his interest. I was sent instead. It was decided not to telephone, telegraph, or even mail anything to you about the situation. The Walls Have Ears, so-to-speak."

"Yes, indeed. I do believe that Mr. Mellenstreet is very ... "occupied" as we shall say."

"I understand, at one time, that you may have some association with the Estate artifacts, and whatever you do know can assist me. Perhaps, because you are a celebrated psychic," I said with a slight comic smirk, "you wouldn't mind telling me what I need to know without me having to ask."

As many before him have said, he said with a kind of arrogant agitation, "You Americans always have to come to the point so quickly. I have expressed my condolences to the estate. I really had nothing to do with artifacts other than to introduce Mr. Carnahan to individuals who were experienced in the world of antiquities. I do not have anything else to say," he stated with an air of exasperation that was intended to be noticeable.

"Do you believe in time travel?" I asked, matter-of-factly.

"I neither believe nor disbelieve in it" he said with a little bit of exasperation. "I consider time irrelevant. It is just a medium to experience events. Reading time is simply adjusting to probabilities based on a current state of affairs, much like a mathematician coming to a conclusion after a long and ponderous equation. The value you place on it has nothing to do with me. I am merely a reader. Apparently, there are enough satisfied clients who bespeak the accuracy of what I have read."

I knew this was a time to be expedient; at least to keep the conversation going. "I know you have been to the Carnahan estate on several occasions," I said politely. He bobbed his head up and down. "Presumably you have seen many of the treasures he possessed. I am showing you a photograph of one in particular." I brought out a photograph of the Double Triangle scarab. For a moment I could tell that his eyes lit up, but then he kept his head down until he regained his composure.

"Regardless of what you may think of the psychic sciences, Mr. Cushner, and regardless of what you may think of me, I am a spiritual counselor. My business and purpose is to attempt to mend the many breaks in a person's emotional and spiritual stability by reading into what they are projecting. They either cannot see it, or seeing it, cannot deal with it. Aside from this, I do believe in the weightier concepts like spirit transmigration and the like, but have nothing to do with them in my daily practice. This is simply my business. I do keep away from séances and the like. I must, of course, deal with the future on a routine basis – this is what my clients pay me for – to get a glimpse of where they will be in a month, a year, or longer. My accuracy is not subject to doubt."

I was going to say something, but this would have simply proven his statements about Americans and being direct. Intuitively I felt just to be quiet and see what he said next.

He continued, "I would strongly suggest, however, that a person would need a great deal more training and appreciation of the true nature of what he was doing, than to learn about spirit or physical teleportation one day and practice it the next. There could be something very simple and very direct that you are missing" he said pointedly, hoping to end the conversation.

"That may be. You have no doubt heard the reports from your contacts. These people simply seemed to appear out of thin air, as the saying goes. They had the triangular marks on their palms and forehead. The meteorite scarab was at the exhibition. It came from the Carnahan Estate."

"I must confess, Mr. Cushner, that I am not fully versed in either these current events or those ancient practices and cannot engage in a scholarly or experiential discussion about them. What went on, or did not go on in your city or at the Carnahan compound is simply beyond my ken. There is really nothing else I can tell you."

He looked at me, slowly got up and walked over to an oak wall unit. He lifted the top from his tobacco humidor, and began inserting pinches of his custom blend into his well-browned sneering-faced meerschaum pipe. Next came the pipe tool ceremony. A push here. A jab there. A cut of a nasty little shred which refused to cooperate. Then the lighting of the pipe.

A look of deep satisfaction spread across his face as the first plumes of smoke billowed to the ceiling and mushroomed in spirited swirls throughout the room. He looked up in admiration, as if to say, "Another job well done, old boy!"

- Michael Kushner

I thanked him for his time and left. I knew he would probably make some calls and I did not want to overstay my welcome - if there was any left. Since Daphne was now tangentially involved, I tried to keep it as light as possible. She could always claim that someone who was involved with the Carnahan estate had linked her name without authority and forged her name. There were many who wanted more information and would stop at nothing to get it.

I left feeling totally alone and helpless; caught between millenniums - being buffeted by a series of inexplicable events and circumstances, like a piece of paper in the midst of a terrific windstorm. True spirituality on the one hand; practical magic on the other. I thought of Philosopher Varro who said that "not all who own a harp are harpists." What was going on in plain sight that I was missing? I wondered if I had the quality and the stamina to keep up with the events in which I had irreversibly enmeshed myself.

I hailed a taxi and took it to Great Russell Street. I alighted at the front entrance of the British Museum - tribute to Great Britain's colonial past.

The Greek government has been attempting, fruitlessly, to retrieve the Elgin Marbles, the sculptures of the Parthenon - the casts which have taken their place were a national disgrace; and, the Greeks also wanted the remains of the temple of Artemis at Ephesus - the temple of "Diana of the Ephesians" of the Acts of the Apostles - one of the Seven Wonders of the Ancient World. Egypt would like to cart away the Rosetta stone, since it is the key to its past. One can only assume that had Britain successfully integrated China into the Empire, the Great Wall would now be surrounding Hyde Park.

I presented my letter of introduction to Robert Marsham, the Director. At one time, many of the Carnahan artifacts had passed through the British Museum for cataloguing and explanation. My tenuous connection to the Carnahan estate at least bought me an entrance. But, that was all. I was promptly and civilly told that anything to do with any unexhibited artifacts similar to the Double Triangle, "if any there would be" would be scrupulously safeguarded. The untimely disclosure of any unique discovery could cause more harm than good. In other words, "I should have known better than to ask." My argument that the fact that any such articles might be the key to unlock the investigation of the millennium, or of all time – literally, was of no avail – unless it mattered only to him, privately. By his tone, it was evident that when those in charge are dealing with the gold, marble and lapis lazuli splendors of dead peoples and civilizations past, the plight of the living is secondary; in fact, it was an absolute nuisance. After making his point, Mr. Marsham promptly guided me to his door, but seeing that he was being summoned to his intercom, with a flick of the fingers on his right hand, he motioned that I was free to show myself out.

I figured that I had at least a few more minutes before Mr. Marsham discovered that I had not left the administrative offices. So, at the receptionist's desk, which contained the nameplate for Sophia Clairebon, I asked for Arthur Shindley in the Department of Oriental Antiquities. His name had also come up several times in relation to the Carnahan artifacts.

I found him to be very agreeable; almost lackeyish. Light brown curly hair, cut too short to suit the curls which made them even more uncooperative. A person of details, going off on tangents at a moment's notice. I told him that I was interested in anything he could tell me about the Carnahan expeditions in the Middle East, and Carnahan's acquisition of priceless antiques. He seemed to have no problem in conversing with me on the topics. I think he presumed my presence in the sequestered area was a license to release whatever information he had.

"A spectrograph examination was done on the amulet. I remember it well. A unique piece in many regards. The examination revealed something not visible to the naked eye. There was writing, of a sort. Hieroglyphs of a type not readily translatable."

"Sidney Azur came up with a completely unbelievable – if not unverifiable – translation; one which I feel is preposterous and without foundation. By comparing some of the forms to the relatively well-known tablets from other Middle Eastern and Asian cultures, he was able to present a quasi-plausible theory to the staff. The center point of his theory was that the amulet was not used in any funeral rite, but was intended for use during life, and this is where it gets very ethereal – enabling the user to transport himself to higher, so called "astral planes." You see, what the amulet was all about, – and please forgive me this – was "transmigration." He said this very slowly and phonetically, as if it would take this emphasis to really sink in. "Upon completion of whatever had to be done, the soul returned to the body. Physical transmigration; actual time travel! Utterly fantastic and unbelievable really, but very tantalizing. In a more practical vein, it gives the modern archeologist the supposed ability to go back in time to actually experience the time period in which he is interested. How would you like to enter the Gardens at Babylon or the Court of Solomon? If time is endless and simultaneous, as the theory goes, we should be able to do this now, for events happening there are also happening in the now; just not here or there. In any event, just talking about his theory makes me feel winded."

"Is Mr. Azur available?" I asked.

"He will be in Jerusalem and Cairo for the next month. Pity!"

"Why there?"

"This is something really spectacular, and not meant to be revealed in any way or manner. The spectrograph imaging revealed very slight pinpricks beneath the letters. At first it seemed like normal distress marks from being in a wilderness site for so long. On magnification it began to look as if there were a clear pattern to the marks. On further magnification it became apparent that the marks were not distress marks at all, but infinitesimally small pin pricks. When followed, the indentations revealed the four letters which are the basis for all spirituality in the Western world. The letters were clearly Hebrew script; the Yud/ Heh/ Vav/ Heh of the Hebrew alphabet; the YHVH Tetragrammaton; the letters symbolizing the unspeakable name of G-d. The King James translation is Jehovah. Mr. Azur needed to speak with the specialists in Israel, and follow it up with further research in the land from which the Exodus occurred. Then, as if this were not enough, in the very center, and completely invisible without the aid of a very powerful microscope was the letter Aleph (א), the first letter of the Hebrew alphabet. The other letters then appeared to be dancing around it."

I pretended to be surprised, amazed and flabbergasted. This was the reaction he expected. I needed to open this door, and to do it quickly. I then asked, with a very serious expression, but also somewhat jokingly so as not to alarm him, "What about the method? Was there enough there for someone to inject himself into another course of history?" "Do you have any reports I could see?"

Before he answered, Mr. Marsham walked by and abruptly stopped at the door. He announced rather stiffly that I was out of place at best and was unwanted otherwise. Mr. Shindley was shocked and stultified by the encounter. I felt badly about that, not wanting to have caused him any discord. For the second time, Mr. Marsham promptly escorted me to the corridor leading from the administrative offices to the museum. He motioned to the receptionist as if to say that I should not have re-entry. He bade me a happy tour of the museum. I find it fascinating that some people think they are fonts of such power, that lives can be directed by mere gestures.

After I entered the museum area, I found a "teley" as quickly as I could and called Kathryn to tell her what was going on in London. When we finished the conversation I turned towards the door, and realized I had left it slightly ajar — a small breach allowing my supposed confidential conversation to softly filter out into the common area. Arthur Shindley quickly walked by, pressed a paper into the crack and walked off without a glance. I quickly unfolded the paper. It contained a short article about Mr. Azur being in Jerusalem at a function hosted by the Jerusalem Museum. I now had a place and could get the number. The General Information desk had a world-wide directory of major museums. I tried calling, but unfortunately, all of my calls to Mr. Azur went unanswered.

I took the tube to Charing Cross and took an airy stroll along the Victoria Embankment. I then flagged a taxi and had him drive me around Trafalgar Square and then into Soho. Three days later I left the land of mist; this land inhabited by the descendants of the Druids and the reputed beneficiaries of Joseph of Arimathaeus.

Arimathaeus. Why did the name sound familiar? But, not the whole name, just a part. Ari? Why did Ari seem familiar to me? "Ari" means lion in Hebrew. Was there a lion of G-d that I would meet? But, no, not Ari. There was something else I just could not put my finger on.

XXVII

The morning after I returned from London, I learned that both Jacob Lake and Timothy Bonticlaire had been indicted for bribery, conspiracy, and extortion relating to the convention project. The Haverfield boy had "materialized" in the vicinity of the convention project. Although not a direct connection, this focused a lot of citizen attention on government corruption, cronyism, and unlawful patronage. This led to a critical demand for an answer to the mysterious appearances, as well as a call to clean up government.

People's medieval fears began to run amuck. Every minuscule detail of the appearances was reported and became an instant lead. The witch hunt was on. Burn the flesh to save the soul. Excise the evil spirit no matter what the price. Expiate to the unknown in a sea of burning cinders to light the path for the spirit of G-d.

Mr. Mellenstreet's involvement was leaked. This may have been intentional to take the heat off the police. It may also have been the product of reports from other participants in the initiation ceremony. Apparently many were appalled about the ritual event or wanted to shield themselves from being accomplices, and either went to the authorities or told others who did. Mr. Mellenstreet was nowhere to be found. Since he was one of the primary objects of the investigation, he was considered to be at large. Both he and the Trustees of the Carnahan Estate were under Grand Jury indictment. Search warrants had been issued for the Carnahan estate. My concerns were for Daphne and my hopes for her welfare. All the press needed was a story about a small town formerly named Winthorp, and now called Pink's Cane! The link between John Winthorp and the town was also disclosed and added fuel to the fire.

Unfortunately, poor Mrs. Mellenstreet couldn't get a moment of privacy. Every move she made was watched telescopically, and critically analyzed. She couldn't even leave her home for a brief respite. If she did it would have been assumed that she would be having a rendezvous with the husband. She could get neither rest nor privacy to be sure.

I think that I understood her better now when she said that she tried to get closer to her husband. Something prevented the connection. Either he wasn't born with the proper receptors to receive the message of intimacy, or they were clouded over by the veils of living in his narrow focus of this material world. Obviously, he subconsciously yearned for the power he now possessed. In this state of mind, his wife was merely a person who needed or wanted him. This made it easy for her to become dispensable in his eyes.

Unfortunately my practice has revealed that there are too many Mellenstreets in the world, whether they are my clients or just others involved in my clients' lives. In fact, forgive the reference, but they are as common as dirt. There are some who believe they are fated to be the beneficiaries of heaven's grace on earth – and that everyone must recognize this fact, whether they like it or not. In their intense self-absorption, they are in intense pain and hence, transmit nothing but pain. In their artifice, manipulation, and control they have sucked the joy out of life and turned this world into one solitary prison cell, in which they are perpetually in solitary confinement. They just do not know it, and will fight the realization with every breath of life in their beings.

Perhaps some have more scruples than others, but eventually their desire and self-interest clouds and blinds their vision, not just to a straight and narrow path – but a singular straight and narrow path leading to a singular object, and only to the object – the power of self-aggrandizement, and a heavy dash of money for good measure. I have never found a class of people who are more fearful of death. This, then, is symbolic of the entire world drunk on its own ego mash.

The "appearances" ceased. In a week or two, interest would subside and fade away. A testament to a human's ability to forget. Yet, this ability is essential to basic survival. There was still coverage about Ponti Moon, but growing more sparse. And what about him? Did I really see him, speak to him, or was it a mirage? Stella was calling. What could I tell her?

I thought, *what if there is another ceremony?*

I knew he was here, but not really here. I knew there was only one way to find him.

I realized the adage that the only way to find someone or

something is to go through the way of unknowing, where there are no guides, no maps, and no guarantees. This adventure always had the earmarkings of the astral, mystic, and the fantastic. Such is the stuff of personal explorations for which no explanation is possible. If one survives, there is a knowing that is only understood in the self, and which can never be translated into words. If one does not survive, then one could still grow quite rapidly into that knowing which all of the great mystics have called the impersonal self; that which is neither bound by nor guided by the ego. In either case, the soul would be in its element. Maybe, just maybe, I would be in mine.

I reflected again on Uncle Duke saying that I could never lose my home. I knew that this would test the accuracy of this statement to its limits. I also reflected on him telling me to always know where I was going and that I could never get lost. Right now, I still didn't know where I was going or how I was going to get there. I didn't have a clue. And, if I did get there, how would I get back? Sometimes you can ask the same question over so many times that the answer just does not matter anymore.

In my innocence, or ignorance, I had the courage to go into this unknowing. Now, all I needed was the process. And quickly.

All I knew was that Mellenstreet was creating a cardinal sin: going back in time to use a past life to somehow aid his 20th Century persona, thereby creating a split – a schizophrenia, if you will – in his consciousness. Perhaps, however, he was the true voyager and I was merely hungering over pipe dreams and engaging in flights of fancy. Had I not gone back to a former time? Had I not breathed the present air of the past and felt its dust upon my feet? Had I not tasted the life of its time? Would I too like to thrust my soul back into this early day – turn life into the true carnival – carnelevarium – bidding farewell to the flesh. I had no doubt my name would soon be linked to the Moon and the Mellenstreet investigations. Soon I would be known as a shrink who doubled as a celestial P.I. What advertising! Petey, the corner newspaperman, would eat it up.

XXVIII

Fall is in the midst of its grand display. The maples are resplendent this time of year. Their leaves vibrate in stunning colors, bejeweled in nature's psychedelics. A wonderful, hopeful time of the year. Walks with heavy sweaters; dried leaves cascading in a soft wind of romance that beckon you to search for warmth. It is a dangerous season. It is a vulnerable time. This is the time of powerful conjunctions; of planets, seasons and people. But, the tremendous poignancy and inner awareness bred by this season is both uplifting and depressing. Soon the vibrancy will give way to the predestined celestial turning and inevitably descend into the next season. Like the final burst of the sun's rays prior to the onset of night, fall is the final grace before the introspective stillness of winter. If winter is anything, it is deafening silence!

This evening I decided to take a stroll through the Harbor Station Park – one would say, careless, to say the least. I did not tell Kathryn. No lights, no homes – I was a moving target. But, at this time, for some reason, I felt safe and protected. Everything seemed to fit into its place very neatly. For some reason, I felt no need for worry or concern. Encased, I lost the movement and the motion of the city. No more crowds and eclipsing buildings. Now there were trees giving shelter. I felt in-between, so-to-speak; like the space in between words; a silent conduit.

It was dark; very dark. A night chill radiated. No stars to guide. No moon to light the way. Only the senses to guide me, inch by inch, until I finally arrived at an exit. Still, I was not afraid and did not even think of turning around.

It is here that I can feel the cool breeze drifting from the lake, and say farewell to the works and days of man, and the machinations of mankind; the gorging pylons of civilization digging deep into the primordial past and impaling it – hiding it in neon lights, gasoline engines, and various economic fictions to which we pay homage. No sense of progression; just continuity from generation to generation.

It is here that the dome of night soothes the gaping wounds and the haunted eyesight. When the night establishes its interlude, its space in the day, this is the time to surrender, to meander and stray from what we know to what we seek; and, this must be done through the darkness of what we do not know. Away from the daylight illusions – Away... .

I have heard contrary reports of those who have crossed over to the other side, and have come back here. Some have spoken of bright lights and peace. Others have spoken of resolution, but after going through a transitional zone; a zone where all feelings were magnified because the blanket provided by this age was gone. During one of our conversations, Daphne warned of astral travel. She said a minor pain could seem the equivalent of a heart attack. She also said that the logical mind does not work in the middle zone, and that one has to rely totally on feelings. The common theme is that once there, all are given the choice as to whether they want to come back to this realm. This conundrum was becoming all too familiar – as I have slightly experienced already. As Daphne again warned, the possibilities of physical death were very high.

I safely left the park and went home.

I was alone this evening. Tired, very tired. I lay down to take a short nap before making a late dinner. I closed my eyes and began breathing slowly, rhythmically and deeply. I did not want to fall asleep since I knew I would wake up by midnight and be up for the rest of the night. I resisted sleep, but did not want to rise either. Slowly, I reached an equilibrium where I was neither totally awake, nor asleep. I was very relaxed and breathing deeply. I felt my cares drifting away as if the magnet which attracted them was shut off. Then there was total stillness. A Surrender. Then there was... .

Fantasy thoughts of an imaginary city began to filter through my mind. But, there is more of a presence about it, as if I am really there. Sort of. Maybe. Maybe more so.

What was a thought is now a feeling. A softness in the air. Welcoming. Puzzled. Like the riddle of being a man dreaming he is a butterfly, or, perhaps that he is a butterfly dreaming that he is a man.

I have never seen this place before. High up in the mountains, but very warm. The sun is out and there is a feeling of peace in the air. A large, well-populated city. I am in the heart of a mercantile area. Above and to my right, I see a magnificent temple complex built in the shape of a huge dome. Like a fine, highly polished stone, but not dense like marble. Radiant. Giving off colors like a rainbow, but having some form within the arc. In the aperture and gateway towards the upper reaches of the arc, I see people standing alone or with others, each being still until a vibratory sound announces the time to move. While the marketplace has the feel of any other meeting place teeming with people, the rainbow arc temple has the feel of being removed; in this time, but not this place. In its airiness, is a sense of fullness and wholeness.

Someone approaches me. "Welcome" he says to me with great love in his eyes. He speaks to me, but not in words. We look at each other. Our eyes meet for but an instant. I know I know him, but cannot remember from where. Then I begin receiving thoughts in words not my own, as he is describing what I am seeing. Because of the way it is related, I will always remember each and every word as if they are etched in my memory, forever. Here is what he said.

"My friend. I know you have come a long distance. It was actually just a glance away. All who come here are broken in some way, or think they are. All who leave here are whole again. The path that led you here shall also be your path home. This way is not generally available in your arena."

He smiled deeply and continued. "In your arena, much emphasis is placed on being honest with oneself and with others. But, honesty at one level is not honesty on the next. Because you feel something in your world, you deem that it is true on all levels. This is not always true. Most of the feelings, beliefs and limitations you experience in your arena have no bearing on these higher levels. In other words, they simply do not exist. They are not universal standards that cross all boundaries. This is the first step in understanding your divinity. These events only have significance in the small, condensed world of your life. As you breathe into expansiveness, they fade into oblivion. Take your place among the visitors and be washed in the Great Light. And, as you do, know that it was but a small step and an even smaller turn which brought you here."

And in this great washing, I thought, what of atonement? No one in this realm has led a perfect, unblemished life. What then, of all the small and great acts and omissions which mark our life? To which, my Mentor answered, "that is between you and the Creator, as in fact, is everything, always."

"Take this with you when you leave. Knowledge for the sake of knowledge is a fool's errand. Experience for the sake of experience quickens the grip that limits you. Only be of the Light and go forth on every errand in which it sends you. This is the true Noble Quest, for it is written in Light, and sanctified from its Source."

I am standing, fully, complete, in the lightness and brightness of the comforting light. For just a mere moment I think how lovely it would be if I were at the top level of the Arc. Before I even completed the thought, so it is. I am at the top of the Arc by the mere thought of it.

As I stand in the light of the Arc, I am watching the other pilgrims as they each turn their palms up as if to catch the light. Then they push their palms forward, as if to project it. There are very definite light forms of triangles on their palms. As their eyes roll up and their heads beam towards the heavens, a definite triangle appears on their foreheads. They stand in perfect repose, confident, still and beaming. Vessels for heavenly light radiating through them. Each person, a temple dedicated to wholeness, and hence, to travel; wholeness being the ultimate stillness in the feeling of the great breadth. And in this light, this sanctuary is the feeling of absolute beneficent love.

Perhaps this was the sign and the standard spoken of in Deuteronomy: "You shall love the Lord your G-d with all your heart, with all your soul, and with all your might. And these words which I command you today shall be upon your heart. You shall teach them thoroughly to your children, and you shall speak of them when you sit in your house and when you walk on the road, when you lie down and when you rise. You shall bind them for a sign upon your hand, and they shall be a reminder between your eyes. And you shall write them upon the doorposts of your house and upon your gates."

Like a mirage in the Arc light, I began seeing an image of another temple taking shape below in the marketplace. It would begin to take shape and then disappear, as if it were real for a sense of time, and then become nothing again, as if it had no existence other than what I acknowledged. I heard the words of the Light Master speak to me.

"Like the image of time, we, too, have other portals of entry if we so choose. Those at the gateway of the Arc have chosen to bypass other structures. Others in the marketplace have not.

The structure came back as if to affirm its existence. As any entity that has been given life, no matter the source, it struggles to maintain its existence. In the structure of time, travel can be to different times, dimensions and realities, or nowhere at all.

In the marketplace my attention is drawn to a radiating structure which I understand supports this science of time travel. It is an enormous man-made complex with heavy gold plates attached to the roof. Like direct desert sun, the sun beams off the plates like laser beams from the heavens. It has seven levels, each smaller than the previous one, gradually ascending into the wide hemisphere of sky, perpetually cloudless, perpetually rainless – yet carrying the guarantee of life in azure blue. Each level is separated by a series of three ramps. The ramps are all on the southern side of the building. One is in the center, and one is at each end. The inner sanctum of the priests is at the uppermost level. Seventy steps to each level, if you choose to walk.

In the Arc, there is only wholeness, comfort and sanctity. In the realm of time, duality comes into play. Being out of time in the Arc, I can see something is out of place in the marketplace. Violence erupts. Pots are flying and daggers are unsheathed. Soldiers let loose upon the crowd and indiscriminately begin butting anyone unlucky enough to be within reach. When control is not attained, they begin jabbing with spears. I am looking down and see a person who appears to look like Mellenstreet, but dressed in the flowing white robes of a High Priest.

I stay in the Arc of Light and watch Mellenstreet. Cascading white garments blown by a frenzied wind, with a purple headdress. Even in this place of perfect light and wholeness, I can see total pandemonium is erupting below me. He is acting out the drama of time in time.

Mellenstreet is apparently having some heated words with the Captain of the Guards – or so the soldier appears by his distinctive headdress. Fingers are pointed and tempers are flaring. The Captain, without warning, suddenly grabs his short sword from its scabbard and runs Mellenstreet through at the abdomen. Bug-eyed and stunned, Mellenstreet buckles at the knees and falls backwards. He leaves the world with the same bug-eyed, stunned look on his face.

High in the Arc, a vibration is removing me from the other visitors. As the vibrational pitch heightens, I understand it is my time to exit, to come forth into the world again. But, even having been through this glorious healing mode, I do not want to leave this place of perfect repose. What is in store? Another birth. Another sense of separation. Again. It is not my choice as I leave the Arc, this time with clear remembrance as I come back into the world. For I am better, and now I must go to the place I have longed for, but was afraid to seek, by asking the question I have been terrified to ask. And so, I see my life as still and mute – but not the stillness of completion; the stillness of uncertainty, and hence, static and frozen. Like a new born babe, cold and alone.

My first emotion. I am stunned. Then a thought, and with it, fear. Will the intense emotions I am feeling trap me here? I cannot speak. I could not speak even if I had wanted to or needed to. Speech has left me. I cannot even think of speaking. There is no speech. There is only an intense awareness – a subtle recognition of self which is somewhat distinct, but only as a part of a blended mass. A subtle sense of being.

A strong wind surrounds me. It brings up thick clouds of dust. It eclipses my vision. Now, I can see nothing, touch nothing. There is no thing. Like a blind man in a dream.

The eyes that have meandered among the turn-style reflections from the glass of revolving doors, returns from the stare, and tries to fix on the moment of disguise and flight..., but, as the Bible says, these are the moments "from which the end will fly in those days which seek an end, yet, an end will not find them, that long to die, yet death flees from them... ."

In my ears, the collective voice of humankind reverberates. It asks why the flesh was given the power to feel; why the body was given the ability to emote. The voices of the incomplete, the unfinished, the unfulfilled. The piercing shriek of unrequited love, of unreciprocated tenderness, of affections gone awry.

I am no longer myself. I am not who I was or who I have ever been; stripped of identity, save the basic soul principles that have meaning only in the higher realms.

I am standing just outside the main entrance of the Temple of Travel. With both trepidation and relief, I enter it. As I walk to the center the structure grows very dark. I can no longer see any entrance or exit. "Where am I?" I wonder. Then, a realization that I am in some sort of a conduit, but I cannot see any physical boundaries. Now, also, a realization that I have a choice. If I wish to bid farewell to the flesh, I have the power to do so. Should I wish to exit to another time and place, this too, I may do. Or, I can return from whence I came. "Choose!" I hear in my mind, as if a foreign thought was being transmitted by a loudspeaker. No one and nothing can help me decide. It is now my decision. The responsibility for my self and my spirit lies in my own hands, as it always has and always will. A moment approaches. I can feel it. Then, a wise voice speaks to me. It tells me, "Bid farewell to thought at this time. It is a wall, not a way."

And now, the vision of two equilateral triangles. The bases are on top and bottom and the tips are pointing towards each other with a slight space in-between. But the forms are not stationary. They are pulsing as if with energy. They begin to glow as if afire, brilliantly intense. I have to turn away since the quality of light is nearly unbearable. Then, as I look again, the forms begin to move, first point to point, and then point into the other form. When they are complete, the Star of David, the Seal of Solomon pulsates in front of me. On all sides, up and down, inter-dimensionally, I am in its center.

The form becomes multi-dimensional. Then, as if by invitation, a channel, a doorway appears in the center. It is up to me now, whether to accept the invitation. Now, I understand that the middle way is not a middle in the sense of harmony. It is a portal. It is middle in the sense of back and forth, up and down, right and wrong. It is the place of constant choice. The admonition "choose wisely" has a persistent, pervasive presence.

As if seeing a vision in a vision, I see myself running. I am lean. Very lean. Skin pulled tight against the bone. Without clothes except for a loin cloth and ox-skin sandals. It is the desert. There is no water. There are no trees. There is no shelter. There is no disguise. There is only sand and heat. The Sun emerges in fiery glory.

I am running. Running from? Running to? Motion. Step after step. The only sound I hear is that of sandy soil crunching beneath my feet. There is no thought. In the desert, there is no room for thought. There is no need for thought. In the desert there are no barriers. There is only the way.

I feel the stretch of muscles; the inhaling and exhaling of hot air. My lungs feel a slight sense of burning. I breathe deep.

The sun rises higher. It is the sun of the desert. An enormous glowing dome that rises like a celestial battleship on the horizon, that fills the horizon and becomes an incandescent fireball. Heat without barrier, without shelter.

The sweat begins to pour down my forehead. I have been running for a long time. Maybe forever. Why? Running from? Running to? Now, exhausted. Alone. Merely an element in the elemental barrenness of the desert. I fall into the desiccated soil. Moisture from my body drips into the ground. It will arouse a memory in the dead soil, but be too little to have any effect.

The salt stings my body. I am losing the last moisture in the world. In the desert I am a river. There is no life to accept it. A blast furnace breeze attacks me. I am beginning to be covered by the swirling sand.

I get up and start to move. Breathing becomes more difficult. It is no longer the ways and means of life. It is a burden.

I must take short breaths because of the heat of the air and the filaments. Cannot suck in the searing air.

Growing weary. Very, very weary. Pains in my thighs. Souls of my feet are burning. Burning. My dry skin cracks.

"Breathe!" I command myself. Breathing is no longer an automatic process.

The distance silently settles behind me. The expanse ahead of me does not lessen. Each breath is a life of its own. My pace is no longer steady. It falters. It is erratic as is my breathing. Pain encases me. Heat distills me.

Soon there is no sweat. There is nothing left to sweat.

My dried skin becomes like parchment. It is blank and my life seems to evaporate.

There is only heat.

It is midday. The Sun is directly overhead. I lie in a deep trench, my knees pulled up tightly against my chest. The earth is mummified and I am its food.

Panting. Dehydrated. My tongue swollen. My eyes bulging. The run is only in my mind now. Where was it before?

And then, as if by desire, I am given flight; but not away from myself; deeper, yet deeper still within myself. This then is the cause for removal.

I watch myself from above, as if released. There is only the run, in life, and in... .

I have great clarity and see a great moving pictorial of days and lives in which I participated. There is still a choice to be made.

A vision comes to me. I am standing. No, I am seeing. There is no one present. A barracks is in front of me. Its wood has been stricken of paint, if there ever was any. It has been completely dehydrated by the elements. The wood is sick. It is decaying and dying. There are no people. There are no odors. The wind whips through unencumbered. There is no one and nothing to resist it.

Around the perimeter are barbed wire posts with inverted tops facing inward. The wire was recently replaced or is ageless.

Everyone is gone. Dust rises on the slightest provocation. There is no vegetation to keep the soil in place. Whatever vegetation existed there was trampled or eaten long ago.

There are no birds and the sun is setting. The setting is undramatic in this place. More an act of inertia than of resolve.

The wind whips around me. I feel an instant of terror. Of fear. Not the fear of dying; but that of living; of existing in this place. This place....

I remember that I cannot get sick. To get sick is to die. Either death by sickness or by their hands. Sickness is death. Living is fear, but it is not death.

There are no people here. There are no memories here. There is only fear and handfuls of ash.

There is something that needs to be said. I refuse to listen. The door to the barracks is open. It does not invite. It does not coerce. Like the door to a dungeon, it is inevitable if you have put yourself in position.

That is enough. I refuse to enter. I only wish to recall. I only wish to awaken. Why can I not wake up?! But, there is no instant awakening. And now, I can only recall... .

An American in a prisoner of war camp; mingled with the enslaved masses of Europe and Asia. The shaven heads, the thin cloth, the tattered ruins of nations and races.

Skin pulled tight against the bone; pulled tight not by exercise and health, but by starvation. And not systematic starvation, but brutal, forced labor with not so much as a maggot for nutrition. The maggots are long since departed.

I look and now see one laying in a doorpost, unable to move, a sardonic grin exposed by the receding skin of a face, populated by bulging and empty eye sockets.

There is only life; there is only... .

Now is the time to choose. You are ready to choose. Choose!

"No matter what the odds, must make it" I think to myself. "Even if the bullet penetrates the heart, must still make it. Let nothing stop me. Nothing can stop me. Nothing. Nothing. Nothing! No... .

The third Ludendorff offensive is in full bloom and Paris is threatened. It is left to the newly arrived members of the American Expeditionary Force to break the stalemate that is devastating the House of Europe. Already, it is reported, that an entire generation of young men has been lost. I am older than most and signed up against the wishes of my aging parents and my beautiful wife.

At first we were merely assigned to hold the line, but we are too brash and impatient for mere "babysitting" duty. We came here to clear the way for democracy and a better world. On a more visceral note, however, many of my compatriots have really come just for a taste of glory, and the possibility of a really good fight. The tension is building and we just want to get the show on the road.

We first met the enemy in a heavily wooded area northwest of a place called Chateau-Thierry, called the Belleau Wood. Once this had been the hunting preserve of the Chateau of Belleau, located close by. Now, it is a sniper's paradise and a machine gunner's heaven. The woods, once routinely cleared of underbrush and thinned of trees, has been neglected for four years. It appears to be thick inside, like perpetual night.

We are nervous. This is our first test. We Leathernecks have been hungering for this show, officers and men alike. We have come to show the world what we Americans are capable of. We have come to prove that the United States of America has a special mission among the nations of the world.

Our courage is inspired by the death and destruction around us. France has become a nation of refugees, in their own country. Old men, women and children clutter the roads oblivious to the fact that we were coming in to save them from the Boche. Only when we yell "Vive la France" do we seem to infuse new life into these helpless and homeless fugitives.

We all have a lot of discomfort and anxiety. We know where the Germans are and we know that they know exactly where we are. We know they also know, that in terms of trench warfare protocol, it is our turn to attack.

At 3:45 a.m. on June 18, 1918, we are for it and go over the top. It is a moonless night. At once the world of peaceful crickets chirping turns into the Fourth of July. Machine gun fire rakes the area sending us for cover. Multi-colored flares loom overhead. Daylight in the middle of the night. Still we crawl on until we reach one pocket of machine guns. They have not expected our company. We kill anything that appears to be dressed in grey.

We are only at the fringes of the forest and receive orders to regroup and hold the line. We are not given orders to charge it. This is a stalemate like all the other stalemates in this cursed war. We now know only too full well, why is it is called a cursed war by soldiers on both sides, and the hapless civilians caught in the way. Although we rebuffed several counterattacks, and continued our advance as best we could, we only have a few yards of real estate to show for it. So much bloodshed, for what?! It has been a long and exhausting day of fighting and waiting. We are all hungry and dirty. We have had our first skirmishes, and feel good about our success. We are soon to realize, however, that what we have been through is but a mere trifle compared to what is to come.

Again, we are ordered to advance. As we make our assault en masse deeper into the forest the German response is furious. Rat-ta-

tat-tat of machine guns comes from every direction in millisecond bursts of hot metal. German artillery trained on our position gives us a taste of the apocalypse our European brethren have tasted for four long years.

In the deep, dark forest, we lay with any meager protection we can find, waiting for the withering volleys of machine guns to subside. Our only hope now is to wait for nightfall and regroup. Heaven only knows how many more counterattacks there will be before then. The dead and the dying are like litter in this pocket of Hell.

Private Smothers lies close to me. He has the unmistakable growl of a man with a belly wound. We both knew what is to be. The only thing I can do is hold his hand and talk to him. He worries for his pretty wife in Idaho and the farm. We talk, it seems, about the most trivial things, because at this moment they form the backdrop for a world that has become absurd and we are basking in its madness.

It is one thing to be speaking in heroic political or historical terms about the role of America in the new world. It was quite another to be in the midst of a dark, menacing forest on a hot, muggy night, threatened by snipers, machine gunners, and these damn bugs.

We have to lie low, really low, and can only talk in whispers. Any major movement brings a terrific response in gunpowder and metal. In short, Harry Smothers is slowly dying, we have no medical care to give him, and we are otherwise cut off from the rest of the company.

Our first assault into the forest has not given us the success we had hoped for and bragged about. But then, what did we expect? Perhaps we, too, believed the newspaper reports too seriously which indicated that the Hun would merely see the sight of us and "high tail" it back to Berlin.

We learned too quickly that war was not made of Waterloos and Trafalgars, but of millions of these long, lonely nights where nothing seems to happen but the passing of life – even if one survives.

Then the machine gun bullets start passing over us again. Harry no longer makes any sound. I take a letter from his inside breast pocket. It contains a picture of his wife and family. I am determined to write to them.

It seems like the bullets are passing over us by only a few inches. The ping of snipers is getting closer. It is a time to make a run for it, no matter what. It's time to get the hell out of here.

A more protected thicket lays a few hundred yards ahead. For some strange reason it seems familiar; almost inviting. Like I have been here before. It seems the safer alternative to head for the forest, find my compatriots if I can, and regroup.

Mortar shells begin to pop into the air and squeal in their descent. They land with dull thuds and explode with tremendous concussions.

It was almost like one instant later, I, a living, breathing human being, am no longer, and I, – well, I, who was him, or used to be, am hovering over him, oh so airily. I am like a bird, so free, circling myself. The exuberance of being an elevated and liberated soul, released from bondage. One moment here. One moment, here, in a different, more expansive and fulfilling way.

Form reformed by the machinations of mankind. A human form in the likeness of some great being metamorphosed.

There is some choice I have to make. I am enjoying the drift and want to continue drifting for eternity. But, whose dream is this anyway? I am reminded that it is not my dream. I am only a participant in the dream of the Master Dreamer.

Poland and Ukraine have exploded with the news that a savior is among us. He claims not to be, but we treat him like so anyway. Our lives were threadbare and downtrodden, but he has given us our redemption. And, he gave it to us using what we already had. He has shown us how to be happy just by being alive, and how to go about our sometimes pitiful lives, surrounded by hate, with joy and grace. He is known as the Baal Shem Tov, the Knower of G-d's Good Name. He has shown the descendants of Abraham, Isaac and Jacob, in literal bondage in Eastern Europe, how to be joyful and go about our tasks with thanks to the Divine. G-d Bless Him!

The Chateau is very pleasant this time of the year. The workers are busy with the first harvest and everyone has many tasks to accomplish. The bounty this year will finally ensure a profit.

Satisfied, I take a brief respite before a diamond-shaped glass window. The second story apartment overlooks the fields to the west.

The pompous Prince of Picardie gives another ball this evening. Tiresome, but necessary in this "social circle" into which I was born. Boring to be truthful. My wife has been readying herself for it all day. My daughter as well. My son works in the wheat fields to gain a firsthand knowledge of what it takes to operate this manor. One day this shall all pass to him, quite deservedly. My Jean-Paul Alexandre is everything that I could have desired in a son. Strong, yet gentle; proud, yet humble. At 21 he is now the talk of many women of his generation. And not a virgin among them, to be sure! This generation takes so much for granted.

My wife is a head-strong Jewess who likes to get her own way, ... and usually does; courteously and diplomatically, of course. Truthfully, I am deeply in love with her and find great amusement with many of her antics – unless, of course, she attempts to strike up a conversation about politics. I absolutely forbid such talk from a woman and a wife, especially amongst our closest friends. Everything gets back to Louis, and his whims are capricious, to say the least. Her father was a merchant who sold silk and velvet to the court. I met her there at one of my rare court attendances. I have not much use for courtiers and the lesser lackeys.

My hair has turned fashionably grey and is tied back with a simple velvet ribbon. I have tried to adopt the empirical standard of Occam's razor in my life, and believe that the simplest things have the most truth; although, I must confess, I have always had a liking for silk.

The ball is exciting, if not predictable in the guest list. What new affair is happening this week? Oh, Lord, how shall I survive these tiresome idiots?

Now we are dancing, my lovely Stephanie and me. How I love to dance with the love of my life. Turning, turning, turning; looking into each other's eyes. Turning... .

At the bus depot there is a circle where ends and beginnings of each bus route occur as a regularity. There is a choice I have to make. Then a drifting sensation, again.

I am young. My body is lithe and strong. Sparta threatens again. It is war. It has always been war. When has there not been war with

Sparta? When have they not tried to exterminate us, and we them?

My breastplate and shin guards are firmly in place. I carry a short sword and a shield with a double holder. Tonight I am on guard.

In the morning we will do battle. The camp fires signal each encampment. There will be no surprise. Tomorrow, we shall either live or die.

I think of Tamara; her long dark hair and wide brown eyes etched in my mind. I wonder whether I will ever see her again. My heart yearns for her now as it has since the first time I saw her in the marketplace.

We would spend much time alone by the water.

I survived. Soon a peaceful coexistence is established between Sparta and Athens. I knew what I had to do. I still remember his face. In the ferocity of hand-to-hand combat, it all happened so quickly. Most of all, I remember his eyes.

I found his house; he, the Spartan I met in battle.

I presented myself next at the door of his parent's home and tapped twice on the door. A comely woman answered. She asked who I was and I could not answer. Speech had left me. I wanted to flee, but was immobile. Then she knew.

I have a choice to make.

It is all flowing so quickly now: the Kingdoms of David and Solomon, the exodus from Egypt, the snows of Tibet, the forests of India, the early cultures of North America before and after Lemuria and Atlantis. Like light radiating on the cascading motion of polished mirrors, first this image, then the next, and the next ... and awareness can only follow that light...

A free-floating stillness. No enclosures. Wistful wafting among the elements of the universe. No form. No substance. Travel everywhere at every moment. There is no distance. There are no barriers. The world is less than a thought. And in the thought is the ability to listen. G-d's first and only commandment is that we listen. It is G-d's dream that we are living, not ours.

It is often said that we feel separated from G-d, and that our lives and motivations are based on being reunited. It is often expressed as seeking G-d's love and feeling our inseparable connection with something more than mortal lives, times and conditions. The mirage of losing ourselves can sometimes be resolved by the equivalent mirage of seeing ourselves in others, using our relationships with others as backdrops for reconnecting with the eternal in ourselves, and therefore learning to see the perfection in all and everything.

There is a choice to be made. A compulsion. Choose!

The Sun purges. The Sun refines. In the desert, there is no confusion. In the desert there are no barriers. In the desert there is no thought; there is only being. The rest is immaterial.
"O Lord, thou purgest me."
"In the end, there is only... ."

I am sitting as a young child before a man I do not know. I do not even know myself. He looks at me and says, "My young friend, be kind to yourself. That is blessing enough for the world. Some stories must be left alone to write themselves. Our lives must similarly be left alone. Too much control, manipulation and desire creates tension in the organism, and the life force is literally squeezed out.
And so, I just watch and am feeling great comfort in watching. The scene I am witnessing has literally vanished. It is as though I am watching a movie on a gigantic screen on all sides of me, above and below, and they are now instantaneously becoming clear. And in this clarity, I feel a deeper peace than I have known before. Such peace, that I know I will never want to leave it, though, I know that this, too, is also some kind of an interim state.
A kindly spirit is talking to me. I look up at him. He is shimmering. I have seen him before. I had a remembrance that he was sitting in a cylindrical object. I see again, but now it is more akin to a light beam, and so is he.
He speaks to me but not in words. I have no capability to speak any longer. My life is only that of which I am conscious. When this fades, I shall be gone.
"There are three paths. They all lead to the same destination. There is neither winning to be gained nor losing to be feared. There is

only the path to be followed. You must choose one, but it is not your choice. You are only the vessel. Allow yourself to make the choice which has been made for you. This is how you choose wisely. It is your will to do so. You have unleashed yourself from material time. Being in limbo is not an acceptable option in this realm."

"I do not know what to choose. What path?"

And now, I again see an image of Ponti Moon, but he is no longer Ponti Moon. I am staring at the face, in partial recognition, only to realize that I am actually looking at someone who is much more familiar. I am looking at me! I just never recognized myself before. But, now, I am staring straight into my eyes, into the depth of eyes which I have never witnessed before. How beautiful they are! How much I love myself! How much I want to open the gates in my life and let the light shine, and by doing so, help others open their gates.

Then I heard these words: "The Lord's grace be with you. Remember, in the thought of G-d is the love of eternity, which is only another expression of love. There is a place of only praise. Choose it. The golden key is there for those who would use it. Take the Key! Life and Death have been offered you. Choose Life. That is the choice. And know this, my friend. For every moment of Death that you breed, Life will confront you. If you flee from it, it will not harbor you, it will assault you. It will encumber you until you accept it. Choose Life. For every moment of Life you extend, you are greeted by eternity with open arms. Hence, the sense of spaciousness, well-being and grace."

At one point I realize that I have named myself, but I cannot remember the name. I know that naming was important because it does something, although I cannot remember what. I stop thinking about it, and just let it go.

Images of people greet me warmly. I recognize them, but cannot remember from where. An image appears and becomes ectoplasmic. We can see and feel each other. From a primal sense, I know there has been both joy and pain in our relationships. In our embracing, I feel something more than the human heart being enlivened. It is a dropping of the crusty layer of emotional scar tissue and the radiance of something deeper and more primal than even a soul, for it pre-existed even before any sense of division of the G-d substance. I can now remake any scene or event. G-d is letting me come home!

I feel so exhilarated. I know that just moments ago I was so tired, but that does not exist right now. I have worked ceaselessly to understand the environment of humanity. I have done nothing more than survive with enough comforts to make the efforts of survival worthwhile. But, my energy, my drive and my life force are on the wane. This is all because of trying. And so, as The Fool, I condense the energy of trying into a single golden pellet, place it in my right hand, and cast it gleefully into space.

Without restraint, I begin to feel; to feel deeply. Whereas, feeling itself was repressed in an effort to avoid pain, and as a consequence, block joy. In this instant, the joy and pain, and any attraction to them, are gone. I feel cleansed and washed to the essence of my being. Emotions wash into and through me like laser light rays coursing unimpeded through vestal space. I feel the flow of movement, but nothing else, because nothing is restrained.

I am meeting and embracing my deceased parents and all of my ancestors and descendants for eternity. I see our history as the history of one person lived over successive generations.

Now I am observing space, planets, and solar systems. I am transported to a planet and shown interlocking lines of vibrant blue light, the ley lines of the planet.

I see a battle re-enacted. The fighting is fierce yet bloodless. Ordinance passes unimpeded through the airy body forms of the combatants, until, realizing the futility of the struggle, they give up in humor and jest. As they walk off the field of battle as one, they became invisible.

I see the unmitigated efforts to propel hate, and the lackluster trajectory of the propulsion. I see heaviness surrounding the propulsion but, the material of hatred seems to be storable forever.

I am shown the artistic portraiture of panic and am placed in a room decorated with its effects. What a curious place, I think. It looks like a common room in a common house. Close. Claustrophobic. Unsettling. Designed to instill dread and anxiety.

Then, another shift as I go all the way through the panic room. My being feels lighter, more relaxed; breathing deeper. In the middle of this way, is a sense of deliciousness; a tingling of delight; a joyful explosion. My being feels as if it were a large smile and I was a messenger of good will throughout the heavens. I feel stars twinkling in what would have been my eyes. I feel like love in movement. Around me, what had been dark is illuminated. I am like the sun, bursting with internal heat and radiating brilliant beams.

Could it get any better than this? I think. And, as I think it, comes an explosion of a supernova. Galaxies are created. New life in the eternal creation drama.

A fierce wind pushing against me. Buffeted, not sure what to do. I cease resisting and embrace it. I became it, and it was no more.

The creation epic for the earth has played out. I see the interplay between the stationary and aggressive forces. As a filtering ether, I am allowed to go back as an intermediary. The scenes now played out in me. I, as love, could encapsulate all and everything in my aura. The space capsule of love is where miracles occur.

A free-fall floating possesses me. My eyes neither open nor closed; neither seeing nor blind; neither aware nor stunned; neither moving nor arrested. Neither living, nor dead.

Here in the passing – interval between silence and confusion; what we think and what we know – between the conversation and the derision; between the need and the want – the surrender, the meander – the passing of Silence.

As if in a movie theater, I see rapid fire images.

Stylized iron gates, and soft dim lights over gilded portraits of stilled men, peering from wooden frames.

The lovely sculpture of Lady Sennuy. Old Kingdom. Egypt. From the expeditions at Kerma, in the Sudan. Whose high polish at such an early date showered the modern world with her peculiar sense of charm.

Form captured in rigid stone. The passion of Saint Teresa, struck by Cupid's golden arrow – desiring this more than life itself.

Euphonious evoked life out of clay. What am I to say?

I shall become a clay maker and mold life.

Time to wait, for a moment, until someone is departed, as one awakens into a darkened room, and for a moment cannot identify that which is known to be. There. Now. Eyes closed. Stepping into a restricted area, pillared and well-kept, an ageless aristocratic scene. White brick in the night; washed white in the great tribulation. Phantom in its pervasiveness – Penetrating – Untouchable.

Turn from the inner stare, and to the moment; Turn... .

We have constructed crystal mansions, and have mused among the evening's phantoms – a moment between this and that; a coin tossed into the passing hat.

So many times we have witnessed this moment.

A loosely woven fabric that tears and bleeds, and swings in the wind, and bends at the knees... .

Over the sultry air of silent seas, we have met the perception, and have been poled out to the quays. We ascended the steps to the flat, to find our tattered image blown forth and back.

"A new heart of flesh will I give you if you choose it. A new spirit will I put within you... ."

"The choice is yours."

"So be it. May the light of the Source be with you and guide you on your chosen journey."

I never knew there was so much comfort in stillness.

XXIX

Sometimes what happens to people in early life is too hard, too painful, too awful to shake off or even deal with. Sometimes, simply the accumulation of common "growing up" events creates enough stress that there is an emotional departure from the soul. The events leave imprints. Our lives are the recasting of these forms sculpted long ago; fueled by anxiety to avoid some vague fear which remains undefined, and in its nebulousness, remains lethal. That which is lethal, is often said to be mortal. Some have said that imprints of past lives also leave indelible imprints that function as hereditary habits.

So, in this grasping and groping, we search for that which has not been altered. It is as it was and ever shall be. Simple in thought, but nearly impossible in experience. Ah, yes! Our old friend: Thought. Friend and Ally; foe and challenger; champion and victimizer.

I often wonder how thought ever came into being. Was it a byproduct of coming into this consciousness? So much has been written about it, so many systems have been created. The Garden of Eden is considered a parable about thought coming into existence in this realm. So much joy and so much pain is experienced on account of thought. But, what really is thought? Where does it come from? Where does it go? Is there a big "Thought House" in the sky that sends thought forms to all of us little receptors? Who knows?! But, I do know this. Until thought becomes your friend and supports you, it can be, and often is, your worst enemy. It is often said that strangers would never treat you as badly as some family members would. In the same way, the manner in which a person treats himself by virtue of the thoughts he or she thinks, is often insidious and reprehensible.

Ultimately, you need to be reminded of how precious you are.

Now it is almost like I am watching a movie. Maybe I am. But it is happening in swirling snippets that all seem to fit together as in a dream that makes absolutely no sense, but is easily understood and makes perfect sense until you try to understand it. In the tunnel or the channel I was in, this was perfectly fine. Something about it made me feel safe. There was no need to run. It was as though all of the run was out of me, and I was content to just stay. And watch.

Like watching ethereal spirits at play, I watched a drama unfold. They were no physical bodies to actually see; only distinct light shimmering presences; each with a somewhat distinct presence or aura, but all of the same fabric of light, so to speak. The less I try to peer, the easier I am able to take it all in. The less I try to focus, the more I understand and appreciate.

There are beautiful swirling conjunctions of light, followed by exits of a stream or two of various fragments, followed by other entries of other streams. A continuity of light play. When light was caused to move, I am told, is when it became aware of itself. This, then, was the beginning of our creation epic. And with the movement came a beautiful sound. A pervasive humming, low in the background, but immersed and absorbed throughout as if it was the meta by-product of the light. And the narrator, who was speaking to me, told me a story. This was not the same Voice, but the presence of truth telling me what I could listen to without reservation.

There was a time before time; long after creation, but long before the emergence of substance and humanity. A pantheon of spirits existed. They were as a thought, or so you would consider them in your time. Yet they had existence, inhabiting the space which is now filled by the planet Earth, and this solar system.

In many respects the earth retains their remembrance in the same way an old house retains vestiges of its former owners. This is an aspect of the universal law that no act is without meaning, significance, or continuity. Once existence, any existence, fills space, it remains for eternity – until converted to another form.

Since light is the basic building block of your realm, these spirits are still among you in one capacity or another. Some made the decision to adopt a form of materiality when it began to quicken in their universe. Others desired to remain pure Light spirit and elevated to higher quarters. A few even accepted corporeality when the flesh came into being, and so entered the world of time. All existence is a continuum - and the continuum seeks endless expansion.

Each of you interacts with your light in a unique way, as the makeup of your light is unique unto you. Many have tried to explain these light forms, some with more success and accuracy than others. Each region has its own version of their characteristics, powers and importance; but, the differences are merely academic.

As Light, these "spiritual" beings came into existence as pure thought forms. Having no mass or density they were once and everywhere simultaneously. Their ability to communicate lay in their thought, which was truly mobile – instantaneous air transmissions.

The ability to interact and communicate led to many happy conclusions, and some not so happy. Light naturally seeks the wholeness in itself and will join with any light anywhere for this purpose; unless it forgets it is light and has become form. Form as you know it does not exist, but for the belief that it must. Form encapsulated brought forth a continuing descent in the lightness and omnipresence of Light. The concept of darkness came into being. Darkness cannot exist; but with it came the power to imagine. The power to imagine generated the ability to desire, and hence to seek control.

The birthing mother seeks to give, endlessly. This is the true reality.

But, as the spirits cohabited in the darkness some felt was upon them, they even instigated amongst themselves for higher positions. It was like they created a vacuum in this realm of creation which gave the appearance of separateness, and the appearance that they were all-powerful. Generally, they became privy to all the emotional manifestations which would be inherited by the form later known as human beings. They could be loving, helpful, vain, petty and jealous – this is the prerogative of all life forms.

With the coming of the first physical forms, there was a type of coexistence between the physical and non-physical worlds. Taking on the human form and accepting the flesh also opened up a whole new world of options for these pure spirit forms. In accepting the earth cycle, however, they did not all lose contact with the astral plane. In fact, they used and retained this contact with much ease.

The material world was slowly evolving within the same sphere as the astral. At first, it was more of a coexistence than a meshing. The two planes were neutral enough to be mutually exclusive, each existing and operating on its own level. Even with the advent of animal forms, the proximity essentially went undisturbed.

The arrival of the human, however, challenged the spirit world for a variety of reasons. First of all, humans were akin to the spirit world, being creatures of thought and imagination. Through innate spiritual abilities, they had the capacity to breach the membrane into the spirit world. Humans were also able to transcend the pure spirit world, in a manner of speaking, because they had the use of the flesh to express feeling and emotions never before imagined or experienced in the spirit world. Feelings and emotions were beyond spiritual comprehension because they emanated from and existed in the blood, a base and heavy element, especially as compared with pure thought. In those times, however, the earth's atmosphere was less settled; less cohesive. Even as human beings came, they were of a lighter density than today.

The conjunction of worlds created a density that began to physically challenge the astral world. There was disruption in the pantheonic union of spirits. Soon the option of elevating to higher astral planes, or accepting corporeality, or a form of it, would present itself.

Materiality continued to quicken into new life forms. Some spirits chose to stay on and came to animate the vegetable and mineral worlds; so even today we speak of the spirits inhabiting supposedly inanimate objects like rocks and trees. Others, elevated to regions closer to the source and outside of physical bounds. Yet, they still remained accessible to those on the physical plane who sought their advice and guidance.

Soon it became a common practice to try to please these co-called gods. As such, primitive societies became increasingly susceptible to the whims of the spirits. The spirits, on the other hand, fully accepted the worship as if they were fully entitled to it. They fulfilled the symbiosis by living vicariously through their fleshen followers.

Gifts of obeisance originated with fruit and vegetable forms. As man's perspective of the power of this new pantheon grew, so did the gifts progress to actual sacrifice.

Those trained in what was to become known as the psychic arts attempted to bypass the lower spirits forms and project to the spirits who had traveled to the higher spheres. Many unwittingly dwelt solely in the lower realms, thinking they were not. A few, as we know, were able to project higher. They retained the remembrance of shedding the physical self, thus allowing the spiritual self to be transported to the higher planes. They also retained the knowledge regarding the indivisibility of the body and the spirit, and even physical transmigration from one time to another. This knowledge enabled them to physically transport the entire self-backward or forward in time, at will.

My attention diverted. There is a magnificent vertical light ray. Inside a vague luminous image briefly appears and then recedes. The appearance of a man on a throne; a brief image in radiance . A beautiful, cylindrical throne. Replicating in light, the image of carved stone, but radiating in a sapphire blue. A handsome man. A kindly face. A generous heart. He looks very familiar, but has an ancient, primordial look about him. There are aspects of his face which look sweet and feminine; others more chiseled like a male. I do not know what to think of him or her, or it. I do not know how to not classify by gender or some other category. The image fades again. It was and is lighter than form. The form fades so quickly into the light which it is. Again and again. Each time the form looks a little different. Then, it is no longer human, but animal, then vegetable; then inanimate. So much fun to watch shape-shifting in a pillar of light.

Then, again, a human form; but less a form than a representation of a feeling. A seriousness as the light-form is deeply reposed in thought as if its thought is all there is and there is no other reality save this.

The light brightens and expands. There is great comfort when all form recedes and there is only light. It is only in the form that discomfort and even the prototype of fear arise.

The humming begins to coalesce and turns into other sounds, some flowing, others staccato. Others flowing into and out of the pictures. A knowing comes to me.

But then, I notice that I have been myopic, for the eternity of light surrounding him is birthing light in continuous waves that go from one horizon to the next, to the next, to the next, to endless horizons without end. The eternal mothering of the universe from which spawns all life and assures continuity. Without the mother the Source of All That Is would be without a vehicle to produce.

I focused. The energy seems to harden, and with it comes the sound of speech, but by a different spirit speaker. In this little vehicle, this odd form of communication, comes a sound. But, it must suffice, for other forms have been forgotten in this land of light-form. The spirit speaks with some deep and unwavering intent.

"Come my friends" I heard. "The density quickens. We shall do more by leaving than by entering the chain of events which has been foretold."

In the same light which accepted to become condensed and concealed, many shadows dart here and there. Not the same radiance, but light forms still. And in the movement in this arena comes another sound from another speaker, but not necessarily the sound of sweet and gentle things. More of a stout and broad-chested bellicosity. And as in the light radiance, comes a form; both definitive and ephemeral. A feeling grows within me that this is a powerful force, but as ephemeral as the wind. Powerful when here; but then gone as if it never existed. Any attempt to focus on it brought no success; like trying to catch the wind.

This void, sometimes filled, sometimes empty; sometimes moving, sometimes still; the channel for all communication for communication can only flow in a void where the filling surrenders to its essence and becomes no more, for a time. And in this, also the visage of beings who represented different aspects of this void, this air, this wind. Some gentle and caring; others belligerent and unyielding. And in the conjunction formed when they met, true chaos and pandemonium. Since, in the eternal scheme of things, none could ever wrest control from or exert control over the other, forever; but in the nature of their movements would be an eternal drama to be played out in unimaginably varied forms and designs; only to be swept back into the vortex from which they came at some moment when the creator of moments so deemed.

A soft gentleness caresses me in a mother-love touch. Then a harsh butt and push as if I were in someone's way and was stopping the flow of progress. This eternal tension and the forms which portrayed them. And then, the bellicose one coming closer to a being form, so as to be seen. Claiming the crown in the same way that Napoleon crowned himself Emperor. While active, his supposed position of power stems from his purported control of the air and the wind. He announces himself as having the power to direct and control thought communications. He portrays his power as the power to unite or divide, at his whim. He wills himself to become a link between spirits, and soon, the creatures of substance. His bellicosity and manipulation set the stage for his own demise, so to speak, for the extreme of his own attributes only and always opens the door for the softer energies to emerge.

Aris was the name chosen by the bellicose spirit to identify itself. He neither accepted the flesh or other earth form, nor did he elevate to the astral world. He merely meshed himself with the air, a common element which suitably exemplified his personality. In this way, he was able to fuse his fickle, ephemeral, and, at times, bellicose spirit with the element he knew so well and which he had controlled for so long. He, therefore, became the links or the divider between the astral and physical planes. Air has substance without form and travels universe upon universe by simply being.

In this collage of light and shadow, other spirits merged into form, receded into other forms until merging with the spirit of forms: rivers and other bodies of water, the seasons, and other natural elements.

I looked above and below. It feels like I was in some "middle zone;" a portion of space which is neither controlled by earth's gravity, nor is governed by higher astral planes. It is truly, neither here nor there. It is a zone of unrestraint, of incompletion; somewhere between temptation and fulfillment. I know that with further compression, somewhere beneath me was the zone of the planets and the earth.

Now the narrator is talking to me again, but seemingly more distant. Now the narrator feels like an unreality. By focus, however, I am able to come closer to the words.

> *"Some spirits remembered their calling even though they chose to take on the flesh and enter the world of time. They retained the knowledge of their source and continued to communicate with the higher astral planes on a continuous basis. At first, all remained stable. Soon, however, many began assimilating to the different*

earth ways. Lightness gave way to weight and heaviness. Brilliant knowing gave way to logical meandering. Communication with the higher spheres began to slacken and diminish; the knowledge of these new earth souls lying dormant within them. Yet, the higher sources continued to try to communicate."

The dramas in the middle zone became the shadow backdrop for the dramas in the arenas where light was more and more constricted; the physical realm. The very ethers remained a communication passageway, of sorts between the realms. But, there was neither rhyme nor reason as to whether communications came or went through unblemished, or muddled.

Fewer and fewer preserved the remembrance of their source or preserved the knowledge regarding the ability to communicate with the astral world. Soon this knowledge became the knowledge of secret things or secret societies.

The advent of religion would attempt to explain things for the common person at a much later date. Various formulae were concocted by priests or religious bureaucrats which were intended to breach the physical bounds. Each formula, however, was no higher than its source, and each was less potent than the former.

Pagan society had the ability to recognize the existence of these spirits. But, it did not understand these spirits' true position in the ultimate scope of things. In the mystery, the spirits with whom they connected in the middle way were soon classified as "gods." Communication with these spirits, at first constant, eventually to grow more distant.

As society grew in number and complexity, communication even with these earth-bound spirits began to slacken. Communication became the stuff of legend and myth. Life became more of a mystery. The initial understanding of the beginning was long lost in distant memory that seemed more of a fantasy. As a result, dependence on these "gods" became more and more important. And the relationships became more fickle.

Those they thought controlled the air and wind achieved a position of authority and grandeur. They were called upon regularly to blow in the rain clouds to water the fields, to wind-cool scorched faces in the middle of summer, and to fill the sails of merchant ships and vessels of war. *They were considered the major benefactors of earth and its populace.*

At times they would govern the weather suitably, corresponding to the desires of the masses. At other times they were more fickle and would cause rain to fall in a limited amount to quicken the desire, but not produce the necessary results. At other times, they were destructive, deluging entire regions in torrents of downpour. But, balance was restored only by intervention. Intervention by whom, I thought? *This is what you must experience my young friend; and once experienced, it will be learned. Like all others who dedicate their lives to control and manipulation, these spirits did not realize that they were and are mere players in a much bigger scheme, and that, in truth, they were the pawns.*

Even though many had not taken the flesh, they could involve themselves in the world of flesh and blood at their desire. This they continued to do whimsically and indiscriminately.

As a result of their presumed power, and presumed fickleness and vanity, much effort went into trying to please and appease them. Vast cult centers were dedicated to them. And, because they were directly associated with water and growing crops, the essentials for the continuation of physical life, they became regarded as fertility deities.

All this time, a spirit with the name of ABA went through his rounds in the larger sphere. Aris did not go about his business completely unbridled. Those above him in the higher spheres kept him within bounds. Higher sources, however, had also decreed that it was humankind's purpose, having taken on the flesh and having entered the world of time, to find its way back to the realization of unity and G-dhead.

You have heard of the legend that in early times certain individuals who were trained in the spiritual arts communicated with each other telepathically. They did not participate in daily commerce and avoided any notoriety. They practiced vows of silence since the divisive powers of speech had already been made manifest.

Your legends differ as to the number of these rare souls. Some say nine, others eighteen or thirty-six, etc. The principle was that each of these groups had to be numbered in multiples of nine. Nine is a magical number that represents fruition before the creative acts which spawn a profound new creation. By their telepathic connection, they created a web around the world that helped to keep the world in balance, notwithstanding the divisive eruptions of empires as well as the explosive thoughts of individuals throughout every region of the globe.

At an early point in time, a group of these ancient ones resided anonymously in a region which encompassed the western half of Asia and the entire Middle East. As spiritual alchemists, they understood the principles behind the creation epic. As Bezalel would do at a much later date using the energies behind the letters of the Hebrew alphabet, this group combined the energies which existed in certain symbols, and caused an enormous pyramid to be constructed. The pyramid was formed of successive levels of fine gold-colored Light, each level smaller in size that the one immediately below. The sanctuary on the uppermost level had exterior walls covered by more highly polished plates of golden Light, as well as enormous plates of precious jewel-colored Light. Sunlight beaming off the golden Light-form gave it a solar appearance, as if it were the very Sun on the earth. As the Sun reflected on it, the solar beams of light from the Sun above, and the reflection of light coming from below, gave the appearance of a direct connection between the heavens and the earth.

These mystics, these holders of truth, were not totally immune to the earth cycle. Although many are reputed to have lived for thousands of years, slowly, each began to fade into the ethers. One by one the priests died. It was only their thought projection which kept the temple in existence. Upon the death of the last, the temple vaporized as if it had never existed.

All of these groups of priests and priestesses were descended from higher spirits who had taken on the appearance of flesh and coupled with the beautiful daughters of the earth. Their only goal was to keep the remembrance of the astral worlds alive. Taking on human form, and accepting the flesh, opened up a whole new world of options for these pure spirit forms. While they accepted the earth cycle, they also maintained contact with the astral plane. If fact, they used and retained this contact with as much ease as we use a telephone today.

These priests retained the knowledge regarding the connection between body and soul; body being from earthly elements, and soul having descended from the highest soul. They were adept in thought projection and physical transport through time.

They knew the future of the world. They were able to project a globe of our earth and on it watch events passing before them. They foresaw the continued antagonism between man's actions and his spirit. They took upon themselves a task. Throughout the cycle of time, they vowed to come together in later incarnations for the purpose of bringing humanity closer to the spirit world, and hence, the Source Of All That Is.

As a sign of identification, they altered themselves genetically and created the genetic formula which appears as a triangle in the palm of each hand. A further convergence of lines formed a triangle of sorts between the eyebrows. If their arms were spread out and slightly lowered, a pattern would be formed where their arms would be the sides of an equilateral triangle leading to the eyebrow mark. The center point of this larger triangle would be the heart.

These marks are unique unto them to this very day. The main purpose of the identification was for use in later generations. Through their advanced mental powers, these palm prints would serve as a portal of sorts, and enable them to think back to their early incarnation and remember their purpose and power. The eyebrow marks would make them identifiable to each other.

They kept their knowledge to themselves because it would have otherwise been misunderstood by the general populace, who were not, and still are not, ready to accept the knowledge – and the responsibilities and obligations – which go along with it.

Society began to resemble the thought-form labyrinth. One thought branching into many, and these many into multitudes; and the multitudes into sub-forms and sub-sub forms. As society became more complex, the Holy Ones, in later incarnations, decided to no longer stay isolated. They mixed with the general population and were gathered into the wheel of incarnation. In later generations they did come together. They were not always great men or women, sometimes only touching one soul or two. In every generation, however, it became harder and harder for any form of purity to remain.

The energetic lines among the Holy Ones remained strong and steady for countless generations. If they met, even for a moment, there was an instant recognition. Remembrances occurred in dreams and daydreams. This helped restore the faded knowledge of who and what they were. They tolerated the mass' subservience to many gods, and the deification of nature and natural elements. In a subtle way, they remained a light to the vast seas of humanity who had long ago forgotten its origins.

They knew who they were, and found each other in many incarnations.

When the spirit accepted the flesh, there was no guarantee that the flesh would remain subservient. This became the challenge: using thought to interact in the human realm, but remaining aloof of the illusion that thought had any purpose or power.

Eventually, one of the priests did succumb to temptation. He became part of the establishment of augurs, saying only what was desired to be heard; seeking his own advantage, no matter the impact or the truth. His condition worsened; he blamed everyone else for what was happening to him. He dreamed of power and reveled in manipulation. He tasted the blood of animals and reveled in it. He fell prey to the shadow of veiled light, and worshiped lower forms. He became motivated solely by greed. Very covetous. He would always, unconsciously, remember this life. As a result, he would continue to condemn himself until he would literally find the secret which would release him from his own error.

The Narrator stopped for a moment as if to look around and center its thoughts. Then, it continued:

The weight of the illusion of time becomes more and more of a factor. The density of time winds together tighter each moment each day, until like a watch, which it resembles, the illusion of time ceases to be. And with it, the end of the necessity of thought. Thought is only a function of the illusion of time. It has no other purpose or function, and ceases to be in any state of timelessness. And with it goes the need for speech and all other divisive attributes of the world of time.

Over time, the priests knew that some form of recordation would be necessary to preserve their knowledge. They began inscribing messages on amulets and scarabs. The source of these amulets and scarabs, as well as the symbols on them, was said to be the astral world. These charms served as a constant reminder of their origin.

Notwithstanding the uniqueness of the symbols, further measures were taken to prevent the information from getting into the wrong hands. While the inscriptions were written in one manner, acronyms and anagrams revealed the true message. Thus poetry and later general writing were born. As a further manner of protection, when each member died, his amulets would be collected and buried in secret vaults. The location was never disclosed to the uninitiated.

And as time went on, more and more was lost. What was remembered was treated as a myth or legend.

In your time the atmospheres of the two worlds, the astral and the physical have come closer and closer, exerting pressure on each other. The result is that the earth's atmosphere is much thicker and denser than in earlier times. An ancient person could not survive in your atmosphere for any extended period of time. A person of today would also find it difficult to adjust to the lighter feeling of earlier atmospheres.

There are those who have learned to teleport themselves through the channels of time, being of one time but intervening in another.

Like any mammal that lives in water, however, they must come up for air frequently. A body of this age could not go back to a prior time indefinitely, unless one learns how to prove that time itself is a fiction and has no existence. Such a person would have no existence as we know it, and would be eternal. Such a person would be akin to a living god.

"The conjunction of our worlds is at hand," was a thought form propelled by ABA as he spoke to his counterpart, EMA.

"Many of our brethren who did accept the flesh are now returning, having completed their tasks, and having reached their goals. They have fully experienced the physical form and the physical being. Some will not be allowed to finish and will complete their education elsewhere."

"We must now begin to remove all impediments to the meshing of our two worlds. It is now the order of things. The conjunction of our worlds is at hand," he said as they faded, one into the other and became One. They were then absorbed into the essence from whence they came.

XXX

It is said that all of human history, human motivations, culture, society, and thought itself, is nothing but the desire for love and nurturance. With it there is no need for anything else for you are in G-d's domain. Without it, you are always looking, and no matter what you find or do, nothing – absolutely nothing – fills the gap.

Apparently I am asleep, but feel awake and alive. Sort of, outside of myself. I can see her looking at me lovingly as I appear to be sleeping. No, she won't wake me. I know this, so I can just remain at peace here. She knows I need the extra sleep and she will go down to the office to just see what is going on.

I have no boundaries and feel anywhere, everywhere. It is a grand, graceful feeling.

She is now in my office. Neat and tidy as usual. Everything in its place. A monument unto itself.

As Kathryn enters my office, the phone rings. "Hello. This is the office of Dr. Michael Cushner."

"This is Mrs. Mellenstreet," said the voice on the other end of the phone line.

"Ah. This is Mrs. Cushner. I thought I recognized your voice."

"Have you seen the headlines this morning?" Mr. Mellenstreet asked.

"No," Kathryn responded.

"I ... I think you ... should" she quivered, which then broke into sobs. Click of the phone. A dead line.

Unseasonably warm, even sultry today. Petey the corner man was affixed and singing his daily litany, always the prototype town crier.

"Hehwo Miss Kathwyn" he said, partly bowing and removing the stogie stub from his mouth. "How'ah you today?" His tongue peeped out of the entry way so opportunely created by the absence of his two front teeth. She felt a brief respite. Petey would certainly not be so nonchalant if there was anything to hide.

"I'm fine Petey" she said not staring directly at him. "What's news today, Petey?"

"Aw, a whole new twist to the Mellentweeeet thing. Haven' you hooud?"

"No Petey; No I haven't. Please tell me quickly."

"The night watchman at the muse'um was going about his business las night. He went by the new Moon exhibit. He heard a dwip-dwop and stopped. He put on his flashlight and caught a gwimpse of a body. He quick wang the alahm and tuuned on the wights. Well, don' you know, it was Missah Mewwenstweet, stawk naked – I mean not a stitch on. He was pwopped up against one of the exhibit cases. And this is weally som'thin.' He was wun cleah thwough with a swoahd, he was. Wun cleah thwough.

"What do you mean by a sword?"

"A swoahd! Like you see in gwadiatah movies, ya know. And his eyes were extwa wide open. 'Bug-eyed' is how they said it in da papah. Here let me show you."

"No, that's alright Petey. Here's a quarter. I think I had better read this for myself."

"Say, where's Mr. Cushneh? Haven' seen him lately. Aw ok?"

XXXI

I can see quite clearly now. What I thought was a cylinder is actually condensed light. Light rays compressed and appearing solid. As I get closer I am able to enter into it – so to speak – as one would see a rainbow in the distance, but it would lose color as one got closer to it. But when you get closer to it, there is an unmistakable feel of tingling vibrations – uplifting. In this enlivening presence, I feel myself getting lighter, and actually rising. It is as though my mass is being aerated and losing subjectivity to the principle of gravity.

The vibratory tingling is getting so strong, I have lost touch with my self. I am beginning to wonder what self I am trying to feel. Lifted from the pressures of habituated earth living, and removed from the details of modern life, I feel whole and transcendent.

The pains and pressures down below have become inconsequential and nonexistent. "I" feel so large that if the Universe were my home, it would be too small.

A feeling of sublime happiness comes over me – happiness just because – feeling unrestrained and glorious. Love and warmth are radiating from me as though the supply is inexhaustible and the continuity is eternal.

Where could this have come from, and why did I not feel it before?

I feel a sense of worry that this will be temporary, and with this, I feel a slight density and heaviness, as though a foreign ingredient has entered my space. Allowing the flightiness to take over, I release the clutching, and once again begin to rise.

If I could think like the Creator, if just for a moment, what would I think? I know what it is. I would think beautiful, powerful thoughts of radiating love. And, if I could feel like the Creator, if just for a moment, what would I feel? Just the same. I would radiate feelings of love, like the light beams which radiate from the love of G-d, and know neither limitations nor boundaries.

If I am made in this image, then why not – if for just a moment. But, even here, even now, I am confused. How to access this? Not knowing any better, I started to talk to myself. Talking to myself just like talking to a friend. Easy. Casual. Just speaking. Telling myself how I am feeling. How I would like to feel. Recognizing the thoughts

I am thinking, the feelings I am feeling. Slowly, I begin to get quiet – ever more quiet. And I begin to realize this talking to myself, speaking the truth to myself, quieted my consciousness. And the quieting of my consciousness makes me feel lighter, and lighter still. And as for a quickening moment I realize I have made contact with my heart's desire. I feel so free.

It is so easy. How could it be this easy? Why did no one tell me? Why did the countless pundits express countless methods in countless programs over centuries and millennia?

If I am in the image of creation, having been made with the stuff of creation, then communication should be nothing less than direct. As direct as talking to myself, and opening a door for the eternal to enter me. The eternal which is always waiting, always waiting for the open door.

I can see creation as an expression of the Creator to create endless sparks of divinity which have never been seen before and will never be seen again. Yet, all of the sparks look and feel the same. Creation looks to be nothing more than a graduated recharacterization of energy in the scope of boundaries which were – at once – changeless and changing.

I feel cleansed and energized and alive. I want only to fly forever.

Then, nothing but the feeling of sublime happiness; a feeling of wholesome well-being.

A sapphire blue light penetrates everything, and I Am housed in it. I hear sublime voices singing – "Happy are those who dwell in Your House. They shall praise You forever."

I now understand the meaning of "House." It is the Light that emanates and wants for each of us to receive it. I Am Returned. I am Exuberant.

The vibration is soothing, but intense. I Am as I Am. I want for nothing. In the Light, I am everything. Life in the Light is glorious. In the Light, Life is as it was meant to be. Free. Light. Expansive. Vibrant. Emanating. Enlightening. Exuberant!

In a sense of disorientation, I begin to look at myself from outside. I am suspended in space in a beam of light. The beam from below goes straight up into the heavens to a point and cascades down in an ever widening arc. The beam from above goes straight down into the material earth and cascades up into a widening arc. An upward pointing triangle and a downward pointing triangle; intersecting. The mixture of heaven and earth forming an intersection which pulses as the heart of our universe, and is the animating force. As the effervescent air is pulsating with life, it impresses itself in a three dimensional pumping action. Rivers of energy going up and down, reminiscent of the image of Jacob's ladder in the Bible. I now understand the concept of Angels going up and down.

A living, breathing Star of David; the Seal of Solomon come alive; it becomes the arena for all life in this realm. Vibrating. Pulsating. The mythical Tree of Life comes alive in form.

In the Center, in the arena of pure creation represented by the Aleph א, are the images of Kathryn and me. For I have opened the door and Love is always waiting.

XXXII

Am I talking or am I thinking that I am talking? "I had a dream last night about us dancing. But, it wasn't here, and it wasn't now. It was before. We were dressed beautifully. You looked elegant in your beautiful white gown and your long, flowing hair wrapped richly in a majestic diamond pin, exposing your long, graceful neck."

"I must have been dreaming more. I feel more alive than I have ever felt before." Without saying it, I can feel energies flowing up and down like a continuous washing and clearing. I feel open, vibrant and abundant. Like I have been away and have returned jubilant and rejuvenated.

But, with the passing of a thought, there is a slight heaviness, as though I am slowly moving to some destination. It appears that I am approaching an entrance, but the lights are so bright, it is hard to tell. I can only squint in the direction.

My vision has not fully adjusted to these new conditions. Everything is still in a blur. No clear definitions. No clear forms. Perhaps there are no forms here. I am not sure.

I can see only vague, fluid images. I think I have a sense of feeling. Yes; definitely, there is feeling. Things are coming to me slowly. There is brightness everywhere. It is a strange new land I have chosen. I have much to learn.

I have a sense of feeling, like I am something in relation to what I am seeing. I do not understand. How could there be forms now when everything was brightness just a moment ago.

I look and see the contours of a form. No name. But, something blowing softly on it. Cold. A little cold.

Whatever is looking at me is rotating so that there is more to see. I become hungry to take in more. I do not understand, but I hunger for more, much more.

There is a sound, a vibration, a cadence.

Movement around me. Startled. A slight fear. Anxiety from the mystery, from the unknown heightens, and then leaves as if an ancient malady is finally released.

Beautiful music in the background. Like a circle, it goes round and round. It fills me with memories. But, of what; of whom? Then, a thought. I recognize the sound but cannot name it. I do not know if it is here or somewhere in my memory and it is just playing for me right now. It is beautiful. Wistful. It wafts like the wind and hungers like the heart. I was moving, but now I am still. The music captures and suspends me.

My memory goes back to the scene when I was holding a beautiful woman and we were turning, turning....

And then, a deep stillness in the turning. And in this stillness, a sense of being. The "joints" in a bodiless entity move smoothly through the vision which moves them. As if, in a dream.

XXXIII

The serenade continues. It haunts me with memories.

A sound. A cadence. A remembrance from other times past. It fills me. The white light enshrines.

A face now appears. It is not the face of any form that I recognize. It emanates Love. Not the love of any particular person or thing; but Love for its own sake. This is what I hunger for. It is without time or place; but here, I am beginning to recognize it as a definite time and place.

I gaze with open, interested eyes; like an infant who sees what it cannot describe and is happy in this bliss. Eyes which want to receive whatever they gaze upon. I gaze into the face of my love. It is bright and beautiful; radiant. Its image grows clearer and understanding starts coming back to me, slowly. This is where the circle meets its beginning. I reach out and embrace the form which holds my life in a loving embrace. A spoken word. A touch of the hand.

A lark ascending is flowing though my entire being. I follow it into the arms which reciprocate my intensity.

Slowly, I became aware that I am aware. My eyes begin to open, slowly. Everything is blurred, but comes into focus. I heard someone say, "You overslept. I am so glad, you needed the rest so desperately." I look up and see Kathryn looking lovingly at me.

XXXIV

With a new Heart comes a new Life. The principle is that if one thing changes – no matter how large or how small – everything changes.

The paper reported a grand opening and reception at the Hall of Antiquities. Ponti Moon played the grand host at the festivities. While the wait was long, the weather was perfect. A slight autumnal breeze graced the crowd and made their wait almost pleasurable. It was, almost, heaven sent. I was told even Petey attended. Even though smoking was not allowed, the security was instructed not to comment on his stogie. Mr. and Mrs. Mellenstreet were in the cover picture in the Evening News. They reported being delighted at the exhibit and intended to come back no matter how long the lines.

A fortnight after the exhibit a large envelope was delivered to the Evening News. In it were photographs of an expedition in a far-away land taken decades before most of the newspaper readers were even alive. There was also a picture of an amulet with an inscription in early Hebraic script. A translation was enclosed:
"The world was created in thirty-two paths of understanding which emanate from the whole. These emanations, however, are merely an illusion, for nothing which exists moves without having already completed its movement. It is an illusion if you say, but it is better not to speak. Creation is reflected only by the light it radiates. G-d's first creation in this Realm was Light. Light contains the essence of all other creations than can be created. The movement of light creates sound. In this Seventh World, everything is light and sound. Time is nothing but the bending of the light channel. Light holds Sound in its womb, and this is the meaning of "In the Beginning." Light, Sound and Time create a sequence which insists that we disobey what we see. In this way, we remember who we are. One portrays as three, and three must be disregarded for the one. In stillness we hear the movement leading to the light of redemption. In redemption, time is extinguished. Points of no space can only rest on each other in utter stillness, for they are not in time and there is nothing between them but space, silence and the Presence of the

Divine Emanation whose name I am not permitted to utter. All knowledge lies here, for it is the knowledge which cannot be known. I commit this to you, I Moshe ben Rafael, the son I Am of an Angel."

The translation was signed Professor Ezra Suberstein, Archeological Authority, Carnahan Expeditions.

The package revealed the time and place of discovery: 11:00 a.m., November 11, 1918; Megiddo. Signed Roger Ensign, director of the Andrew Carnahan expedition."

At the bottom of the package was a glossy picture of a meteorite with the image of two equilateral triangles nearly touching. Text in Hebrew above and below the symbol was translated by Professor Suberstein to read, "Be Still. And Know."

Only by walking through the cauldron as if it does not exist, can there be true redemption without consequences. Only in timelessness, can there neither be beginning nor end.

XXXV

As I look at the soft light streaming in my balcony window, I think of it as a thread coming and going; connecting. Something real that I can touch; but something imaginary that I can never grasp. Like the wind, that which is elemental and eternal is uncontainable.

If I allow the light to lead me, it will transport me to other times and places, many of which I have never seen or been. If I speak to the light it will tell me things I did not dare to know.

The Light has a story to tell. I am merely reading it, like a witness to a holy event.

I will never be able to look at the light like I used to. Forever more, it will be the medium that transcends boundaries, but provides the locus for all birthing in this universe. It is a container without boundaries.

In all human events, the only important thing is to remain large; to remain in the flow of the Creator's energy circuiting through you, and therefore to remain in the beam of light from which you were created in the first and the last.

There does not seem to be much point in choosing what has already been chosen for you; but, this seems to be an important lesson in our realm. In this rather voluntary way, the Dreamer, the Dream, and what is dreamt become one. Another triplicity which is separate in theory only, as is any separation.

What value are experiences that keep you in the cycle of winning/ losing/ glory and fear? If each of these has the opposite built into it, than the ingestion of one will necessarily generate the other. This is an adverse diet.

This is just an idea. In the end, ideas are only ideas and fade like air passing over an ocean. Doctrines are meaningless. The only salient detail is whether the spark of love has been kindled, stoked and allowed to radiate. If Love is endless, all else, which is temporary, is meaningless. How much meaningless data fills your days?

I did learn something very important on my adventure:

Michael Kushner

> Thankfulness leads to happiness
> Happiness leads to love
> Love simply leads

XXXVI

Autumn. 1902. The trees are resplendent. Everything is basking in the glory of this abundance. Life feels full and complete. Is there anything not yet created that is waiting to be created? With the impressive cache of inventions now in use, it does not seem so. Still, I wonder. Even a few years ago, who would have thought that buildings could be illuminated by electricity, and not just candle light or gas light. What marvels yet wait to be created?

My name is Michael Cushing. I must admit I have always enjoyed being of a certain social class which enjoys freedom and respite from the work-a-day world. I do have too much time on my hands and the free time does allow frequent flights of fancy.

I enjoy the clothing of my station, the air of gentility, and the social gatherings. I knew I was born to wear tails and a top hat. Society Gala Balls such as these are one of the ways the wealthy "let their hair down," so to speak; but in a way that is dressed to the nines and almost as gilded as humanly possible. In these settings, even the gossip is tolerable. I love to dance.

It is a good time. A promising time. I am tall, handsome, and blessed with angular, aristocratic features. All doors have always been open to me. I feel the abundance of this world. Yet, I have wondered if there was something ...more.

Tonight, however, something is different. As I look into Kathryn's eyes, I feel different. Her eyes, always so bright and clear are sparkling like doorways to galaxies yet to be discovered. I feel a sense of release and relief as though events in a time whose time has not yet come have been resolved and I am better for it; even though I have not participated in it. Or maybe I have and just do not know it.

The crystal chandeliers sparkle as though the crystal has come alive. Each seems to be telling a story in a language which was long hidden even before the Tower of Babel.

The night air, the night reveries. The day offers a dress rehearsal. The night witnesses the spiraling of men and women in union in a waltz which defies description. But, yet, it is the sense of light which exudes from even the darkness, from just enough champagne to still the senses, which captures the soul. In this stillness is the only real freedom we shall ever know.

I do so love the tenderness as we touch in deep affection and respect. As we turn, it is as though all the cares of the day are whisked away, unable to resist the centrifugal pull from a core in which they truly have no business.

At times I have given thought to the past and the future. I have fantasized about lives I may have lived in times before, and what I might like to be and do should I return. Perhaps I would like to be an explorer of sorts. Adventure has always interested me. But now, in this glorious, graceful turning, all fantasies are irrelevant, for the indescribable beauty and harmony I feel eclipses any fantasy. In short, I feel this immense love flooding through me and spiraling from me and showering us in the unlimited elegance and richness of a moment I feel to the core of my being. I wonder if she is feeling the same, but the sparkle in her eyes answers that very innocent question.

And so, it is a turning toward; not a turning away. A turning, growing ever more close. The proof is in the joy, and her rich, green eyes are portals to true happiness. Now it is the turning in ever more elegant circles that has captured my being. As we turn I slip into it, so to speak, and forget everything of who and what I am. I feel so alive. I feel so at home.

My love's enchanting perfume reminds me of something. I dreamt last night of strange places and even stranger buildings. Mostly, all I remember is the light. Direct and strong, yes. But comfortable. A softness which invited. I felt protected. I saw myself, I think. I knew it was myself, but I was different. There was a building which looked like a pyramid ... of all things! ... And, For Heaven's Sake – there was even a rainbow – the pyramid was in a rainbow!

But, then, I was walking through a thick, dark forest. An enchanting, alluring aroma seemed to come out of nowhere. It made me feel so alive and at home.

I came upon a field of bright flowers, orange poppies I think and stopped, stared, and became very still. Someone somewhere told me something I understood then. It was something about being still. I cannot remember it exactly. But I understood it very clearly then and did not dwell on it. Something about silence and stillness. I wish I understood now what I did then. That's the funny thing about dreams.

As I heard this, I turned slightly. A ray of brilliant light shot through an aperture between the thick, dark leaves and hit me squarely in the eyes. For a moment, I was stunned and completely blinded.

And then, I was ... wide Awake.

About Michael Kushner

Michael E. Kushner was born and raised in Buffalo, New York. He has journaled for most of his life, and uses journaling as a spiritual meditation.

Mysticism, religion and spirituality have always been very important aspects in his life. He has explored the mystical traditions of many groups and cultures. The science of mind has also always been very captivating to him.

Michael has practiced law in Albuquerque, New Mexico for more than 30 years. He has also lived on the Big Island of Hawaii, which he dearly loves.

He has always loved music. Throughout high school and college he played drums. He has now opted for the more soothing sounds of cello, oboe, piano and Native American flute.

Recent Releases from Casa de Snapdragon

Tango Sunday
Janet K. Brennan
ISBN: 9781937240165
Genre: Short Stories

Tango Sunday is a collection of fictional short stories about life on the edge. True to Janet Brennan's style and philosophy, she titillates the reader with good doses of revenge, ghosties, life in the spiritual world and death. Author Brennan aptly demonstrates in these dark and twilight zone tales that "Life simply is."

Anasazi Ruin
Jon Hovis
ISBN 9781937240110
Genre: Historical Fiction

"Anasazi Ruin" follows the life of a young man during the high point of life in Chaco Canyon in 1100 A.D. The story follows his life as he grows to follow in his father's footsteps and beyond as the life as he knows it is changing for the worse. Get an insight into pueblo life and culture as you read this intriguing book as it details the fall of the greatest empire to ever exist in this part of the world.

Art Effects
Connie Gotsch
ISBN 9781937240103
Genre: Investigation

A painting disappears from the Mesa City Art Museum and art objects vanish from galleries and restaurants around town, an investigative reporter with the Mesa Vista Times, begins an investigation. This was the final book by Connie Gotsch and will keep you turning the pages.